ALSO BY MARGARET LOUDON

The Open Book Mysteries
MURDER IN THE MARGINS
A FATAL FOOTNOTE
PERIL ON THE PAGE

WRITING AS PEG COCHRAN

Gourmet De-Lite Mysteries
ALLERGIC TO DEATH
STEAMED TO DEATH
ICED TO DEATH

Cranberry Cove Mysteries
BERRIED SECRETS
BERRY THE HATCHET
DEAD AND BERRIED

Farmer's Daughter Mysteries
NO FARM, NO FOUL
SOWED TO DEATH
BOUGHT THE FARM

Murder, She Reported Series
MURDER, SHE REPORTED
MURDER, SHE UNCOVERED
MURDER, SHE ENCOUNTERED

WRITING AS MEG LONDON

Sweet Nothing Lingerie Series
MURDER UNMENTIONABLE
LACED WITH POISON
A FATAL SLIP

Peril on the Page

MARGARET LOUDON

BERKLEY PRIME CRIME
New York

BERKLEY PRIME CRIME
Published by Berkley
An imprint of Penguin Random House LLC
penguinrandomhouse.com

ISBN: 9780593099308

First Edition: March 2022

Printed in the United States of America
1   3   5   7   9   10   8   6   4   2

Book design by Gaelyn Galbreath

Peril on
the Page

ONE

❧❦

Penelope Parish loved her position as a writer in residence at the Open Book bookstore in Upper Chumley-on-Stoke, England. She never knew what to expect. One thing she certainly hadn't expected when she'd crossed the Atlantic and set foot on these shores was to be involved in a murder. So far she'd been involved in two. But that was all behind her now and she could focus on writing her book and helping Mabel Morris, the owner of the Open Book.

At least that's what she told herself.

Today they were getting ready for a book launch at the bookstore. Stepping into the Open Book was like stepping back in time, with its low ceiling crisscrossed with wooden beams and the large diamond-paned front window. It was located on Upper Chumley-on-Stoke's high street, where the storefronts were the original Tudor and all the shops had hand-carved wooden signs hanging out front.

The book launch had been Penelope's idea and she had

her fingers crossed that it would go off without a hitch. Mabel had been a bit skeptical at first, but had finally come around and was now as enthusiastic as Penelope was about the event.

Odile Fontaine, an art teacher at the Oakwood School for Girls just outside Chumley, had written a book called *You Can Paint* and the book launch was being combined with a wine and paint party.

The event had stirred up considerable interest, and a photographer for the weekly newspaper the *Chumley Chronicle* had phoned to say she planned to attend and take pictures.

Odile was a member of the fiction writing group Penelope had recently started and was a teacher at the Oakwood School for Girls. The headmistress, Maribel Northcott, had invited Penelope to conduct a seminar for the students there. Penelope was quite pleased that her master's degree in Gothic literature was finally being put to good use.

Of course that same degree had driven her to write *Lady of the Moors,* which, much to her surprise, had become a bestseller, so perhaps the money on her education had been well spent after all, in spite of what her mother was always saying. It was the writer's block that she'd been stricken with while working on her second book that had pushed her to apply for the writer-in-residence position at the Open Book, hoping that a change of scenery would spur some creativity.

Life in Upper Chumley-on-Stoke, a medieval town about an hour from London, had worked its magic and Penelope's second book was due to be published at any moment.

Pen was arranging a stack of Odile's books on a display table when Mabel approached her.

Mabel ran a hand through the fluffy white hair that

made her look more like a grandmother than the former MI6 analyst she'd been.

"I've cleared a space for the easels to be set up," she said. She frowned. "They are bringing the easels, right?"

"Yes. Odile is taking care of everything—the easels, paints, aprons for the participants, and the wine." Pen looked toward the bookshop's tearoom, which was run by Lady Fiona Innes-Goldthorpe, or Figgy, as she was more familiarly known.

"Figgy is providing some desserts—cakes and cookies, that sort of thing."

Mabel nodded. "Good. Best to have something to soak up the wine." She looked around. "It appears as if everything is in order, then," she said, giving a relieved smile.

The bell over the front door tinkled and Odile Fontaine, the subject of that evening's book launch, swept in. She was a fairly tall woman—although not as tall as Penelope's nearly six feet—big-boned, and had a purple beret perched on top of her head of long curly red hair threaded with strands of gray. She removed her cape with a dramatic flourish, sending it swirling in an arc around her that nearly toppled the sign on one of the display tables.

She was wearing a bloodred skirt, which flowed around her ankles, with a purple tunic over it and a necklace of large mustard yellow beads that looked hand carved.

Penelope took the cape from her and hung it on the coat stand near the front door.

Odile had brought an almost palpable sense of excitement into the store with her as well as a whiff of cold air. It was mid-October and the Michaelmas term was underway at the Oakwood School. The leaves on the trees were turning and the residents of Chum, as the town was affectionately known, were digging out their cozy sweaters and boiled wool jackets.

Odile swept over to Penelope and greeted her with an air kiss on each cheek.

"Have you read my manuscript yet?" she said. An armload of silver bracelets jingled as she straightened one of her books on the display table. "I'm hoping to send it off to a publisher soon."

Not content to just publish a book on painting, Odile had taken up fiction as well and had penned a four-hundred-page contemporary romance. Penelope silently groaned. She'd been meaning to get to it and had actually read a few pages, but it was such a slog that she'd given up and had spent the time wondering how she could persuade Odile to stick to painting instead.

The door opened again, sending a chilly breeze through the shop that ruffled the pages of the flyers sitting out on the front counter. A young man stuck his head into the store.

Odile glided over to him, her long fluid skirt swishing about her legs.

"I've got the gear," the young man said. "Where do you want it?"

Penelope hastened to join them. She glanced out the window and saw a large van with the Oakwood School crest on the side double-parked in front of the Open Book.

"There's another entrance behind the shop," she said, and directed the young man to an alley that ran alongside the Open Book and led to a back door that opened into the storage room.

"Cheers." The young man gave a sketchy salute, turned around, and hopped into the driver's seat of the van just as the driver of the car behind him began to lean on his horn.

"That's Grady Evans," Odile said, as the van pulled

away. "He takes care of the grounds at the school and does odd jobs for Rodney Simpson, who is in charge of maintenance. I asked him to cart my supplies over here for me."

The door opened again and a gentleman walked in. He had thick gray hair brushed back from his forehead in a wave and round tortoiseshell glasses. He was wearing a tweed coat with a velvet collar and leather gloves, which he pulled off as he walked toward Odile and Penelope.

Odile smiled and put her hand on the man's arm.

"Penelope, this is Quentin Barnes, my significant other, as the young people say." She smiled up at Quentin. "He teaches history at the Oakwood School." She turned to Quentin. "Quentin, this is Penelope Parish. This event was her brilliant idea."

Pen crossed her fingers. She hoped her idea would turn out to be brilliant.

"Will you be doing a painting?" Penelope said to Quentin.

"Heavens, no. I'm just here for moral support and to say good-bye." He gave Odile a peck on the cheek and glanced at his watch. "Unfortunately I can't stay long. I have a conference in Bristol that starts early tomorrow morning, so I'm heading out tonight." He turned to Odile. "I'll be at the Bristol Harbor Hotel if you need to reach me."

"Well, I hope you can stay for a bit. I've got some of that wine you fancy." Odile took his arm and led him over to the display table where her books were piled up, waiting to be signed.

A few minutes later Pen heard Grady knock on the back door and ran to open it.

Grady sidled through the door with several easels tucked under his arms.

He was tall and sinewy, with dark brown hair long

enough to flop onto his forehead. He was wearing faded and worn jeans, a plaid flannel shirt with the sleeves rolled up, and work boots. Penelope could see goose bumps on his arms.

"You must be freezing without a coat," she said.

Grady shrugged. "I left my jacket in the van. I'm okay." He nodded at the easels he was holding. "Where do you want these?"

"We've cleared a space at the front of the store," Penelope said.

"Righto."

Penelope led him toward the area where she and Mabel had decided to hold the event. They'd shoved some display tables out of the way to create a large enough space for the painting party.

"Why don't you lean them against that table over there." Odile pointed to a spot. "You can help me set them up after you bring everything in."

Grady nodded. "I'll go get the rest of the gear." He loped off through the store toward the back entrance.

Moments later he came back with a handcart piled with cardboard boxes.

"Let's have those over there," Odile said, pointing to a spot off to the side. "Now we can begin to set up the easels."

Grady, who had briefly paused and was leaning against one of the display tables, reluctantly shoved off and began placing the easels according to Odile's instructions.

"What do you have here?" Mabel wandered over and peered into one of the open cartons.

"Paints, palettes, aprons." Odile ticked them off on her fingers. "And that last one there is the wine." She whirled around to face Penelope. "Do we have glasses?"

"Yes, no problem."

"Hello!" Figgy called as she wheeled a tea cart over to them, its wheels rattling as she pushed it across the floor.

Her short dark hair was gelled into spikes and looked as if she'd run her hands through it haphazardly, and she was wearing one of her vintage thrift store finds—a flowered peasant dress with an empire waist—a style that had been popular in the nineteen seventies. She'd paired it with black ankle boots and large hoop earrings.

Penelope glanced at the tea cart and her stomach rumbled, reminding her that she hadn't had dinner yet. She'd been working on her third novel and had become immersed in it—something that sadly didn't happen every time she sat down to write. Her writing room at the Open Book—a small space barely bigger than a closet with a desk and a chair and nothing else to distract her—was windowless, and she hadn't seen the sun going down and darkness descending. She wondered if there was time to dash across the street and pick something up from the Chumley Chippie.

"I've made some shortbread cookies, Jaffa cakes, and jammy dodgers," Figgy said, pointing to the various platters.

"What on earth is a 'jammy dodger'?" Penelope said. "It sounds like a position on a baseball team." Penelope put on an announcer's serious voice: "And John Smith has been drafted for the jammy dodger position with the New York Yankees."

Figgy laughed. "It does rather sound that way, doesn't it? They're shortbread cookies with jam filling. They're quite lovely." She pointed to the tea cart. "There's a Victoria sponge as well and some slices of Madeira cake." She frowned. "I think that should do."

"It certainly should," Pen said, pushing her glasses up her nose with her finger. She glanced at the tea cart again, longing to grab a slice of the Madeira cake. It had become one of her favorites since arriving in England. It was like a pound cake, but moister and with a hint of lemon flavoring. According to Figgy, the Victorians used to serve it with a glass of Madeira in the afternoons and that was how it had acquired its name.

Grady, meanwhile, had set up the easels and the folding chairs Mabel had rented for the occasion and Odile was organizing the paints and palettes.

Penelope glanced at the clock. The wine and paint participants should be arriving any minute now. She nixed the idea of running to the Chumley Chippie. A slice of Figgy's Madeira cake would have to do.

Fortunately for Penelope, she had been blessed with the sort of metabolism that made it hard to gain weight and it didn't help that she often forgot to eat until hunger finally drove her to think about having a meal.

The shop door opened again and two women entered, their faces red from the cold and their hands fluttering in excitement.

Odile introduced herself and invited them to choose a spot and take a seat.

India Culpepper was the next to arrive. She was wearing the English gentlewoman's uniform of a waxed jacket, plaid wool skirt, twin set, and a strand of yellowing pearls. She was distantly related to Arthur Worthington, the Duke of Upper Chumley-on-Stoke, and lived in a cottage on the grounds of the Worthington estate.

The family money, handed down through generations of Worthingtons, hadn't reached India to any substantial degree, and her sweaters were likely to be darned and her shoes rather worn at the heels. Figgy kept her supplied with cookies and cakes from the tea shop at no charge, and Mabel often hunted out used copies of the books India wanted to read.

But India was a proud woman, as befitted the aristocrat she considered herself to be, and never complained about her lack of funds.

Penelope guessed that India's interest tonight didn't lie in wine and painting but rather in the contents of Figgy's tea cart.

Gladys arrived next, her face red from rushing across the street. where she and her husband owned the Pig in a Poke, Chumley's butcher shop. She took off her coat and squealed when she looked down at herself.

"I've forgotten to take me apron off," she said, laughing and slapping her thigh. She whipped it off quickly and hung it from the back of the chair she'd chosen next to India.

Several more women arrived, chattering like birds and fluttering around the shop. One of them went over to talk to Odile.

The bell over the front door tinkled as it opened and everyone's head turned in that direction. Several of the women gasped in surprise when the Duchess of Upper Chumley-on-Stoke walked in. Charlotte Davenport had married the Duke of Upper Chumley-on-Stoke in a magnificent ceremony at Worthington House that had been the talk of the town from the moment it was announced. Not all the talk had been positive, though—not only was Charlotte an American, but she was a romance writer, and neither of those things sat well with a lot of the residents.

Charlotte was as unpretentious as they came. She and Penelope had developed something of a bond as Americans and fellow writers and had become friends.

From the moment Worthington and Charlotte had said *I do*, everyone in Chumley, as well as reporters and photographers from all the tabloids, had been on the watch for the proverbial baby bump. There had been a couple of false alarms, but now Charlotte was very visibly pregnant, much to everyone's satisfaction and delight.

Charlotte looked effortlessly elegant as usual with her long blond hair swept into a simple knot at the nape of her neck. She was wearing a waxed jacket, jeans, and a fitted navy-and-white-striped Breton sweater that accentuated her baby bump.

The women smiled at her nervously as she took a seat on the other side of India.

Finally Odile clapped her hands and everyone took their place. Quentin didn't join the group but instead wandered around the Open Book, stopping every once in a while to pull a volume off the shelf.

Figgy opened the bottles of wine and began handing out glasses to the women. Odile accepted one, took a sip, and put it aside as she concentrated on leading the class through a painting that looked like a piece of modern art.

Figgy poked Pen as she stood watching. "It looks rather like a faked Mondrian, doesn't it?"

Pen looked at the squares and rectangles of red, yellow, and blue separated by black lines.

"It looks like a Rubik's cube to me."

Figgy laughed, then picked up a bottle of wine and went to refill Gladys's glass.

Penelope noticed Quentin walking toward the door as he buttoned his coat and pulled on his gloves. He waved to Odile and left.

The audience continued to follow Odile's instructions and slowly their paintings were taking shape. Pen noticed that Gladys had the tip of her tongue between her front

teeth as she concentrated on her canvas and Charlotte's jaw
was set as she attempted to copy Odile's strokes.

The photographer from the *Chumley Chronicle*—a
middle-aged woman with graying hair wearing a stretched-
out red sweater—roamed around, snapping pictures of the
event, occasionally pausing to grab a cookie off the tea
cart.

Suddenly Odile swayed and put a hand to her head. Penelope eyed her with concern.

"Are you okay?" Pen said. "Do you need some air? Perhaps the smell of the paint . . ."

"The paints hardly have any odor," Odile said. "It was
just a slight dizzy spell. Nothing to worry about."

"Do you want to sit down for a moment?"

Odile made a face and waved Penelope away as if she
were a pesky fly. She adjusted her beret and turned back to
the assembled audience.

"Where were we?" she said in her throaty voice, pausing
dramatically with her paintbrush in the air.

Penelope glanced around the room again. The women
were dutifully copying Odile's brushstrokes with varying
degrees of success. India's hands shook slightly and her
lines were wavy, giving the whole thing a watery impres-
sionist look, like something seen through a rain-spattered
window.

Everyone seemed to be enjoying themselves and Penelope sighed with satisfaction.

Once the paintings were finished and left to dry, the ladies gathered around Figgy's tea cart, their eyes wide with
delight at the array of goodies. Slices of Madeira cake or a
couple of jammy dodgers in hand, they wandered among
the easels, admiring one another's handiwork.

Much to everyone's delight, Charlotte circulated with them, complimenting their artistic abilities and daintily munching on a shortbread finger.

"I've been craving sweets ever since . . ." Charlotte said to the women clustered around her. She cradled her belly gently with her left hand.

Gladys threw back her head and laughed. "I was the same with my daughter Elspeth—only with me it was Vegemite. I had it on toast every morning and for my tea and I even dipped crisps in it. I went through any number of jars of it. Bruce—he's my husband—thought being in the family way had made me barmy."

Their laughter was cut short by a cry from Odile. Pen looked over at her and was horrified to see her sway wildly and clutch at one of the easels, sending the painting soaring, and then crash to the floor in a heap of red and purple fabric. Her beret flew off and landed several feet away.

The photographer, who had been busy munching on a piece of Madeira cake, gave an abrupt cry, grabbed her camera off a chair, and hastened over. She immediately began snapping pictures, oblivious to the crumbs leaving a trail down the front of her sweater.

"Please, don't," Pen said to her and held up a hand to stop her. She knelt beside Odile. "What is it? Are you ill? Should we call a doctor?"

"I'm dizzy," Odile said. "My head is spinning."

Mabel came over and crouched down next to Pen, her knees giving a loud crack that sounded like a shot.

"And I have the most abominable headache," Odile said, rubbing the back of her neck.

"Has this happened before?" Mabel said in a crisp, no-nonsense voice. "Do you have any medication you're supposed to be taking?"

Odile shook her head. "Just so dizzy," she said again.

"When did you start feeling ill?" Mabel said.

"After I got here," Odile said. "I felt fine before. I don't know what's wrong."

Several of the women had wandered over and were clustered around Odile.

Mabel peered at Odile more closely and then turned to Pen. "Her pupils are awfully dilated. They're positively enormous. Take a look."

Pen looked at Odile and nodded her head. "Shall I call an ambulance?"

"I think you'd better," Mabel said. She frowned. "I hope it's nothing serious."

As Penelope stood up and pulled her phone from her pocket, Odile's eyelids fluttered, closed, and her head flopped to the side.

TWO

❧

After Odile was taken to the hospital by ambulance, the festive atmosphere in the Open Book deflated like a punctured balloon. Mabel rang up the customers' purchases of *You Can Paint* with a serious face and, one by one, the women donned their coats and trickled out the door.

Charlotte said good-bye to Penelope and Mabel and went out to the car that was waiting for her at the curb. She waved as she was whisked away.

Mabel let out a sigh that fluttered the curls that had fallen onto her forehead.

"That was something," she said to Penelope, running a hand through her hair. "We've never had an author collapse before. Although there was that one time when an elderly gentleman who had written a book on World War Two history became quite weak and shaky, but a couple of Figgy's shortbread cookies and a cup of tea with plenty of sugar in it soon set him right again."

Mabel went to the door, flipped the sign to Closed, and turned the lock.

"Anyone for some tea?" Figgy called from the tearoom. "I'll put the kettle on."

"That's not a bad idea," Mabel said. She reached under the counter and pulled out a bottle of Jameson. "And I'd say a shot of this would not be amiss."

They gathered around a table in the tea shop as Figgy poured out cups of tea. There were still a few slices of Madeira cake left on the tea cart along with an array of cookies.

Penelope grabbed a finger of shortbread and began to nibble on it. She still felt a bit shaken by Odile's collapsing.

"I do hope Odile will be okay," she said, brushing some crumbs off her sweater.

Mabel broke off a piece of her cookie and crumbled it between her fingers. "I hope so, too. The event was such a success. It's a shame that she took ill like that."

"I'm sure Odile will be fine," Figgy said, reaching for the bottle of Jameson and adding a drop to her cup of tea. "Perhaps she was coming down with something—a virus, maybe—and it made her dizzy. I know the last time I had the flu it left me feeling dreadfully wobbly."

"We did sell a lot of Odile's books," Mabel said brightly. "I'm sure she will be pleased about that." She nibbled absentmindedly on her piece of shortbread. "I do wish we could find out how she is. I doubt the hospital will tell us anything."

"I can call the school tomorrow and see if they know anything," Pen said, reaching for a slice of cake.

"Good idea." Mabel got to her feet. "I guess it's time we close up. I don't know about you, but I'm exhausted." She stretched her arms over her head. "Well done, Penelope. In spite of everything, I believe the evening was a success."

Pen bit her lower lip. "I'd feel more like celebrating if we knew Odile was okay."

"I agree," Mabel said with a sigh.

Figgy began to clear up the tea things. Penelope grabbed another slice of cake before Figgy wheeled the tea cart away.

Mabel already had her jacket on and was tucking a scarf into the open neck.

"Coming?" she said to Pen, her hand on the bookstore light switch. "Are you ready to go?" she shouted to Figgy, who was flipping off the lights in the tea shop.

"All set." Figgy grabbed her jacket off the back of one of the chairs and slid into it.

Mabel's keys jingled as she pulled them from her pocket. She had her hand on the doorknob when the telephone rang. The three of them froze and looked at one another.

"A customer checking to see if we're still open?" Pen said.

"Or someone forgot their gloves or left a bag behind," Figgy said. "You wouldn't believe the things I find in the tea shop at night when I clean up—pens, notebooks, cell phones, dummies."

"Dummies?" Pen raised her eyebrows.

"I think you call them pacifiers in the States," Figgy said.

Mabel shook her head. "I don't know. I have a bad feeling. I'd better get it." She went around the counter and picked up the telephone receiver. "Hello. The Open Book. May I help you?" she said somewhat breathlessly.

Mabel listened, her head cocked to the side, her face blank. Penelope studied her expression, trying to discern if the call was something ordinary or if it was indeed bad news. She had a sinking feeling in the pit of her stomach that it was the latter.

Mabel hung up the telephone and stood for a moment with her hand on the receiver, her face blanched white.

"What is it?" Figgy said after Mabel was silent for several seconds.

Mabel shook her head. "That was Quentin Barnes—the man Odile introduced as her significant other. He just heard from the hospital. According to him, Odile has died, I'm afraid."

Both Penelope and Figgy gasped.

"How awful!" Pen put a hand to her chest. "Maybe we should have done something? CPR? I feel terrible."

Mabel squeezed Pen's shoulder. "It's not our fault. We had no idea her illness was so serious. We called for the ambulance and that's all we could do."

"Was it her heart?" Figgy said. "The poor thing."

"Quentin said they were trying to figure that out. He's still on the road to Bristol. He asked that we contact the headmistress at the school and let her know."

"That would be Maribel Northcott," Pen said. "I'll look up her number." Pen pulled out her phone. She frowned. "It seems I only have a telephone number for the school itself. I suppose it's worth a shot."

Pen punched in the numbers with shaky hands and held the phone to her ear. After several seconds she shook her head.

"I got the answering machine. It looks like we'll have to wait till the morning."

"I don't think we should wait," Mabel said. "Let's go over to the school now and see if someone can tell us where Maribel lives. I suppose she lives on campus somewhere?"

Pen nodded. "All the staff have apartments there."

"I hope you don't mind if I beg off," Figgy said with a yawn. "I'm positively knackered. It's been a long day."

"It's after nine. You go on home," Mabel said, making a shooing motion. "We'll see you in the morning. It will be here before you know it."

Mabel closed up the shop and she and Penelope headed out. It was cold—Penelope's breath made a cloud of condensation in the air. The streetlights were on and cast pools of light on the sidewalk and the night-lights in the shuttered shops dimly illuminated their front windows.

Pen was shivering by the time they got to Mabel's car.

"I'll turn the heat on as soon as the engine warms up," Mabel said, putting the key in the ignition and starting the engine. "It shouldn't take long."

They drove down the high street, through the town, past Kebabs and Curries and the new Tesco, which were still open. They passed the Book and Bottle, the local pub where all the residents gathered—even Worthington joined them on occasion.

Another half mile and they were in the country, where hedgerows bordered the narrow lane and shadowy fields were dimly visible on either side.

Suddenly a cloud drifted over the moon and darkened the road ahead. The bushes and trees alongside the lane took on a sinister aspect, and Penelope shivered again although the heat was going full blast now. She was grateful when several minutes later they saw the sign for the Oakwood School up ahead.

The ivy-covered buildings were dark with yellow light shining through a window here and there. Mabel pulled up in front of the main building, where a sign with the school crest and WELCOME TO THE OAKWOOD SCHOOL FOR GIRLS was written in gold. She pulled into a space and parked the car.

Mabel looked up at the darkened façade. "Let's walk around and hope we run into someone who can direct us." She glanced at her watch. "It's nine thirty. Everybody can't be in bed already."

Penelope was reluctant to leave the warmth of the car and shivered when the chill night air hit her as she opened the door. She took her gloves out of her pocket and pulled them on.

A flagstone path, silken with moss, led to a central quad ringed with buildings. Pen noticed that several of them were still ablaze with lights despite the hour and she suspected they must be the girls' dormitories. One of the windows opened suddenly and the scent of tobacco smoke drifted toward them.

Obviously some things never changed, she thought. She remembered when she was in middle school and a friend had talked her into trying a cigarette. Fortunately she'd found the taste disgusting and had never done it again.

They were crossing the quad when the door of the building opposite them opened and someone walked out and began heading down the path toward them. It was a young woman hugging a laptop case to her chest. She passed under a light and Pen realized she must be one of the teachers—she was older than she'd first appeared to be.

"Excuse me," Pen said as the woman neared them. "I'm wondering if you could help us."

The woman cocked her head. "I'll try."

"Do you know where Maribel Northcott lives?"

"The head? Why, yes. That building over there. The one with all the lights on." She pointed across the quad. "It's called Sutcliffe House. There's a door around the side that leads directly to her apartment. It has a brass knocker in the shape of a man's head. Maribel says it reminds her of the scene in *A Christmas Carol* where Scrooge's knocker turns into Jacob Marley's face."

"That should make it easy to find," Pen said. "Thank you."

"Cheers," the woman said with a smile and went on her way.

They continued across the quad until they came to the building the woman had indicated. *Sutcliffe House* was written on a plaque set in the brick wall near the door.

"This is it," Mabel said as they rounded the corner. "There's the door."

Pen went up to the door and banged the knocker. The noise seemed shockingly loud in the stillness of the night.

The curtain in the window alongside the door moved briefly and then the door opened.

Maribel was wearing a long velvet robe and slippers. Pen thought she managed to look put together even in her nightclothes.

"Yes?" she said. She peered at Pen. "Penelope, is that you?" She opened the door wider. "Please, do come in. It's quite cold tonight."

Penelope and Mabel followed her into an elegant sitting room with tall windows draped with dark green velvet curtains, which were drawn against the dark night.

The ceiling was high with elaborately carved crown molding, and bookshelves covered one wall. A small round table held a stack of books along with several pictures in silver frames.

Maribel tightened the belt of her robe. "I'm sorry I'm not dressed. I have an appointment first thing tomorrow so I thought I would turn in earlier than usual." She gestured toward a sofa. "Please, sit down."

"We're sorry to disturb you," Pen said as she took a seat.

"I assume it's something urgent," Maribel said with a worried frown, perched on the edge of a chair.

Penelope took a deep breath. "It's Odile Fontaine. She collapsed at the wine and paint party tonight at the Open Book and was taken to the hospital."

"Oh, dear," Maribel said, her hands fluttering near her face. "I do hope she will be all right."

Pen shook her head. "I'm afraid she's dead."

Maribel gasped and her hand flew to her mouth. "How positively dreadful. What happened?"

"We don't really know any more than that," Mabel said. "She became ill and we called an ambulance for her. Quentin Barnes called us from the road. He's on his way to a conference and asked that we give you the news."

"We'll need to contact her next of kin," Maribel said. She stood up and swayed slightly. She put a hand on the chair to steady herself. "I will have to check the records to see who is listed as her contact. I know her parents are no longer alive and I don't think she had any siblings." Maribel started to turn away. "I'll head over to the administration building to look up her records."

"Would you like us to come with you?" Mabel said softly. "This has been a shock to you."

Maribel gave a half smile. "I wouldn't mind, as a matter of fact. Normally I would take something like this in my stride, but I'm just back from burying my sister and it's left me a bit shaky." She ran a hand through her hair. "I'll go get changed."

Mabel sat on the sofa and Pen went over to the bookshelves and began to scan the titles. Maribel had a wide range of reading material, she noticed—books on wildflowers, history, philosophy, and a complete set of Dick

Francis's novels. Pen was looking at one of them when Maribel returned.

She was wearing a pair of jeans with a sharp crease that had clearly been ironed into them and a Shetland sweater.

Maribel noticed the book in Penelope's hands. "I was a bit of a horsewoman when I was younger," she said with an embarrassed laugh. "I have a soft spot for Francis's mysteries. I've heard that the queen herself is also quite fond of them."

Pen closed the book and slotted it back into position on the shelf as Maribel got out her coat and slipped into it.

"I didn't know Odile well," Maribel said as they walked across the quad toward the administration building. "We weren't close, but I admired her teaching skills. The students in her class were quite devoted to her." She stopped suddenly. "They're going to be dreadfully upset at this news. I shall have to tell them at assembly tomorrow."

"Odile was certainly a forceful personality," Mabel said, pulling her coat closer around her. "I can see how she would have had an influence on the girls."

Maribel gave a ghost of a smile. "That she was. She was passionate about her art; although frankly, I could never make heads or tails of most of it myself." She paused. "Perhaps we should plan an exhibit of her work here at the school. A sort of memorial." She waved a hand. "No need to think about that at the moment. Everything in its own time."

They followed Maribel down the path that led around the darkened administration building to the front entrance. Maribel took a key card from her pocket and swiped it. The lock clicked and the door opened.

She stopped just inside the doorway and swept her hand along the wall until she found the switch. The hallway was flooded with light and Penelope blinked at the sudden brightness.

Maribel pulled a ring of keys from her pocket, selected one, and inserted it in the lock of the door nearest to them. She pushed it open and flicked on the lights.

Pen recognized the admissions office from a previous visit. The desk at the back belonged to Maribel's secretary.

Maribel led them through the outer office to the door that led to her own private office. She opened it and turned on the lights.

"I need to get the keys," she said, as they followed her into the wood-paneled room. Maribel walked over to a highly polished desk that Penelope thought looked like an antique, opened the drawer, and took out a set of keys.

"The files are in the outer office."

File cabinets lined the wall next to the secretary's desk. Maribel chose one and opened it. She rifled through the files and finally pulled one out. She laid it down on the desk, opened it, and began to go through the papers inside.

"Here we go," she said, holding up a sheet that looked like a printed form. She pulled a pair of reading glasses from her pocket, perched them on the end of her nose, and began to read.

She frowned.

"What is it?" Penelope said.

"There's no next of kin listed. Odile left the space blank." She put the page back in the folder and closed it. "I don't know who needs to be notified. This is most distressing. Who is going to make the arrangements?"

"Perhaps there might be a clue in her apartment?" Pen said. "An address book or some letters or anything that might give you a hint as to who to contact."

Maribel cocked her head. "That's an excellent idea.

Someone needs to be notified immediately. The hospital will want arrangements made as soon as possible."

"Maybe we should go look now?" Pen said.

Maribel hesitated. "If you're not too tired . . . I know it's late. But I know I'll sleep better once this is handled."

"I'm a night owl." Pen smiled.

Mabel nodded. "Me, too."

"I'll get the master key, then, shall I?" Maribel squared her shoulders. "Odile is . . . was in Parker House. It's not far."

THREE

❦

The quad was quiet as they headed toward Odile's apartment and fewer lights were shining from the windows. They passed a building where they suddenly heard a burst of laughter followed by someone whispering shhhhh.

"Everything seems so peaceful," Mabel said.

Maribel chuckled. "You should see it during the day. Students rushing back and forth to class, music playing, laughing, and shouting." She shook her head. "I do miss it when the girls go home for half term. Although with all the international students enrolled now, more and more of them are staying on campus between terms. It's not that easy to fly back to Hong Kong or Singapore for only a couple of days."

Odile's apartment wasn't far and within minutes they reached Parker House. Maribel swiped her key at the door and led them into a hallway where the walls were covered in dark-green-and-cream-striped wallpaper.

Odile's apartment was the first one on the right. It took Maribel a minute to get the key to turn, but after jiggling it a bit, it finally did, and she pushed open the door.

The apartment was not quite as grand as Maribel's. The sitting room was smaller, the windows not as tall, and the molding not as ornate. The sofa was covered with throw pillows in exotic prints and draped with a richly colored paisley shawl. Opposite it was a chair upholstered in a bold black-and-white zebra-striped print.

Paintings and various pieces of art nearly covered the walls, and the faint odor of oil paint hung in the air. Soapstone carvings of various animals—elephants, giraffes, and rhinos—were displayed on a small table. Pen picked one up. The stone was cold and smooth in her hands.

"These are lovely," she said.

"Odile brought those back from Africa a couple of years ago," Maribel said. "Her trip there was such a bright spot in her life." Maribel's voice caught in her throat. "This is all quite dreadful."

She dashed a finger under her eyes. "I suppose we should get back to business. I'll check her desk first," she said, gesturing toward a small alcove where a delicate wood escritoire was nestled.

Maribel opened the drawers one by one, then sighed in frustration.

"Nothing," she said, swiping a hand across her forehead. "No address book, no letters, nothing at all, I'm afraid. It's almost as if Odile had no life before she took the teaching position here."

Penelope wandered into the small kitchen, where a simple wooden table with iron hairpin legs was pushed against one wall. An oddly shaped ceramic bowl sat on top.

The room was tidy except for a half-full bottle of wine

on the counter and several plates, some cutlery and a wine-glass in the dish drainer. The plates and cutlery were already dry but water still beaded on the wineglass.

Poor Odile, Pen thought—having her dinner and not re-alizing it would be her last meal. The idea gave her goose bumps.

"That's that," Maribel said when Penelope rejoined her and Mabel. "There's nothing here. I looked again just to be sure."

"Perhaps Odile kept her contacts on her cell?" Pen said. "I don't see a phone here so I assume she took it with her to the Open Book. If she had it in her pocket, surely someone at the hospital will find it."

"Let's hope," Maribel said with a grim expression. "I'm beginning to think we knew even less about Odile than we realized."

The next morning, Penelope pulled the covers over her head to stifle the noise that had woken her. What was it anyway? It sounded like ringing.

Ringing! She threw back the covers and grabbed her phone.

"Hello?"

"It's Beryl. Did I wake you?"

Penelope pried open one eye and glanced at the clock on her bedside table. It was eight o'clock. Beryl would think her a slug if she knew she was still in bed.

"No, no. I'm up. I've been up for ages."

"You don't sound like it," Beryl said testily.

Beryl was Pen's older sister. Under normal circum-stances, Beryl would be at home in Connecticut in her massive Georgian house with its exquisite landscaping and décor that had once been featured in *House and Home* magazine, most likely heading out to her Pilates class, followed by an afternoon spent planning her next dinner party.

But these were not normal circumstances. Beryl's husband, Magnus, had been arrested for perpetrating a large-scale Ponzi scheme, and Beryl had fled to England to be with Penelope, lick her wounds, and evade the tabloid reporters who had flocked to her house.

Thanks to Penelope's contacts, the Atelier Classique in London had secured a work visa for Beryl and had hired her to model clothes for their customers. Penelope had found her an apartment over Icing on the Cake on the high street, where Beryl complained the aroma drifting up from the bakery alone was causing her to gain weight.

Beryl reminded Penelope that they had planned to call their mother that evening.

"You won't forget, will you?" Beryl said.

"Nope."

"I'm off, then. I'm catching the eight-thirty train to London. Bye."

Pen sighed and clicked off the call. She sat on the edge of the bed and shivered as her feet hit the cold floor. Mrs. Danvers, her black-and-white tuxedo cat, had been sleeping at the end of the bed and meowed her displeasure at having her sleep disrupted.

The cottage, loaned to Penelope by Mabel, was on the high street not far from the Open Book. It was what was known as a two up, two down. Two of the rooms were upstairs—a bedroom and a spare she sometimes used as a study—along with a small bathroom that boasted a rather unreliable supply of hot water. The ground floor consisted of the other two rooms—a kitchen and a small sitting room.

Pen dressed quickly in a pair of leggings and a long red sweater she'd bought at the Knit Wit shop in town. When it came to clothes, she opted for comfort over style, unlike Beryl, who was always perfectly put together and was constantly urging Penelope to update her wardrobe. So far, Penelope had been able to resist her sister's attempts to take her shopping. The outfits she'd been forced to buy for the Duke and Duchess of Upper Chumley-on-Stoke's wedding festivities were pushed to the back of her closet in favor of her old standbys.

Mrs. Danvers accompanied Pen down the stairs to the kitchen, where the ancient Aga was belching out much appreciated warmth. Pen plugged in her electric tea kettle and popped some bread into the toaster.

She checked Mrs. Danvers's food and water bowls as the cat wove in and out between her legs. There was a bit of kibble left in the food bowl, but Penelope topped it up anyway. Mrs. Danvers disliked it when her bowl wasn't completely full.

Her tea made and her toast buttered, Pen sat at the rough farmhouse table and ate while she flipped through the latest issue of *Tatler*, which she'd picked up at Tesco when she last did her shopping.

There was a small item in one of the gossip columns on Charlotte with an "inside source" claiming to know that the Worthingtons were expecting a girl. Penelope knew that wasn't true—Charlotte and Worthington had decided against finding out the baby's gender before the birth.

Penelope finished her breakfast, cleaned up the dishes, and got ready to leave for the Open Book. Her laptop was on the table in the sitting room.

The sitting room was Pen's favorite place in the small cottage. It had a large open fireplace flanked by bookcases, rough wooden beams across the low ceiling, and a bay window that afforded her a view of the high street.

She enjoyed sitting in front of the window and watching the activity on the street. She'd come to recognize a number of her neighbors—Mr. Patel, who walked his dog every day before heading to work; Mrs. Clark, who opened the door opposite Pen's in her bathrobe to collect the morning paper; and Mr. Harrison, who passed by at precisely seven fifty every morning on his way to the train.

The window was streaming with rain today, and it looked more like dusk outside than morning. Pen longed to make a fire in the fireplace and curl up on the sofa with a book, but she wanted to set up a new display at the Open Book and she also wanted to talk to Mabel about the store newsletter that was due to go out soon.

Pen reluctantly donned her coat, picked up her laptop and tote bag, and headed out. She closed the door to her cottage and unfurled the umbrella that she'd purchased at Marks and Spencer in London. A gust of wind immediately grabbed hold of it and threatened to turn it inside out. She clung to it as she headed down the high street. She had purchased a used car upon her arrival in England, but it had unfortunately been totaled in her attempt to escape a killer. She thought it a small price to pay; but on mornings like these, she really missed her MINI.

She was wet and cold by the time she reached the Open Book. She glanced at the front window of the shop as she headed toward the door. She'd created a display of Regency romance novels arranged around an antique tea set and was quite pleased with the results. As she stood and admired it, she noticed that the glass in one of the diamond-shaped windowpanes was missing and a piece of cardboard had been taped over it.

"My sainted aunt," Mabel said when Penelope walked into the Open Book. "You look as if you're half drowned. Come in and get warm."

Penelope stuck her umbrella in the stand by the door, took off her coat, shook it, and hung it on the coat-tree.

She rubbed her hands together. "I'm freezing, too," she said as she approached the counter.

"Hot tea is coming," Figgy shouted from the tea shop. Moments later she trundled a tea cart over to the counter. There was a fresh pot of steaming tea and a motley collection of mugs, along with a plate of Chelsea buns.

"You are a lifesaver," Pen said, filling a mug and wrapping her cold hands around it. She took a cautious sip—steam was still rising from the cup.

"What happened to the window?" she said to Mabel. "It looks like one of the panes was broken."

Mabel made a face. "The pane was broken when I came in. The glass was scattered all over the carpet. The work of some young hooligans with nothing better to occupy them, no doubt. They're not content with saving their mischief for Guy Fawkes Day. I've called the police to make a report for the insurance. They'll send Constable Cuthbert around, I should imagine, although there's not much he'll be able to do. Fortunately, nothing else was damaged and nothing was stolen."

The front door opened and a cold breeze swept through the store. Several wet leaves blew across the threshold and stuck to the carpet. Penelope was surprised to see Detective Brodie Maguire walk in.

"Looks like they've sent the big guns," Mabel said. "I wonder why." She winked at Penelope.

"I don't think he's just here to talk about our broken window," Figgy said. She looked at Penelope with a knowing smile.

Penelope felt her face getting hot and she took a sip of her tea to hide it.

Maguire was wearing an anorak over jeans, a sweater, and a button-down shirt with a slightly frayed collar. His hair was wet from the rain.

He wasn't really handsome but had a pleasant and welcoming face that Penelope found quite attractive.

Maguire smiled as he approached the counter. "Someone called about a broken pane?" He gestured toward the front window.

"Yes, but I didn't expect them to send you," Mabel said. "I was thinking they'd send Constable Cuthbert around to take the report." She picked up a pen and began to fiddle with it. "Now I feel foolish for calling at all, but I will need the report for the insurance company. I didn't mean to cause such a bother."

"Please." Maguire held up a hand. "It's no bother. I was going to come by anyway. We got a report of a teacher from the Oakwood School who passed away in hospital. It appears the death was unexpected, so I thought I'd gather a little more information. I understand it was here that Odile Fontaine collapsed last night?"

"Yes. We assumed she was ill," Penelope said, hoping the red in her face had subsided.

"That's probably all it was," Maguire said, leaning against the counter. "But it seems she wasn't under the care of a doctor. We'll know more after the autopsy results and the toxicology report come back."

"Toxicology report?" Pen said with a frown.

Maguire smiled. "Standard procedure in a case like this."

Pen noticed that he was eyeing the Chelsea buns Figgy had brought over.

"Would you like one?" she said, offering him the plate.

"I wouldn't mind." Maguire's expression was sheepish. "I haven't had any breakfast yet." He reached out and picked up a bun.

He took a bite and was silent for a moment as he chewed.

"Can you walk me through what happened last night?" he said finally. "You served wine, I understand?"

"Yes," Mabel said.

"Who poured the wine?" Maguire licked some icing off his fingers.

Figgy looked startled. "I did. Why?" Her tone was defensive.

"Just curious," Maguire said. "I'm trying to get a picture of the sequence of events."

He was eyeing the remaining bun. Penelope held the plate out.

"Here—please have this one if you'd like. We've already had some."

"Was Ms. Fontaine feeling ill when she arrived?" Maguire said, picking up the last Chelsea bun and biting into it.

"Not that we know of, but she did complain of feeling dizzy and having a headache at one point."

"And then she collapsed?" Maguire said.

"Yes." Pen nodded. She snapped her fingers. "Just like that. We were all quite startled. I called an ambulance immediately."

"I'm sure there's nothing sinister about it," Maguire said, turning to Mabel. "Now tell me about your window."

Penelope went off to work on a display she was putting together of art books with Odile's *You Can Paint* prominently showcased. She'd ordered a palette and a brush to be the centerpiece of the display.

She was looking for a way to prop up the palette when she felt a hand on her shoulder and turned around. It was Maguire.

"Hi, there," Pen said.

"Hi, there, yourself," Maguire said, his face crinkling in a smile. "I heard about that woman collapsing here last night and I wanted to make sure you were okay."

"I'm fine," Pen said. "A little sad, maybe, even though I hadn't known Odile long."

Maguire brandished a small notebook. "I got all the details from Mabel about the broken window. I'll make sure a patrol car comes by from time to time tonight. That ought to deter any young punks out for mischief."

"Thanks."

"Unfortunately, I have to go." Maguire squeezed Penelope's shoulder. "I'll call you later."

FOUR

❧

Penelope had a bit of a lift in her step that afternoon as she left the Open Book after her book group for the taxi that was waiting at the curb. She was headed to the Oakwood School to conduct her first seminar on Gothic literature. She'd been preparing her notes for a week and had them tucked safely in her tote bag.

She had a few butterflies batting around in her stomach, but she told herself that she knew the material and she knew teenage girls—she'd been one herself, albeit a number of years ago.

Her taxi driver was even more ancient than his cab with a bald, dome-shaped head. His ears stuck out and had gray hair bristling from them. Pen had learned that the residents of Chumley referred to him as Mad Max, although she couldn't imagine why.

"Where to?" he said in a voice hoarse from cigarette smoking.

"The Oakwood School for Girls," Pen said as she settled into the back seat.

"Posh place," the driver said. "Bunch of toffs, if you ask me." He gave a gurgling cough. "I've driven a couple of those lasses to the train station and such. I can't say I much care for them. I've learned that the more money people have in their pocket, the less likely they are to share it."

So, the girls were poor tippers, Pen thought. She smiled, hoping that would be a sufficient comment.

The driver gave a long rattling cough. "You're that American, aren't you?"

He made it sound like an accusation, but by now Pen had become used to being seen as something of an oddity in Upper Chumley-on-Stoke, where many of the residents hadn't ventured as far as London even though it was only an hour's train ride away.

The driver kept up a sedate pace and Pen was becoming impatient when they finally left the town behind and were headed into open country.

At that point, the high street petered out into a single lane, barely wider than a footpath, bordered on both sides with hedgerows. The fields beyond were beginning to turn brown, and sheep stood in clusters, picking at the dying grass.

They had almost reached the school when they encountered a van with *J & W Electrical* painted on the side coming from the opposite direction. The taxi slowly came to a halt with a loud grinding of gears, then the driver carefully pulled off the road as far as he could. Penelope closed her eyes as the van squeaked past them with barely inches to spare.

Finally they reached the gates of the Oakwood School. Pen directed the driver to the administration building, where he pulled over and shifted the car into park. She settled the fare, being sure to include a generous tip, tucked her tote bag under her arm, and got out.

Walking into the school as a lecturer, granted a temporary one, as opposed to simply a visitor seemed different to Pen. She had a feeling of belonging—the same feeling she got at the Open Book. She found herself humming as she walked up the steps to the door.

Maribel's secretary, Tina Resse, nicknamed T. Rex by the students, was at her desk. Pen was again in awe of the perfect placement of her stapler, tape dispenser, and pencil sharpener, all precisely lined up perpendicular to a stack of folders.

Tina looked up when she heard Pen walk in.

"Penelope," she said in rather icy tones. "I have some forms for you to fill out right here." She tapped the folder at the top of the stack.

She opened the file, took out several sheets of paper, and fastened them to a clipboard. She handed it, along with a pen, to Penelope.

Penelope had met Tina months ago when she had been poking around, trying to find out who had killed Worthington's former girlfriend. She had let Tina believe that she was a reporter from *Tatler* in order to get her to talk. She cringed now, thinking about it. She didn't blame Tina for being somewhat frosty toward her.

Penelope filled out the papers, signed them, and handed them back to Tina, who acknowledged them with a raised eyebrow.

"Everyone is gathering for an assembly in the Stewart-Calthorpe Assembly Hall. I believe Ms. Northcott would like you to attend." She gave Penelope a tight smile.

Penelope picked up her tote bag, said good-bye, which was barely acknowledged, and went outside. The quad was bustling with students all streaming in one direction. Penelope joined them as they headed to the assembly hall.

A paved path led from the quad to another cluster of buildings. Unlike the other buildings, the Stewart-Calthorpe Assembly Hall was a modern structure that looked as if it would be more at home in a big city than in the midst of ivy-covered buildings.

The lobby had a soaring ceiling with a large crystal chandelier hanging in the center. The space was filled with clusters of chattering girls in plaid skirts and gray blazers, who were slowly moving toward the door to the auditorium.

Pen followed them and found a seat off to one side. She was slipping off her jacket when someone said, "Excuse me."

Pen smiled and moved her knees out of the way as a pretty blonde with large blue eyes and a lush figure wearing a white uniform began to make her way past. She looked down at Pen and held out a hand.

"Layla Evans." She gestured toward her uniform. "As you can probably guess, I'm the school nurse."

"Penelope Parish. I've been invited to give a seminar on Gothic literature."

Layla smiled and a dimple popped into her right cheek. "Welcome to the Oakwood School."

"Thank you. Are you related to Grady—"

"We're married," Layla said. "Grady is my husband." She smiled again. "Nice to meet you, Penelope." She moved down the row to a vacant seat in the center.

Pen was reading over her notes when another woman slid into the empty seat next to her. She had rather nondescript coloring—hair that was not quite blond and not quite brown—and was wearing a Black Watch tartan kilt and a turtleneck sweater that coordinated with the blue in the plaid.

She smiled rather timidly at Penelope. "I'm Helen Dingley," she said. "English literature."

Penelope introduced herself. "I'm to be the guest lecturer on Gothic literature," she said.

"Oh," Helen's hand flew to her mouth. "You've written *Lady of the Moors*, haven't you?"

Pen nodded.

"I positively adored it," Helen gushed.

Penelope felt her face begin to redden, but just then Maribel walked out onto the stage and tapped the microphone. Slowly the chattering voices faded away and there was only the occasional rustling sound coming from the audience.

As soon as everyone settled down, Maribel cleared her throat and began to address the teachers and students. She led them in a brief prayer, a moment of silence, and then read off a number of notices—the service of dinner would be delayed due to a plumbing problem in the kitchen, there would be a performance by the Oakwood String Quartet that evening at seven o'clock in the assembly hall, and bicycles were not to be ridden on the quad paths.

There was a burst of chatter, and Maribel once again held up a hand for silence. She smiled at the audience and gestured toward where Penelope was sitting.

"I'd like to introduce Penelope Parish, author of *Lady of the Moors*, who has graciously agreed to conduct a seminar on Gothic literature for us." Maribel consulted her notes. "There will be a book signing in the Jane Austen Room tomorrow at eleven o'clock. All are welcome."

The audience clapped politely.

"And now I must impart some terribly sad news," Maribel said in suitably grave tones. "Unfortunately, Odile Fontaine, who has taught art at the Oakwood School for five years, was taken ill last night. She was rushed to the hospital but unfortunately she passed away."

A low moan went through the audience. Maribel had been right—Odile had obviously been well-liked, Pen thought.

"We don't have any details yet about a memorial service but we will let you know when we do."

After a suitable moment of silence, Maribel continued.

"I'm afraid that's not all the bad news I have for you today." She paused, wet her lips, and continued. "The Oakwood School's precious first edition of Jane Austen's *Pride and Prejudice* is still missing."

The noise from the audience began as a murmur and then rose in volume as the girls whispered among themselves.

"If anyone has any information that might prove helpful, please contact me or anyone in the administration. I'm hoping the culprit will come forward soon and spare us the necessity of going to the police. I'd like to keep this among ourselves if at all possible."

Helen leaned over and tapped Penelope on the arm.

"Serves them right," she said, her mouth drawn down in a bitter line. "Last time I saw it I noticed signs of foxing— brown spots—on some of the pages." She clamped her lips together. "And you know what causes that, don't you?"

"Um, no," Penelope said. "What?"

"Moisture." Helen nodded her head in satisfaction. "And humidity. It's mildew, you see, caused by being stored in the wrong conditions." She shook her head. "I told Maribel that that plexiglass case in the Jane Austen Room was going to be a problem. And now look what's happened. The book is missing."

Penelope failed to see the relationship between mildew and a book going missing, but she didn't say anything.

"The volume needs to be taken to an experienced restorer for treatment."

Helen would have gone on, but Maribel was motioning for everyone to get to their feet. They sang the Oakwood School song as they filed out of the auditorium.

The quad was full of laughing, gossiping girls as Penelope crossed it, headed toward Corbyn Hall. Her palms were a bit damp. This was to be her first lecture and she was slightly nervous. She reminded herself that she knew her subject and had nothing to fear. These girls were well-brought-up young ladies and weren't likely to be throwing spitballs like Billy White used to do in her high school English class.

Penelope squared her shoulders as she walked through the door of the ivy-covered building. She found the room assigned to her easily enough. It was a cozy space furnished with several sofas with worn slipcovers, two slightly sagging armchairs, and one upholstered straight-backed chair without arms. She decided she would take that one for herself. It would be hard to convey a sense of authority while being slowly swallowed by an overstuffed couch.

She took out her notes and set them on a small table that she pulled alongside her chair.

A bell rang somewhere in the building; and suddenly a handful of girls burst through the door, curiosity obvious on their faces. They arrayed themselves on the sofas and chairs and sat staring at Penelope, clearly appraising her.

Penelope felt like a specimen under a microscope with their intense scrutiny trained on her. She was relieved when a second bell sounded and she could begin her lecture.

She was about to open her mouth when another student skidded through the door and came to an abrupt stop. She didn't seem in the least bit perturbed about being late.

Pen judged her to be close to eighteen. She had wavy blond hair that fell over her shoulders and green eyes. There was a dark red leaf caught in her hair. She had an athletic build that spoke of sports like field hockey, swimming, and riding.

She smiled at Penelope; dropped her backpack, which landed with a loud thud; and took a seat on the sofa, her posture suggesting she was completely at ease.

Penelope cleared her throat. It was now or never.

"Welcome," she said. Her voice quavered slightly but then got stronger as she continued. "I'm Penelope Parish and I'm the author of the *Lady of the Moors,* a modern-day Gothic novel." A soft murmur went around the room. "Why don't we all introduce ourselves?" She pointed to the girl who had arrived late. "Let's start with you."

The girl gave a slow smile and licked her bottom lip.

"I'm Nicola Hyde-White." She rolled her eyes. "Or perhaps I should say the Honorable Nicola Hyde-White."

She seemed quite full of herself, Pen thought. But she supposed that's what having a title, even if it was only "the honorable," did to you.

They continued around the room until everyone had introduced themselves and then settled in as Penelope began the lecture.

She started with Horace Walpole and explained that he wrote the very first Gothic novel, *The Castle of Otranto.* She then moved on to the required elements in a Gothic novel.

"Setting and atmosphere are very important," she said.

"Does anyone know what pathetic fallacy is?" She waited a moment but wasn't surprised to see blank faces staring at her. "Pathetic fallacy is giving human emotion to inanimate objects of nature."

Pen walked over to the window and glanced out. "For instance," she said, turning back to the class, "using weather features to reflect a mood, as in 'the somber clouds darkened our mood.'"

The girls nodded.

"That's why in Gothic literature you will so often find angry winds, threatening clouds, and menacing skies. It helps to set the mood of a scene and gives Gothics that subtle air of danger lurking just around the corner."

Penelope picked up her notes. "Consider, for instance, this line from the great Gothic novel *Rebecca* by Daphne du Maurier. 'A lilac had mated with a copper beech and to bind them yet more closely to one another the malevolent ivy, always an enemy to grace, had thrown her tendrils about the pair and made them prisoners.'"

Penelope was pleased to see one or two of the girls begin to shiver, their arms wrapped across their chests.

Penelope smiled. "That certainly sets the tone, doesn't it?"

"Excuse me," a masculine voice said from the doorway.

The girls' heads swiveled in unison in that direction. A man was slouched in the doorway, leaning against the doorjamb, one leg casually crossed over the other.

He was young. Penelope thought he must still be in his twenties. He had dark hair left long enough to curl and flop onto his forehead, a dimple in his right cheek, and an impish grin. He was wearing black jeans and a black turtleneck.

He looked at Penelope. "I wanted to say hello and to welcome you." He stuck out his thumb and gestured down the hall. "I'm Adrian Mabry. Music." He tossed his head to get the hair that had fallen onto his forehead out of his eyes.

Penelope introduced herself.

"I won't keep you," Adrian said and turned to go. "Welcome to the Oakwood School for Girls, Penelope Parish. And if you ever need anything, let me know." He winked and headed back down the hall.

The girls giggled and began to murmur. Penelope caught a few of the words—*cute . . . hot . . . dreamy.*

She noticed the girl who had introduced herself as Nicola had languidly crossed her legs and rearranged her plaid skirt so that it was well above her knees.

She smiled to herself. It seemed as if the girls had developed a crush on the very attractive music teacher. Penelope had to admit she didn't blame them.

Shortly afterward the bell rang and the girls jumped to their feet, gathered up their things, stuffed them into their backpacks, and made their way out the door. All except for Nicola, who continued to lounge on the sofa.

Penelope looked at her and raised her eyebrows.

Nicola pulled a strand of hair over her shoulder and began to chew on it.

"Do you mind if I stay here for a few minutes?" She gave Pen a winning smile. "I'm meeting a friend in ten minutes and I don't want to wait outside." She pulled her backpack onto her lap and sat with her arms around it.

"I don't mind but what if there's another class coming in?"

Nicola shook her head. "There isn't. Yours was the only lecture scheduled for the room today. I checked."

Penelope said good-bye, stuffed her notes into her tote bag, and left. Nicola had left her with a weird feeling—

there was something odd about how she had been acting—
but Pen couldn't quite put her finger on it.

A glazier was at the Open Book, fixing the broken pane
in the front window, when Penelope returned from
the Oakwood School later that afternoon.

Mabel was behind the counter watching, her reading
glasses pushed up on top of her head.

"How did your lecture go?" she said when Pen walked in.

"I think it went well," Pen said, slipping off her jacket
and hanging it on the coat-tree. "They seemed interested."
She smiled and shook her head. "Of course they were far
more interested when the cute music teacher showed up to
say hello and welcome."

Mabel laughed. "Some things never change, I guess. I
remember having a crush on my maths teacher. I hated the
subject but I adored him."

Pen tilted her head toward the back of the store. "I'm
going to get some writing done unless you need me for
something?" She raised her eyebrows in question.

Mabel made a shooing motion with her hand. "Go on.
I'll be fine. It's been a slow morning." She sighed.

Penelope headed toward her writing room, stopping
briefly to straighten a couple of books on a display table
and prop one back up on the stand.

The small room Mabel had given her for writing was
dark when she opened the door. She felt along the wall for
the light switch and flicked it on, then set her laptop on the
table, opened it, and powered it up.

Where was she? She read through the last few pages

she'd written on her third manuscript and glanced at her notes.

In the next scene to be written, her protagonist, Eirene, was working for the enigmatic scientist Mr. Bloodworth at his house, deep in the dark and shadowy Maine woods. Bloodworth was researching human gene mutations and Eirene had taken the job as his assistant in an effort to get away from her nasty stepmother.

Bloodworth had suddenly taken to locking the door to the laboratory, which was odd. He'd never done that before. Eirene was determined to find out what he was hiding and on a dark night, with howling winds and only a flashlight to light the way, Eirene . . .

Pen stopped there. Dark night and howling winds? Was that too much of a cliché? It certainly added to the atmosphere of menace, which was what she'd intended. Pen chewed on a ragged cuticle. Finally, she decided to leave it in. Bettina, her editor, would tell her if it was really too over-the-top. She could imagine Bettina's e-mail.

Darling, surely you can come up with something
a little less . . . hackneyed than the proverbial dark
and stormy night?

After an hour, Penelope leaned back in her chair, rolled her shoulders, and took a deep breath. She cracked the knuckles of her right hand and then her left and looked at what she'd written. She was right in the middle of a scene. Should she stop now? She remembered what Hemingway supposedly said—that you should stop when you know what's going to happen next and then you'd never be stuck.

Penelope wasn't so sure about the not getting stuck part

but the method did make a certain amount of sense. She hit save, closed the document, powered off her computer, and shut the lid.

She felt her energy flagging and thought a cup of Figgy's excellent Earl Grey tea might revive her along with a taste of whatever goodies Figgy had prepared that day.

She was pushing back her chair when there was a tap on the door. It opened and Mabel appeared in the crack.

"Detective Maguire is here. He said he wants to speak to us."

"Maybe he has some news," Penelope said as she and Mabel headed toward the front of the store.

Maguire was leaning on the counter, flipping through one of the books Mabel had stacked there.

He looked up and his face brightened when he saw Penelope. He closed the book he'd been looking at and put it back on the pile.

"Why don't we have a cup of tea," Mabel said, shepherding them toward the tea shop. "You look like you could use a good cuppa," she said, glancing at Maguire.

He rubbed his hands together. "That would be brilliant. The wind has an edge to it today."

Two ladies sat at one of the tables, nursing cups of Darjeeling and picking at a plate of shortbread cookies.

Mabel chose the table farthest away from them and pulled out a chair. They had barely sat down when Figgy bustled over with a tray of cups and saucers, a steaming pot of tea, and slices of lemon drizzle cake.

Penelope noticed Maguire's eyes light up. "You are a lifesaver," he said. "Lunch was a butty out of the machine. It was so bad I tossed it in the bin after two bites."

"I'll be mother, shall I?" Mabel said, using the colloquial expression that meant she would pour the tea. She passed the filled cups around. "I assume you have some news about Odile Fontaine?"

Maguire took a slice of cake and broke off a piece. "Yes. We've gotten some results from our tests back. I'm afraid this has turned into a murder investigation."

Penelope and Mabel gasped.

"Oh, dear," Mabel said. "How tragic."

"What? How?" Penelope said, putting down her teacup. "We thought she was simply ill."

"According to the medical examiner, she was poisoned."

Mabel paused with her cup halfway to her mouth. "Dear me."

"What kind of poison?" Pen said.

Maguire pulled his notebook from his pocket and flipped through the pages.

"Deadly nightshade," he read from his notes. "It's some sort of plant."

"Also known as belladonna," Mabel said.

Maguire looked at her sharply.

Mabel held up a hand and laughed. "And that's all I know. I'm innocent, I can assure you."

"Sorry." Maguire ducked his head. "I didn't mean . . ."

"I know you didn't," Mabel said, pushing the plate of lemon drizzle cake toward him. "Here—have another piece."

"I'm afraid I do need to ask you some questions," Maguire said. "I understand you went to Odile's apartment the night she died."

"Yes," Pen said. "We were hoping to find some information about her next of kin."

"Did you touch things? Move them around?"

"We looked through her desk," Mabel said. "But we didn't move anything."

Maguire scribbled in his notebook. "Did you go into any of the other rooms?" He pushed his empty plate away and leaned his arms on the table.

Penelope and Mabel exchanged a glance. "I went into the kitchen," Pen said.

"Do you mind describing what you saw?"

"Nothing much. Just the usual things—a table and chairs, some dishes on the drainboard on the counter."

"Dishes?" Maguire raised an eyebrow.

"Yes. A couple of plates and a wineglass."

"Anything else?"

Penelope and Mabel exchanged a glance again.

Penelope shrugged. "Not really."

"I'd best see about those customers waiting at the counter." Mabel pushed her chair back.

"And I should get back to work," Maguire said after Mabel had left. "We have another case on our hands as well as this one."

Pen gasped. "Not another murder?" Maybe sleepy Upper Chumley-on-Stoke wasn't so sleepy after all.

Maguire shook his head. "No, thank goodness. Just as big a headache though. A break-in at one of those big houses in Birnam Woods—that new development just outside of town. Fortunately, no one was hurt but some jewelry was stolen and the owners are demanding immediate action." He sighed. "And immediate results." He stood up.

Penelope walked Maguire to the door, where he smiled and squeezed her hand.

"Let's try to grab a bite soon, okay?" he said. "I'll try to sneak a couple of minutes away from the station."

Pen stood at the door and watched as Maguire disappeared down the street.

"I'm worried," Figgy said later, coming up to Pen as she was shelving some of the books that had been left out on the tables.

Penelope paused with her hand on a copy of Charlotte Davenport's latest romance. "Oh? Why?"

"I get the impression . . . oh, I know it sounds ridiculous, but I have the feeling that Detective Maguire suspects me of poisoning Odile."

Pen gave a bark of laughter, which she quickly stifled. "You? Why on earth would he suspect you?"

"I don't know." Figgy chewed on her bottom lip. "I suppose I'm imagining things."

Mabel approached them with an armload of books.

"What are you two gossiping about?" She smiled.

"Figgy is imagining herself as a suspect in Odile's murder."

Mabel snorted. "What on earth has given you that idea?"

Figgy shrugged. "All those questions the other day about who poured the wine. I suppose I feel guilty since I was the one filling the glasses. I feel as if I did something wrong."

"It couldn't possibly be your fault," Mabel said.

Mabel put the books she was carrying down on a table and leaned against it. She winced.

"Are you okay?" Pen said.

"Fine, fine." Mabel waved a hand. "A bit of arthritis is all. It acts up when the weather turns damp." She looked toward the front of the shop. "I suspect we'll be having some rain later tonight."

Figgy looked at Penelope. "A penny for your thoughts."

Penelope came to with a jerk. "I've been thinking," she said. "I have a theory." Both Mabel and Figgy turned to stare at her.

"About Odile's murder?" Figgy said, fiddling with a loose button on her dress.

Penelope nodded. "Yes. Maguire asked us what we saw when we went to Odile's apartment."

Mabel and Figgy both cocked their heads. "Go on," Mabel said.

"When I was in Odile's kitchen, I noticed some dishes on the drainboard. There were a couple of plates and some silverware, which were dry. But there was also a wineglass and it was still slightly wet."

Mabel frowned. "Why is that significant?"

"Because it means Odile must have had a glass of wine before she came to the Open Book. And that's where the killer put the poison—the deadly nightshade."

"And . . . ?" Mabel said.

"Then they washed Odile's glass and left it in the dish drainer, making it look as if she'd had a drink by herself."

Figgy nearly jumped up and down. "That's it," she said. "Odile had a visitor and it was the visitor who poisoned her."

"And by washing her glass, they made it look as if she'd been drinking alone," Pen said, somewhat triumphantly. "And that makes it look as if she had to have been poisoned somewhere else."

"True. She'd hardly have poisoned herself," Mabel said somewhat dryly.

"So she had to have had a visitor," Figgy said. "I wonder if it was the boyfriend. What was his name?"

"Quentin Barnes," Pen said.

Figgy sniffed. "I didn't like the looks of him. Terribly pretentious." She frowned. "But if she'd had a visitor, shouldn't there have been two wineglasses?"

"Yes, if she'd had a glass of wine herself, she certainly would have offered one to her caller," Mabel said.

Penelope felt deflated. "I guess my theory doesn't hold water."

"Or in this case, wine," Figgy said with a giggle.

Penelope wasn't ready to give up on her idea, though.

"Okay, how about this. Odile sits down with the killer and they each have a glass of wine. Odile leaves to come here to the Open Book and the killer goes back and washes out their glass and dries it. They then wash Odile's glass—the one with the poison in it—and leave it in the dish drainer. That makes it look as if Odile was drinking alone."

Figgy tapped her lips with her index finger. "But there would still be fingerprints, wouldn't there?"

"Maybe they wiped the glass clean. Maguire didn't say if they found any prints." Penelope pursed her lips.

"Or they could have worn gloves. One thing I did learn during my career with MI6 is that criminals don't always leave fingerprints scattered all over like they do on television. Sometimes a surface isn't hospitable to prints and some people don't leave any identifiable prints at all because the pads of their fingers have been worn down. Like bricklayers who work with rough material all day or even secretaries who constantly handle paper. Although that most likely wouldn't apply to anyone at the school."

"But what about the taste? Wouldn't Odile have noticed a peculiar taste to the wine?" Figgy wrinkled her nose. "I wonder what that deadly nightshade tastes like? Is it a powder? Or liquid?"

"It comes from a plant," Mabel said. "Let's see." She walked over to one of the shelves, ran her finger along the spines of the books, and pulled one out.

She flipped through the pages. "Here we are," she said, putting on her reading glasses. "It seems that the foliage and the berries of the deadly nightshade plant—known as *Atropa belladonna*—are highly poisonous.

"This is interesting," Mabel said, pointing to a paragraph in the book. "Children have been known to eat the berries because they are sweet. The killer must have used the juice from some berries to poison Odile. She didn't notice because the berries aren't bitter and the wine probably masked the taste." Mabel closed the book.

Figgy shuddered. "How awful."

"Now we just need to find out who Odile's mysterious visitor was," Penelope said brightly.

FIVE

❧

Pen retreated to her writing room and spent another hour working on her book. It was coming along nicely—or so she thought and hoped.

She was finishing a chapter when there was a knock on the door.

"I'm about to close up," Mabel said.

Penelope jumped. "Is it that time already?"

"Six o'clock on the dot."

"I'll be right there," Pen said as she pulled her tote bag toward her. "I just have to get my things together."

Mabel smiled. "No rush."

Penelope powered down her laptop, closed the lid, and slipped it into her tote bag. It caught on something and wouldn't slide in all the way.

What on earth? Penelope stuck her hand into her tote bag and felt around. Her computer appeared to be stuck on a rubber band wrapped around a stack of paper.

Penelope mentally slapped herself on the forehead. It was Odile's manuscript. She'd been carrying it around with her all this time. No wonder her bag had been so heavy. Guilt washed over her. She hadn't read more than a couple of chapters. She'd promised Odile she would read it and, even though Odile was dead, she felt she needed to make good on her promise. She vowed to go through a few more chapters as soon as she got home.

Mabel was waiting by the door, her keys in hand, when Penelope emerged from her writing room.

"I didn't mean to keep you waiting," Pen said as she grabbed her coat from the coat stand. She glanced toward the darkened tearoom. "Has Figgy already gone?"

"She just left." Mabel flicked out the last of the lights and locked the door behind her.

Pen said good night and began the short walk home. The sun had disappeared below the horizon and the streetlamps had come on, creating a mellow glow.

The door to Pierre's Restaurant opened and delicious aromas redolent with garlic and herbs drifted out. Pen's stomach grumbled.

She paused in front of Francesca and Annabelle's boutique to admire a chunky knit sweater and then again, farther down the street, in front of Icing on the Cake, where one of the clerks was pulling nearly empty trays of pastries out of the window.

With the sun having disappeared, the night was getting colder. Pen flipped her collar up and quickened her steps and was grateful when she reached her cottage.

Mrs. Danvers was waiting by the door. She appeared to be in a pleasant mood, allowing Penelope to scratch under her chin and even run her hand down Mrs. Danvers's back.

"It's good to be home," Penelope said to the cat as she took off her coat and hung it up.

There was a sizable remnant of a log in the fireplace. Penelope added some kindling and set it alight. Within minutes the flames were licking at the log and Penelope knew that soon it would be glowing and sending warmth into the room.

Mrs. Danvers followed Pen out to the kitchen, where Penelope fed her and topped off her water bowl. Then her thoughts turned to her own dinner. She opened the refrigerator and stared with dismay at the contents. She really needed to make a run to Tesco one of these days.

There was a container of leftover lamb rogan josh from Kebabs and Curries that she hadn't finished. She popped it into the microwave and got out a fork while she waited.

The timer dinged and Penelope took the container into the sitting room, where the fire was now burning brightly. She curled up on the sofa and reached for her tote bag. Guilt over dismissing Odile's manuscript so summarily had stayed with her and she pulled out the sheaf of papers.

She removed the rubber band and began reading as she absentmindedly ate her dinner.

The manuscript was a romance set in an all-girls school that was a thinly disguised version of the Oakwood School. The prose was florid and Penelope found herself laughing at descriptions like "when he whipped off his shirt, she noticed his chest was as hard as flint" and "her womanliness overflowed the bodice of her dress."

Penelope was finding it all so amusing that she didn't realize she was already nearly a third of the way through the manuscript. The romance in Odile's book was an affair between the philosophy teacher and the head's secretary at the fictional Briarwood School. There were a lot of passionate clutches in darkened doorways and sneaking around under the cover of night.

The villain of the story—because there always has to be an antagonist—was the art teacher who knew a little too much and stood between the two lovers, preventing them from being together.

Penelope stacked the pages together again and put them down on the coffee table. She would finish the rest of it later.

She continued to think about Odile's manuscript as she was throwing out her empty container from Kebabs and Curries. Odile's writing was not particularly creative—all her creative skill had gone into her paintings—so Pen wondered where Odile had gotten the idea for the story. The girls' school had clearly been modeled after the real one where Odile taught.

But what if other parts of the story were also based on reality—the philosophy teacher and the secretary in love and cheating on their spouses, the art teacher who knew too much?

Had Odile possibly stumbled upon something that had gotten her killed?

Penelope had just finished wiping down the kitchen counter when her doorbell rang. She glanced at the clock. It must be Beryl.

Mrs. Danvers showed scant interest as Penelope headed toward the door and flung it open.

Beryl stepped into the sitting room. "Oh, good, you've got a fire going. I'm quite chilled."

She slipped off her coat—a luxurious camel-colored wool that matched her dress—and went to stand in front of the fire.

Beryl sniffed. "What's that peculiar smell?"

Penelope took a tentative sniff. "It must be the leftover rogan josh I heated up for dinner."

Beryl shuddered. "I love it, but"—she patted her stomach—"it gives me terrible indigestion. Besides—the calories!"

Beryl stepped away from the fire, moved one of Penelope's throw pillows, and took a seat on the sofa. She kicked off her black suede pumps.

"My feet are killing me." She reached down and massaged the arch of her right foot.

Penelope studied her sister's face. Something was wrong—she could tell by Beryl's expression—the furrowed line between her brows and the downward turn of her mouth. Normally, Beryl avoided making any facial expressions that might ultimately lead to wrinkles or sagging skin.

Pen perched on the other end of the sofa. "What's up?"

"Do you have any wine?" Beryl said.

"That sort of day, huh?" Pen said as she got to her feet.

Beryl was silent as Penelope made her way to the kitchen. She opened the refrigerator, poked around amid the contents, and pulled out a bottle of white wine with a couple of swallows left in it. She couldn't remember when she'd opened it—the last time Maguire came to dinner perhaps?

She poured it into a glass, carried it out to the sitting room, and handed it to Beryl.

Beryl took a sip and made a face. "What vintage is this?"

Penelope laughed. "I think it was grape juice as of yesterday."

"Tastes like it," Beryl said, but she took another sip. "We promised to call Mother this evening, remember."

"No changing the subject." Pen shook a finger at her sister. "We can call her in a bit. But I know something is bothering you, so out with it." Pen took a seat again. "What's up?"

Beryl sighed loudly and fiddled with the ends of her Hermès scarf.

"Yvette informed us today that she is closing Atelier Classique in London and opening up shop in Paris instead."

"Oh, no!"

Beryl swallowed the last of the wine. "I will have to find a new job or else I will have to go home and face the mess Magnus made of our life." Her lips twisted into a bitter line. "Perhaps something can still be salvaged."

"Will you be able to keep your house?"

Beryl shrugged. "I don't know. I doubt it." She buried her face in her hands. "Oh, Pen, what am I going to do?"

"I'm sure you'll find another job." Pen thought for a minute. "What about those advertisements for Molton Brown soap you were being considered for?"

"It's been put on hold for now. Something about the new president at the ad agency reviewing everything."

"Something else will come along," Pen said soothingly.

"But I'd need any other employer to sponsor me for a work visa and I'm not qualified for much of anything. Modeling clothes for Atelier Classique is about all I'm good for."

"I'm sure you're good for more than that," Penelope said, going over to sit next to her sister. She patted Beryl on the back.

"I hope so," Beryl sniffed.

* * *

Today's your big day," Mabel said when Penelope arrived at the Open Book the next morning after a brisk walk from her cottage. "Your book signing at the school."

"If anyone shows up," Pen said. "I thought you might need some help packing up the books."

Mabel picked up her mug and took a sip of tea. "The books are packed and ready to go." She pointed to some cartons stacked by the counter.

"You didn't move those cartons yourself!" Pen said.

"Goodness, no. Laurence helped me." Mabel motioned toward the back of the store, where Brimble, ensconced in an armchair, was thumbing through a book.

"Maribel said she'd send Grady Evans to pick them up," Pen said. "He's the young man who brought the supplies for Odile's wine and paint night."

Penelope had her coat on and was about to call for a taxi to take her to the Oakwood School when the door burst open and Gladys stumbled across the threshold. Her normally ruddy face was blanched a pale white and her eyes were wide and staring like a frightened horse's.

She stood gasping for breath in front of the counter, her mouth moving but no words coming out.

"What is it, Gladys?" Mabel said. "Has something happened?"

Gladys gave a low moan and swayed slightly.

"You'd better sit down," Pen said, rushing over to the stricken woman. She took Gladys's arm and led her to a chair. "Put your head down if you feel faint."

"What on earth has happened?" Mabel said, coming out from behind the counter.

Gladys moaned again.

"Are you ill?" Pen said.

Gladys shook her head.

"Is it your husband? Is Bruce ill?" Mabel said.

Gladys shook her head again.

"Good heavens, woman! Let's have it, then. What's wrong?" said Brimble, who had come over to see what the commotion was about. He looked irritated.

Gladys took a shuddering breath and clenched a handful of her skirt in both fists.

"Someone's thrown a rock through me window," she said finally.

"The window of the butcher shop?" Mabel said, sounding incredulous.

Gladys nodded.

"Who would do something like that?" Penelope said.

Penelope looked at Gladys, but Gladys's glance slid away from hers and she began fidgeting with her wedding ring, turning it around and around on her finger.

Since it was obvious that Gladys was no longer in any danger of fainting and unlikely to need heroic efforts at resuscitation, Brimble clearly became bored and wandered off to the Open Book's selection of history tomes.

"Have you called the police?" Mabel said.

Color was slowly returning to Gladys's face. "No. I was beside meself, wasn't I?"

"We'd better ring them, then," Mabel said, moving back behind the counter and reaching for the telephone. She dialed, spoke with the station, and hung up. "Constable Cuthbert will be around in a tick." She frowned. "It must have been some hooligans out for mischief." She pointed toward the bookstore window. "Perhaps the same ones who broke that pane of glass in our window."

Gladys lowered her brows. "Or it's that vegan group I read about in the *Chronicle*. They want people to stop eating meat. Can you imagine? It would put me and Bruce in the poorhouse. We'd be skint in no time!" Gladys's mouth clamped shut in a thin line.

"I hadn't heard about any vegan group," Mabel said. "Surely they wouldn't go around breaking windows? I'd have thought they'd be all peace and light and happiness for everyone."

Gladys began fiddling with her wedding ring again. Penelope was convinced she knew more than she was letting on. She just couldn't figure out what it was.

As soon as Gladys left, Penelope called for a taxi and was straightening some books on a display at the front of the store when it pulled up outside the Open Book. She was lecturing on the role omens, portents, and visions played in Gothic literature that morning. Maribel had rearranged the schedule because some of the girls in her seminar were leaving campus early that afternoon for a field hockey game an hour away.

There was a bit of a commotion across the street at the Pig in a Poke, where Constable Cuthbert was talking to the clerk from Brown's Hardware next door. Gladys stood in the open door of her shop, an apron tied around her waist and her arms crossed over her chest.

"Looks like there's a bit of a to-do going on over at the butcher's." The driver jerked a thumb in that direction. "Can't imagine what the world is coming to."

Pen murmured something noncommittal and leaned back in her seat. She was going over her lecture in her mind and hardly noticed the wood-paneled van that nearly side-swiped them a quarter of a mile outside town and was surprised when she looked up to see that the driver had turned down the road leading to the school.

He pulled up in front of the administration building with a flourish.

"There ye go, miss," he said, holding out a hand for his tip.

Pen placed the money in his calloused palm, opened the door, and got out.

Several of the girls waved to her as she made her way across the quad to Corbyn Hall, and Helen Dingley called hello as she passed.

The door to Pen's classroom was shut when she got there. She knocked and waited but there was no answer. She pulled the door open and a blast of stale air rushed out. It appeared as if the classroom had not been used since her lecture the previous day.

Sun came in the window where the blinds were partially raised, illuminating the dust motes dancing in the air. Pen cracked open one of the windows to let in the breeze.

She got her notes from her tote bag and realized she'd been carrying around some papers she'd meant to discard. She wadded them up, walked over to the trash can, and dropped them in. She was about to walk away when she did a double take. She reached into the bin and pushed the papers aside. Nestled at the very bottom was an empty wine bottle.

How odd! What a strange place to dispose of a wine bottle. People were unlikely to have been drinking in the classroom, so why carry the bottle with them and throw it away here?

A cluster of students rushed into the room, chattering,

their faces rosy from their walk across the quad. Penelope was getting ready to begin her lecture when she realized Nicola Hyde-White was missing. She'd barely formed the thought when Nicola slipped through the door and into an empty seat.

Her hair was windblown and she was panting slightly.

"Sorry," she said, not actually sounding in the least bit sorry, "but I have to come all the way from Fernsby Hall, which is a bit of a hike. But I'm afraid there's nothing to be done about it." She gave Penelope a smile that said *That's that*.

Penelope nodded, cleared her throat, and began her lecture.

The girls were enthusiastic students and Penelope was surprised at how quickly the time sped by.

The bell rang and the girls began shuffling to their feet.

"We'll see you at the book signing," said a girl with long red hair pulled back in a ponytail, as she went out the door.

Penelope had a few minutes to spare and went in search of a restroom, where she powdered her nose and tried to pat her hair into place. There was no point in trying to comb it—that would only cause her curls to turn into a head of frizz. When she deemed herself to be as presentable as possible, she left Corbyn Hall and headed toward the administration building where the Jane Austen Room was located.

One of the students was in the process of unpacking the cartons of Penelope's books that Mabel had sent over and arranging them on a table. Another table with tea things and bite-size pastries was already set up and Penelope gazed longingly at the pink and white petit fours. She loved the English tradition of elevenses—a break mid-morning for a cup of tea and some light refreshments to tide you over until lunch.

Helen Dingley was fluttering from one end of the room to the other, like a caged bird, getting in people's way and generally accomplishing little. She hastened over to Penelope.

"So glad you're here, dear Penelope." She clapped her hands together. "This is dreadfully exciting to have an honest-to-goodness bestselling author in our midst." She lowered her voice conspiratorially. "We've had our share of obscure poets and literary novelists who'd barely sold five hundred copies of their books, of course, so this is a real treat."

Penelope smiled wanly and thanked Helen.

Helen gestured toward the plexiglass case that stood on a highly polished wooden base in the center of the room.

"It pains me so to see that empty display case." Helen clasped her hands to her chest as if she were having a heart attack or palpitations.

"Has there been any progress in finding the book?" Penelope said.

Helen shook her head. "I'm afraid not. I fear it's lost forever." She put a hand to her mouth to stifle a sob. "Such a treasure. Better care should have been taken with it."

"By the way," Pen said, "something rather peculiar occurred. I was in my classroom in Corbyn Hall." She gestured with her shoulder vaguely in the direction of the building. "I was throwing some papers away and I noticed something odd in the trash."

Helen raised thin, crescent-shaped eyebrows. "Oh?"

"It was a wine bottle," Penelope said.

"A wine bottle? Why on earth would someone bin that in a classroom at Corbyn Hall?"

"That's what I was wondering."

Helen pursed her lips. "I do know that some of the girls have apparently been drinking. Head has been trying to figure out how to deal with it. Frankly, I don't know how they manage to get their hands on liquor. None of them is old enough to buy alcohol."

Pen was about to say something but bit her tongue. No need to tell Helen about the time she'd stolen Beryl's ID her senior year in high school to buy alcohol for herself and her friends and had subsequently become violently ill on peach schnapps. Beryl still thought she'd lost the ID herself and that Penelope had been stricken with a vicious case of stomach flu.

Helen looked thoughtful. "I think you should tell Maribel about it. Something really needs to be done about this. It can't be swept under the rug any longer. The school's reputation is at stake." Her expression was grim.

"If you really think so," Penelope said.

"I do." Helen gave a decisive shake of her head.

Helen fiddled with the ends of the silk scarf tied at her neck. She wet her lips.

"Quite shocking about Odile. I still can't get over it. Has the detective made any progress on the case, do you know?"

"Not much. Or at least not that I know of," Pen said.

Helen gave a funny sort of laugh. "Odile was something of a character, albeit a fascinating one. But one didn't want to get on the wrong side of her. She had a tongue that could give you whiplash." She reached out and straightened the book on display at the signing table.

"Oh?" Pen said.

"And she was something of a prima donna," Helen continued. "'Fetch my sweater for me, darling, would you?' she'd say in that breathy, drawling voice of hers. And of course one leapt to obey."

"I imagine that could get irritating," Pen said, picturing how she herself would respond.

"Odile could turn on the charm when she wanted to, so one found oneself doing little things for her without even minding. At least not too much. She could be irresistible when she wanted to be. I imagine she kept that beau of hers hopping, but Quentin didn't seem to mind. He was clearly smitten with her."

What if Quentin had actually minded being pushed around? Penelope thought as Helen wandered off. Just then Adrian Mabry came up behind her, startling her and causing her to jump.

"I didn't realize you were an illustrious author," he said, tossing back his hair.

"Hardly illustrious," Pen said.

"Nonsense. Of course you are." Mabry stared intently at Penelope as if she were the most fascinating creature in the world.

He really was quite the flirt. Penelope looked away and took a second to regain her composure.

"I hope you didn't believe a word Helen said." Mabry grabbed a shortbread cookie from the tea table.

"About what?"

"All that nonsense about Odile's charm." He put on a falsetto voice. "How one just leapt to do her bidding."

"She wasn't charming? Or people didn't leap to do her bidding?"

"A bit of both, actually. She could be charming when she wanted to be, but lately she had been treating poor Helen like a dogsbody, having her fetch this and carry that. She nearly ran the poor woman ragged. I can't understand why Helen didn't revolt and tell Odile to bugger off."

"Maybe Helen didn't mind," Pen said. "Maybe she wanted to help. Some people are like that. They like to feel needed."

Mabry scoffed. "Could be, but I think there was more to it than that."

"What, then?" Penelope was beginning to find Mabry very irritating.

"I think Odile was holding something over Dingley's head."

Penelope blew a lock of hair off her forehead. "Like what?"

Mabry shrugged and held out both hands, palms up. "I'm afraid I have no idea."

SIX

~◦~

Pen was still debating with herself as she headed down the corridor toward Maribel Northcott's office after her book signing ended. Should she tell the head about finding the wine bottle? She didn't want to get any of the girls in trouble. She felt a bit as if she had a foot in both worlds—she was a teacher, at least temporarily, but at the same time her student days didn't feel all that far behind her.

The door to the outer office was open and Pen stepped inside. She expected to see Tina sitting at her desk, but the room was empty. Pen was about to approach Maribel's closed door when she heard voices coming from behind it.

One was a man's voice and he sounded quite furious and rather like a trumpet blaring. His voice came right through the thick wooden door.

She inched closer to the door. She began to catch snatches of words—"underage" . . . "alcohol" . . . "lack of supervision." As the fellow's rage mounted, he became even louder and Pen heard him say quite clearly that if things didn't shape up, he would remove his daughter from the school and send her to the local grammar school. And if she still didn't decide to work hard and make something of herself, she could get a job in his office doing data entry. He wasn't going to have her sitting around, spending his money, and getting into trouble.

Penelope had the sense that Maribel was trying to soothe him, but her voice was too soft to carry into the outer office.

Suddenly the door to Maribel's office was flung open and the man in question stalked out, his face dangerously red and his fists clenched at his sides. Maribel followed close behind him, looking more amused than anything.

Maribel rolled her eyes discreetly as she passed Penelope and led the irate gentleman through the outer office and out the door.

"Phew," she said when the gentleman had retreated a safe distance down the corridor.

"Come." She gestured to Penelope to follow her into her office. "I think a glass of sherry is in order."

Maribel went over to a small table next to the rose-colored brocade sofa across from her desk. Two small cut-crystal glasses and a bottle of Bristol Cream sherry sat on top of a lace doily.

Maribel poured a couple of sips of the amber liquid in each glass and handed one to Penelope.

She took a drink and then said, "That"—she put an emphasis on the word—"was Mr. Nicholas Hyde-White. Or, more correctly, Sir Nicholas Hyde-White."

Penelope raised her eyebrows. "Is he the father of Nicola Hyde-White?"

Maribel nodded and appeared to contemplate the rainbows glinting from her crystal glass as the light hit it.

"An impossible man," she said. "With an impossible daughter." She paused. "Although I must say that Nicola is a very bright young lady. If only she would apply herself a bit more."

"She's taking my seminar," Pen said, sipping her sherry.

"Oh?" Maribel said. "I probably shouldn't be telling you all this." She looked into her glass as if plumbing its depths. "But I'm sure I can count on you to keep this confidential. Nicola's father was complaining that she's been getting hold of alcohol. And not for the first time." She laughed. "But I suppose you must have heard him. He was quite incensed. Not that I completely blame him, mind you. He has placed his daughter in our care and we have a duty to keep her safe. He pays dearly enough for it."

Maribel took a sip of her sherry. "Sir Nicholas has been very generous to the Oakwood School. He gave the money to build the art studio in the Stewart-Calthorpe Assembly Hall and has provided the funding for the arts program."

"Oh?"

"Indirectly, he is the one who paid Odile's salary." Maribel turned her glass around in her hands. "Odile was quite alarmed by his threats to cease funding the program if we didn't get to the bottom of who was supplying the girls with liquor. My biggest fear is that it's one of the staff. That would reflect terribly on the school. Odile was determined to flush out the culprit."

"I'm guessing she didn't," Pen said.

Maribel shook her head. "At least not that I know of. But I'm sure she would have told me immediately if she had." She frowned. "I let the staff know that I would fire the person on the spot. And that I wouldn't hesitate to pass a word along to my counterparts at other schools. The culprit would have found themselves hard-pressed to get another job."

"That reminds me," Pen said, "when I went to throw out some trash in my classroom, I found an empty wine bottle in the waste can."

"In the bin?" Maribel's voice rose along with her eyebrows. She shook her head and tut-tutted. "I can't fathom one of our teachers disposing of a wine bottle in a classroom. It had to have been one of the girls. They could hardly toss it out in their dorm. It was bound to be noticed." Her shoulders sagged. "We know that someone was buying alcohol for them. The problem is, we still don't know who that person is."

The sun had shifted slightly and was beaming into the room. Maribel moved to the window and adjusted the blinds.

Penelope was thinking about what Maribel had said—how Sir Nicholas had threatened to pull funding for Odile's art program.

"You don't think . . ." she started and then stopped.

Maribel tilted her head to the side. "Don't think what?"

The idea suddenly seemed foolish, but in for a penny, in for a pound, as Penelope's grandmother used to say.

"It's nothing really. But what if the person supplying the girls with alcohol knew that Odile was onto them? They might have been afraid that she would talk and so they felt the need to . . . silence her."

Maribel gasped, and her hand flew to her mouth.

"I never thought of that. But it's perfectly possible. Whoever was doing it had to have known that the consequences would be dire if they were found out. Oh, dear." She turned to Penelope with a stricken look on her face. "That would mean someone from the Oakwood School murdered the poor woman."

Pen said good-bye to Maribel and headed out the door

of the administration building. She was about to telephone for a taxi when she realized she'd left her scarf draped over a chair in her classroom. She sighed and began heading back toward Corbyn Hall.

Classes had not yet ended and the quad was nearly deserted. There was a couple walking together ahead of Pen. A bit of white skirt showed beneath the woman's coat and Pen realized it was Layla Evans, the school nurse.

The man had longish dark hair and when he tossed his head to get his hair off his forehead, Pen recognized him as Adrian Mabry.

The couple was walking side by side, talking, and something about their movements made Penelope suspect they might be more than just friends. She remembered the couple in Odile's manuscript—was this a case of art imitating life and she had been writing about Layla and Mabry?

Penelope decided to follow them for a bit.

They crossed the quad and left the path, which ended at the entrance to Corbyn Hall, to make their way around the building. About a hundred yards beyond the building, the land was wooded and undeveloped.

Penelope ducked into the shadows alongside Corbyn Hall and watched as Mabry and Layla crossed the lawn toward the woods. She headed after them. She had no idea what she would say if they saw her, but they seemed to be oblivious to anything but each other.

They entered the woods and Penelope held back for a minute to put some distance between them. They were making their way through the trees to what looked like a small clearing. They seemed to know where they were going and Penelope wondered if they went there regularly.

After a moment or two, she started after them. As she entered the woods, she stepped on a dry and brittle twig that made a loud snap as it broke in half. She cringed, her heart hammering in her chest, but the couple obviously hadn't heard the noise.

Penelope crept a bit closer. Off in the distance she could see an abandoned hunting blind. She recognized it because an old boyfriend had taken her hunting once—a dreadful experience, even though he hadn't managed to bag anything. It wasn't for lack of trying, though. A beautiful stag had been within shooting range, but Penelope couldn't bear to see such a magnificent animal killed and had pretended to have a violent coughing fit. As she had hoped, it had had the desired effect of scaring the wary animal off. She and the fellow—she thought his name had been Harry—had spent an uncomfortable car ride back to the city with neither of them talking to the other.

Penelope wondered if Mabry and Layla were headed for the hunting blind, but they stopped suddenly in the middle of the clearing. Penelope watched them. Were they lovers or was she imagining things? But just then Layla reached out and smoothed a lock of hair off Mabry's forehead and moments later, Mabry put his hand on Layla's cheek.

"'Shall I compare thee to a summer's day? Thou are more lovely and more temperate,'" Mabry intoned. "The bard certainly had a way with words."

Penelope felt her cheeks flush. She felt tawdry—like a common voyeur. She was about to turn and make her way back out of the woods when Mabry and Layla moved closer together. They held each other in a lingering embrace and kissed.

She had seen enough. It was clear they were romantically involved. Were they the couple that had inspired the love story in Odile's manuscript?

They were taking an incredible chance with Layla's husband also working at the school. Had Odile threatened to tell Grady what she'd found out? And had Layla or Mabry killed her to keep her quiet?

Penelope made her way through the woods to Corbyn Hall, where she picked up her forgotten scarf. She was headed back across the quad when she ran into Maribel again. Maribel's coat was open and she was carrying a key ring in one hand.

She stopped when she saw Penelope.

"I'm off to Odile's apartment," she said, holding up the key. "We'll eventually be having a new art teacher starting and I want to get the apartment cleaned out before half term. The police have already photographed everything and have taken away anything they deemed to be evidence." She gave an apologetic smile. "I'll be taking a few days at the coast then for a bit of a refresher." Her smile faded. "I'm not looking forward to going through Odile's things."

"Would you like some help?"

Maribel's face brightened. "That would be lovely. Much easier with two people. The movers are coming next week to pick up the bits of furniture that belonged to Odile. Odile hadn't left a will, of course, and we haven't located a next of kin, but Quentin has offered to take it off our hands. He's rented a small storage space in Lower Chumley."

They had been walking as they talked and by now had reached Sutcliffe House and Odile's apartment. A pile of cardboard boxes was outside the door.

"I had Grady drop off these cartons," Maribel said as she put the key in the lock. "Odile's personal things need to be packed up. Quentin will come for them later. He has a key."

The door stuck a bit and Maribel had to give it a slight shove to get it open. The apartment looked much as it had the first time Penelope had been there, although now some of the surfaces were dusty with the residue of fingerprint powder and the paisley shawl, which had been artfully draped over the sofa, was in a puddle on the seat cushion and one of the throw pillows was on the floor.

Maribel tut-tutted under her breath. "The police have made a bit of a mess, haven't they? Although I suppose it was unavoidable." She looked around. "Where to begin?"

"Perhaps the desk?" Penelope motioned toward the dainty escritoire. "I'll tackle her things in the bedroom."

Penelope went out to the hall and brought in the stack of cartons that Grady had delivered. She handed one to Maribel and took another one with her into the bedroom.

Odile's bedroom was as exotic as her sitting room. The bed was piled high with pillows in vibrant colors and covered with a spread that was equally colorful and had tiny mirrored disks sewn onto it.

A copy of Odile's book, *You Can Paint*, was on the nightstand along with a glass, which might have held water but was now empty, and a small box of tissues.

The bureau was a hand-painted piece from India made of mango wood with elaborate brass handles. A layer of dust had settled on the polished surface and a number of half-empty perfume bottles were scattered on top along with an antique silver brush and comb set.

Penelope opened the first drawer. It was filled with various bits of lingerie and several pairs of black tights. She transferred everything to the carton and opened the drawer below.

In it, sweaters in a rainbow of colors were neatly stacked.

Penelope took out the first batch and placed them in the carton. As soon as she was finished, she went on to the third drawer.

She was surprised to find that it didn't contain clothes but rather miscellaneous items such as an old camera in a cracked leather case, a lighted magnifying glass, a tangle of charging cords, and a stack of eight-by-ten photographs.

Penelope lifted the photos out of the drawer and began to go through them. They were pictures of paintings—Penelope presumed they were Odile's work—strikingly modern pieces in bold colors. They were photographed unframed and sitting on an easel. She was about to put them in the carton when the last photograph caught her eye. It was a portrait of a woman done in bold strokes. The woman had black hair and strong, dark brows. The colors were vivid like Odile's clothes and décor. This painting was in a gold frame and appeared to be hanging on the wall of Odile's sitting room.

The painting looked familiar to Penelope. She'd taken an art appreciation course in college and she could have sworn she'd seen works just like this. She remembered a similar piece being featured on the last slide Professor Jacobs showed during their final exam.

Finally it came to her. "Maribel," she called, as she ran out of the bedroom and into the sitting room.

"What is it?" Maribel looked up from the box she was packing. She must have noticed the expression on Penelope's face. "Is something wrong?"

Penelope handed her the photographs. "These all appear to be Odile's paintings," she said as Maribel began to flip through them. "All except the last one. And if I'm right—"

Maribel took the photograph from Penelope. "That's

Odile's Matisse painting. She was terribly proud of it. She'd inherited it, she said. Her grandmother—or was it her great-grandmother?—had briefly modeled for Matisse. Matisse had been too poor at the time to pay her but had given her this painting instead." She handed the photograph to Penelope.

"Ever since Odile moved in, the painting has been on the far wall here in the sitting room. She whirled around and pointed at the wall behind her, but it was empty.

"Odile must have moved it," Maribel said. "It must be in the bedroom."

Penelope shook her head. "It's not in there."

Maribel's lips tightened. "Surely Odile didn't hang such precious artwork in the kitchen."

"No, it's not there either."

Maribel frowned. "Where is it, then? You don't suppose the police took it, do you?"

"Stole it, you mean?" Penelope pictured Maguire's honest and open face. "I'm certain they didn't. Odile had to have moved it somewhere else."

Maribel snapped her fingers. "You're so right. Perhaps it's in Odile's studio in the assembly hall." Maribel rubbed her hands together. "Oh dear, this is quite worrisome. Such a valuable painting. I do hope no one tries to blame the school. It's bad enough that the Jane Austen has gone missing."

"I'm sure that won't happen," Penelope said. "Perhaps we should check Odile's studio? You're probably right and that's where it is." She glanced toward the bedroom. "I'm nearly finished packing up Odile's bureau, so there's only the closet to be done."

"That would put my mind at ease," Maribel said. "Otherwise I doubt I shall sleep a wink until it's found."

* * *

By the time Penelope and Maribel left Odile's apartment, with her cartons of belongings stacked neatly by the door, it was after two o'clock. Penelope was glad she'd had several petit fours and a couple of shortbread cookies at her book signing.

Maribel turned to her as they were crossing the quad.

"You must be starving. I'm so sorry. I wasn't thinking. I haven't had much of an appetite myself lately. We should get something to eat."

Penelope patted her stomach. "I'm fine. I filled up on those delicious petit fours and cookies."

Mabel's mouth curled into a small smile. "That's hardly sustenance."

Pen sighed. "I know. I have the most appalling eating habits, according to my sister." She laughed. "Somehow I still managed to grow to be almost six feet tall."

By now they had reached the Stewart-Calthorpe Assembly Hall. The vast lobby was empty except for a man in overalls on a ladder changing one of the bulbs in the chandelier.

"Do be careful, Rodney," Maribel called up to him as they went past. She shuddered. "I don't know how he can bear being up that high on a ladder."

They went through a door at one end of the lobby, which led to a long corridor lined with closed doors. Strains of music—violins and pianos—came from behind some of the doors.

"These are our practice rooms," Mabel said as they headed down the hallway. "Odile's studio is over there." She gestured toward the end of the corridor.

A rather screechy rendition of Beethoven's "Ode to Joy"

came from the last room on the right as they passed it and Penelope thought she saw Maribel flinch.

"Here we are," Maribel said and pushed open the door.

"It wasn't locked?" Penelope said as she followed Maribel into the room. It was spacious and airy and filled with the sunlight that poured in through the large window. A bit of bright blue sky was visible through the skylight.

Maribel's shoulders slumped. "No. Odile never bothered to lock the studio. Her students often used it as well to work on projects." She bit her lip. "That's what has me so worried. It would make it all too easy to steal that painting if it's here."

Pen looked around the room. Three easels were set up and a half-finished painting sat on one of them. It appeared to be one of Odile's abstracts. A palette with drying paint on it was on a table and the smell of oil paint was heavy in the air.

A stack of canvases leaned against one wall. Penelope flipped through them, but the Matisse painting wasn't there.

There weren't too many other places to look. Maribel opened a storage closet that ran the length of one wall. Paint-smeared smocks hung from hooks and various gear was stored inside—blank canvases, tubes of paint, and boxes of brushes.

But no paintings.

Maribel had become more distressed the longer they looked. Her face was pale and her lower lip quivered slightly. She wrung her hands.

"It's not here. The painting's not here."

"Perhaps Odile loaned it to someone?" Pen said in a soothing voice.

"I suppose that could be," Maribel said, stiffening her

shoulders slightly. "But why would she loan out such a valuable painting? She was so terribly proud of it."

She had a point there, Pen thought.

Maribel looked at Pen. "I don't know what to do."

Frankly, neither did Pen.

SEVEN

꘎

Penelope realized she was, indeed, starving on the taxi
ride back to town. She had the cabbie drop her off in
front of the Chumley Chippie. The aroma greeting her as
she pulled open the door made her stomach grumble in
anticipation.

The shop was crowded—for that matter, there was
hardly ever a lull at the Chippie. People began arriving for
an early lunch not much after they opened at eleven o'clock
and continued to stream in until well after two. Shortly
thereafter, customers in search of a midafternoon snack
began to pop in; and that segued into the dinner hour
crowd; and finally, right before closing, those who arrived
after the bars shut their doors in search of something to
ward off the worst of a potential hangover.

Penelope had grabbed lunch or dinner there often
enough that the staff no longer exclaimed at her being

American; and Stan and Mick, who ran the place, now greeted her with recognition.

Stan was behind the counter, taking orders today, while his brother worked the fryer. Stan was the taller of the two and had lost more of his hair. What was left was thin and wispy and tended to flutter slightly in the breeze created by the overhead fan.

"Howdy," he said in an attempt at an American accent when Penelope approached the counter.

"Howdy," Penelope said in return. "I'll have the pollack and a double order of chips."

Stan raised his wiry eyebrows. "Hungry, are you?" He leaned over the counter and the movement strained the buttons on his white shirt. He lowered his voice. "I'd go with the haddock today, if I was you. I don't like the smell of the pollack." He pinched his nose. "Gilbert, he's the one that delivers the fish every day, said it's fresh but I think he's having me on. I know my fish." He poked himself in the chest with his finger. "And if that pollack is fresh, then I'm Tom Jones."

He gave a wheezing guffaw that ended in a strangled cough. "I'm sending it all back when he comes round tomorrow. If he thinks he can put one over on me, he's mistaken."

Penelope laughed politely. "Fine. The haddock it is, then."

She watched as Mick, the younger and slimmer of the two, lowered pieces of battered fish into the fryer, where they bubbled and sizzled and almost immediately began to turn golden brown. He put a batch of chips in another vat of hot oil and stood watching over the two. When the food was sufficiently cooked, he removed the baskets, dumped the fish and chips on a plate, and handed it to Penelope.

"Bon appétit," he said in an appalling accent. He grinned, showing uneven teeth.

Penelope thanked him, grabbed some napkins and silverware, and turned to scout out the nearest table. A group of young men in their twenties clad in overalls and work boots were seated at one table, joking and jostling one another as they ate. A couple of single people were scattered at the other tables, and Penelope was both surprised and delighted to see that one of them was Maguire.

She carried her tray over to his table. He looked up from his plate and broke into a grin when he saw her.

"This is a nice surprise," he said. He put down his fork and leaned across the table to give Penelope a kiss.

Penelope grabbed the bottle of malt vinegar that was on the table and liberally sprinkled it over her fish and chips.

"I've been at the Oakwood School all afternoon," she said as she shook out her paper napkin and placed it in her lap. "The head is quite distressed over poor Odile's murder, as you can imagine. Has there been any progress in finding the killer?"

Maguire looked pained. He ran a hand over his face.

"Not much, I'm afraid. I feel like all I've done is chase down one blind alley after another." He stabbed a chip with his fork. "On top of that, I haven't made much headway on that robbery in Birnam Woods either." He rolled his eyes. "What a bunch of entitled toffs. They think we should drop everything and put all our resources behind finding the thief." He forced a smile. "Tell me about your day. I'm sure it was better than mine."

Penelope took a deep breath. "Everything went well. The school arranged a book signing for me. And I had my second class." She wrinkled her nose. "I wasn't quite as nervous this time, although I could still have used a stiff drink afterward, but sadly the wine bottle I found in the trash can in my classroom was empty." Penelope made a face.

Maguire raised his eyebrows. "In the bin?"

Penelope nodded as she cut a piece of her fish. "I assume that one of the students is responsible. They probably didn't want to dispose of it in the dorm for fear the housemistress would find it."

"Typical teenage hijinks," Maguire said with a smile. He looked at Penelope. "Come on. Surely you got up to a bit of mischief now and then when you were in school."

Penelope tried to protest but Maguire was having none of it.

"Come on. Out with it. What was it?"

Penelope thought of all the scrapes she'd gotten into and tried to decide which ones to own up to.

"My father took the train into the city for work," she began. "New York City," she said in response to the look on Maguire's face. "He used to drive to the station and leave his car in the lot there. It was an old Volvo station wagon he'd had for years."

Penelope could see the car in her mind's eye. She could even smell the old cracked leather that was imbued with the scent of her father's cigar smoke.

"It was a gorgeous day at the beginning of June. The school year was almost over and we were all becoming impatient to be sprung loose. And the beach was beckoning." Penelope poked at the last fry on her plate.

"The four of us—me, Beth, Lauren, and Megan—pretended to walk to school as usual. But instead of going to school we walked to the train station, where we all met up. My father had already parked his car and gotten on the eight thirty-seven to the city."

"Go on," Maguire said, a small smile hovering around his lips. "I think I can see where this is going."

"I'd taken the spare key to the Volvo out of the junk drawer in the kitchen where we kept it, and we took my father's car to the beach."

"Did he ever find out?" Maguire said.

Penelope laughed. "We returned the car to the same parking space before he got off the six seventeen train that night so we thought we'd pulled it off."

"Something gave you away?"

"Yes. We hadn't noticed the sand we'd left all over the floor and the seats. He'd never driven the Volvo to the beach, so it was quite obvious what we'd done."

Maguire grinned. "On a scale of one to ten, with ten being the worst, I'd say that's only around a three."

Penelope snorted. "My father didn't think so. I was grounded for a month. It would have been awful if I hadn't figured out a way to climb out the window of my bedroom and shimmy down the drainpipe."

Maguire threw back his head and roared.

Penelope pointed a finger at him. "Now. How about you?"

Maguire's face clouded over. "I was on a bit of a tear during those years. I regret it now." He sighed.

Penelope sensed his hesitation and didn't push for an answer.

"I should be getting back to the Open Book. I want to discuss next month's newsletter with Mabel."

Maguire looked at his watch and groaned. "And I've got some jewels to find and a murderer to track down." He pecked Penelope on the cheek. "Wish me luck."

* * *

Three people were in line at the sales counter when Penelope got to the Open Book late that afternoon. She raised her eyebrows at Mabel to ask if she needed any help, but Mabel shook her head and continued to ring up Laurence Brimble's books.

Penelope had to smile. Poor Mr. Brimble was going to go broke courting Mabel. He seemed to feel he needed to buy something every time he visited the bookstore—as if none of them could possibly guess what his true purpose was.

Brimble turned from the counter, his new books in hand, when he saw Penelope. He gave her an embarrassed smile.

"Had to pick up the new Tom Clancy," he said, brandishing his shopping bag. He smoothed his mustache with his index finger. "Of course Clancy isn't writing them anymore, but the new fellow has done a good job of picking up where he left off."

"I've heard it's very good," Pen said, although she'd heard no such thing.

"Quite. Also grabbed a couple of history books I want to read. The new Erik Larson has been getting good reviews."

"The one about Winston Churchill?"

Brimble nodded. "Well, I must toddle off. Lots to do. Cheerio!" He waved gaily as he headed out the door.

Mabel had just finished serving the last customer in the line when Penelope headed toward the counter. She leaned on it, a teasing grin on her face.

"Poor Laurence is going to drive himself into the poorhouse buying all those books."

Mabel's face turned slightly pink. "I've told him he doesn't have to buy something every time he comes into the store."

Pen laughed. "I suppose it is one way to get customers."

Mabel looked away and fiddled with a sign announcing Charlotte Davenport's newest book, *The Regency Rogue*, that was prominently displayed on the counter.

"Laurence has asked me out again," Mabel said with her back turned to Penelope.

"What?" Pen's voice went up an octave in mock surprise. "What did you say?"

Mabel turned around. "I said yes, of course. Suitors aren't exactly a dime a dozen at my age, you know."

"You do like him though, don't you?" Penelope brushed a strand of hair off her forehead.

Mabel gave a sly smile. "I like the attention." She looked down at her hands. "Of course I like him. It's just that . . . he's not Oliver. And never will be."

Oliver and Mabel had been in love when they were both working for the British government. Oliver had been sent on a mission to Russia and had never returned. After several years it was presumed he was dead. Mabel had been carrying a torch for him ever since.

Mabel gave a loud sigh. "But that's in the past and it's beyond time to move on." She lifted her chin. "So I will be joining Laurence for dinner tomorrow night at Pierre's."

Penelope whistled. "Isn't this the second time he's taken you there?"

"Yes," Mabel said with a fretful smile. "I do hate to see him spending so much money, but he insists he can afford it and wouldn't take no for an answer."

Pierre's was next door to the Open Book and was the most expensive restaurant in town. The menu was French, the ambiance romantic, and the prices sky-high. Most residents of Upper Chumley-on-Stoke only dined there for the most noteworthy of occasions—university graduations, silver anniversaries, and significant birthdays. The regulars were the new people with money who lived in places like Birnam Woods and made Maguire's life miserable.

Penelope had been there once when Figgy's fiancé, Derek, who had a successful career in the City, had taken them all for dinner to celebrate his and Figgy's engagement.

"I'm happy for you," Pen said, reaching out and squeezing Mabel's arm.

Suddenly Mabel squealed loudly—a sound that was totally uncharacteristic for her. After her experiences in MI6, there were few things that fazed her.

Pen was alarmed. "What's wrong?"

Mabel gave a slight shake. "Something just ran over my foot." She looked down.

Penelope looked at the floor as well but didn't see anything.

"What do you suppose it was? A mouse?"

"We've never had a problem with mice before," Mabel said. "At least I've never seen one. But I can't fathom what else it could have been."

They both looked around, but there was nothing whatsoever to be seen.

"It must have been a mouse," Mabel said decisively. "They're doing some renovations next door at Francesca and Annabelle's and perhaps the poor thing was chased out, having been frightened by the noise." Mabel pursed her lips. "What we need is a cat."

"Mrs. Danvers!" Penelope said suddenly. "I could bring her for a visit. She's a great mouser—she caught one in the cottage and she's left a couple of presents for me on the back doormat."

Mabel snapped her fingers. "Perfect. Why don't you bring her tomorrow? I can pick you up on my way to the shop in the morning."

"I really should get another car." Penelope said, picking a piece of lint off her sweater. She must have put a tissue through the wash again. "I miss my old MINI."

"I'd really rather you didn't," Mabel said sternly. "I feel much calmer knowing you're not out there driving down the wrong side of the street."

It was an hour till closing and Pen decided she could delay no longer. It was time to work on her manuscript. She couldn't leave poor Eirene hanging any longer.

The more immersed Penelope became in her book, the more the characters came to life for her. She actually began to think of them as real people and it pained her to put them in danger. But a writer had to be cruel, she thought, because without danger—whether it was emotional or physical or psychological—the novel would end up being quite dull indeed.

She took her laptop into her writing room and closed the door. Once the computer was powered up, she selected the file with her manuscript in it and read over the last bit she'd written. Poor Eirene. She'd left her tied to a chair in Mr. Bloodworth's laboratory—having been caught sneaking into the locked room. The wind was howling and beating against the windows and the lights were flickering on and off.

Penelope stared at the blinking cursor and bit her knuckle. For once she wished she was the sort of writer who made a proper outline before sailing off into the void. It felt like jumping out of a plane not knowing whether your parachute would open or not. Sometimes the words came easily and other times they had to be pulled out one by one in a procedure she suspected was more painful than surgery.

How was she going to get Eirene out of her predicament? Especially since the idea of the literary damsel in distress had gone out with hoopskirts and heroines were now expected to save themselves. She couldn't have Byron, Mr. Bloodworth's dreamy reclusive son, barge in, and save Eirene. She'd run the risk of having Eirene going rogue and swooning in Byron's arms, thus bringing the story to a crashing halt. Byron would be Eirene's reward in the end, but the girl was just going to have to exercise some patience and wait.

Penelope rubbed her forehead and pinched the bridge of her nose. Could Eirene scoot her chair close enough to the table to grab one of the Bunsen burners? And when Mr. Bloodworth got close enough, she could set fire to his rather wild mop of gray hair.

Rats, Penelope thought. How could Eirene grab anything with her hands tied to the chair? Perhaps she should have Mr. Bloodworth put the rope around her waist instead?

Penelope bit her lip in frustration. After several minutes, she turned off her computer and slammed the lid shut. She knew from experience that the solution would eventually come to her if she gave her mind time to mull it over.

Penelope sighed, closed the door to her writing room,

and went to join Mabel. They still had to discuss the store's upcoming newsletter.

Mabel was talking to an older gentleman wearing a trench coat and a dark brown fedora with a feather in the ribbon that wound around the brim. They seemed to be having a rather intense conversation—he was leaning toward Mabel, their heads nearly touching.

Penelope wondered who he was—probably a customer—Mabel often had passionate discussions about books with people who came into the shop.

Mabel said good-bye to the gentleman and turned slightly. Penelope noticed her face was whiter than usual and her hands were trembling.

She went over to Mabel. "Is everything all right? Do you feel okay?"

"If I could have a glass of water."

"I'll be right back." Penelope put a hand on Mabel's shoulder.

She ran to the storeroom, got a glass from the cupboard, and filled it at the sink. She was walking quickly and some of the water sloshed out of the glass onto her hand.

She handed it to Mabel. "Drink up now."

Mabel raised the glass to her mouth with an unsteady hand. A bit of water dribbled onto her sweater as she drank. She finished the water and handed the glass to Penelope.

"Now tell me what's wrong," Penelope said, as Mabel sagged against the counter. "Perhaps we should go sit down."

Mabel let Penelope lead her over to one of the sofas at the back of the shop. Pen caught Figgy's attention and motioned for her to bring a cup of tea.

Moments later, Figgy rushed over with a strong cup of

English breakfast and a couple of chocolate digestive biscuits.

"Is everything okay?" she said, her face pinched with concern.

"You might as well sit down," Mabel said. "You're not going to believe this."

Pen and Figgy exchanged alarmed glances.

"Drink some tea," Figgy urged. "I've put lots of sugar in it. You've gone dreadfully pale."

Mabel blew out a sigh that fluttered the hairs around her face. She looked at Pen.

"You saw me talking to that man? The one in the trench coat and brown fedora?"

Penelope and Figgy nodded.

"He knew Oliver." Mabel's voice caught and she smoothed the knees of her trousers with the palms of both hands. "He seems to think . . ." Mabel choked back a sob and reached into her pocket for a tissue. "He seems to think that Oliver might still be alive." She reached into her pocket again and pulled out a folded piece of paper. Her hand shook as she handed it to Penelope.

The paper had obviously been creased numerous times and was beginning to wear at the folds. Penelope opened it carefully, fearful that it would disintegrate with her touch.

The letter was addressed to Mabel. It was clearly a love letter. Penelope felt intrusive reading it. She glanced at the signature—*all my love forever, no matter what happens, Oliver.*

She silently handed the letter back to Mabel. She didn't know what to say.

"How . . . how did that man come to have this?" Pen said finally. She dashed at her eyes—they had welled with tears.

"He said Oliver gave it to him the last time he saw him.

He was supposed to post it to me but he was in a terrible accident and spent months in hospital. Poor man suffered a head trauma, so no wonder he forgot about Oliver's letter." Mabel looked into the distance, a wistful expression on her face.

"By the time he found the letter years later when he retired and cleaned out his desk, I'd left London and moved here. He had no idea where I'd gone. He's only just tracked me down now. I don't know if I can do it," Mabel said, wiping her eyes with the tissue again.

"Do what?" Pen put her hand on Mabel's arm.

Mabel waved her hands in the air. "I don't know. Continue to see Laurence, I suppose."

Penelope frowned. "What made this man think that Oliver was still alive?"

Mabel made a face. "He said it was a feeling he had. A hunch." She looked down at her hands. "I've had the same feeling myself, only I've put it down to woman's intuition." Mabel gave a small smile that quickly faded.

"But is that any reason to stop seeing Laurence? You've been enjoying it, haven't you?"

"I don't know." Mabel ran a hand through her hair. "I'll have to think about it. But I'm going to cancel our dinner date. It isn't fair to allow him to spend so much money when my heart isn't in it at the moment."

EIGHT

❧

The sun was setting and the shadows deepening as Penelope left the Open Book and hurried down the high street. She turned up the collar of her jacket. The temperature had dropped and leaden slate-colored clouds moved swiftly across the sky.

She was passing the estate agent's when she felt something cold and wet on her cheek. She swiped at it. Was it beginning to rain? She looked up at the sky and felt more drops on her face.

Several umbrellas popped open over the heads of the other pedestrians hurrying down the high street. Of course she hadn't brought hers. Leave it to the British, Penelope thought—always prepared.

She quickened her step, but fortunately the worst of the rain held off and she made it to the Tesco with only a few spots of damp on the shoulders of her jacket.

She'd promised herself that she was going to cook something for dinner and not rely on takeout from the Chumley Chippie or Kebabs and Curries or bits of leftover cheese and crackers.

The rush of warmth when Penelope opened the door to the shop felt wonderful. The tips of her fingers were frozen as well as the tips of her ears.

"Getting right chilly out there, isn't it?" a female Tesco employee said. She was stacking cans of soup into a pyramid at the end of an aisle. "Wouldn't be surprised if we had a dusting of snow. Although it's still a bit early for that."

Penelope smiled, wrangled a cart from the tangle by the door, and began perusing the aisles. She wanted to make something simple—she still had work to do on her manuscript and she hoped to read more of Odile's to see if any other clues were buried in the story.

She was tempted to buy a couple of the cans of the Baxters soup the woman at the front of the store was arranging, but Pen was determined to cook something and not just heat something up.

In the end she decided on the makings for a pot of chili. It didn't take long to put together and she would have it to eat for several nights. Besides, it was perfect for a damp and chilly evening. As she reached for a can of diced tomatoes, she pictured herself curled up in front of the fire with a warm bowl of chili and Mrs. Danvers purring beside her.

Someone edged past her and accidentally bumped her elbow.

Penelope looked over her shoulder. "Sorry," they both said at the same time.

Penelope smiled when she saw that it was Grady Evans

from the Oakwood School. He gave Penelope a smile in return that suggested he recognized her but wasn't sure why.

He continued down the aisle, an empty shopping basket swinging from the crook of his arm, and Pen put a couple of cans of diced tomatoes in her cart and moved on.

She went up and down the aisles and hesitated in front of the ice cream section. Should she, or shouldn't she? Why not? she thought and grabbed a container of salted caramel.

She tossed the carton into her cart and headed toward the checkout. The store wasn't busy and Grady Evans was the only person ahead of her. He reached into his shopping basket and pulled out three bottles of vodka.

Pen smiled at him. "Having a party?"

Grady looked down at his shoes. "The wife's having a hen party and sent me out shopping," he said as he handed his credit card to the cashier. "As soon as I deliver these provisions, I'm heading to the Book and Bottle myself. I can't stand all that chatter."

The cashier whisked a used carton out from under the counter, put the bottles in it, and pushed it toward Grady.

"Cheers," Grady said as he hefted the carton onto his hip and headed toward the door.

There had been something off in his voice, Penelope thought as she left the store. He was lying. She was certain of it. But why? The only possible explanation was that the three bottles of vodka he'd just bought weren't for his wife's hen party but rather for the underage girls at the Oakwood School.

Had Odile known that? Surely Grady knew there would be dire consequences if he was found out. Would that have been enough to motivate him to make sure that Odile kept quiet?

* * *

The next morning, Penelope reached into the back of her closet and pulled out her black pantsuit. Today was Odile Fontaine's memorial service at the Oakwood School and she had been invited. She had barely known Odile but attending seemed like the correct thing to do, since she was now a part of the school—albeit only temporarily.

Besides, it would give her the opportunity to observe the other teachers and staff. Who knows? She might pick up a clue as to who killed Odile. Not that she didn't trust Maguire to find the killer, it was just that he was obviously stressed handling the murder and the burglary and if there was anything she could do to help, she was going to do it.

The taxi driver dropped Pen off at the administration building. She paid him and set off across the quad toward the Stewart-Calthorpe Assembly Hall. The previous day's clouds had been chased away by a brisk wind to reveal a bright blue sky. Penelope took a deep breath as she walked. The day seemed out of sync with her destination—a memorial service. Yesterday's dark skies and heavy clouds would have seemed more appropriate.

Maribel and Helen Dingley were huddled together in the lobby of the assembly hall when Penelope arrived. Maribel had arranged a small exhibition of Odile's paintings and they were scattered about the space.

"What do you think?" she said, waving a hand, as Pen approached her.

"I think it's a lovely tribute," Penelope said. "Odile was quite talented."

"She will be missed." Helen sniffed and pulled a tissue from her purse. She waved to Penelope and headed toward the door to the auditorium.

Penelope saw Maribel glance at her watch and then announce, "We should be starting. Let's go on in."

Maribel headed through the entrance to the auditorium and then toward the stage, while Pen began to search for a seat. Girls were still trickling through the door, but the pace had slowed and the chatter began to die down as Maribel walked out onto the stage. Pen slid into a vacant seat and looked around. She was pleased to be able to recognize some of the faces.

A large picture of Odile was displayed on an easel to the right of the stage. In the photo, Odile was wearing a bright orange top, blue beads, and her customary beret. A large vase filled with flowers sat at the foot of the easel.

Although the memorial service wasn't religious in nature, Maribel opened with a short prayer. The audience bowed their heads and silence fell over the auditorium.

"Jesus, let your presence manifest in this place. As we gather here to mourn our beloved, Odile Fontaine, may you bring healing into our hearts."

As soon as Maribel finished, one of the students walked out onstage. She looked nervous as she approached the microphone.

"Odile Fontaine was a wonderful teacher," she said, her voice cracking slightly. "She inspired us."

She went on for another few minutes and then Quentin Barnes took the stage.

"I probably knew Odile better than most," he said with a smug smile. "She was a brilliant artist who chose to share her gift with her students."

Finally, the service came to an end and the audience rose to sing the Oakwood School song. The girls filed out quickly and were gone—racing across the quad, talking, laughing, Odile already forgotten.

The staff lingered in the lobby, admiring Odile's art-work and talking among themselves.

Maribel was talking to Quentin Barnes. When she saw Penelope, she motioned her over.

"I believe you've met Quentin Barnes," she said, as Penelope approached.

"Yes. We met at the bookstore."

He smiled at Penelope. "I'm having a few people round to my place for a drink. I hope you'll join us."

"I'd love to," Pen said.

Quentin looked at his watch. "Shall we say in half an hour?" He glanced at Maribel. "Maribel can show you the way."

Penelope headed to the library, where Maribel promised to come get her when it was time to head to Quentin's apartment. She hoped that working on her book would take her mind off the case. In the end, she spent twenty minutes going over her notes for her book and fretting over how she was going to get her character Eirene out of her predica-ment. Sadly, Maribel arrived before Pen had had any brain-storms.

"It's not far," Maribel said, as they headed across the quad. "He's in Leighton Hall."

"This must be so difficult for Quentin," Maribel said as they neared the ivy-covered building in the distance. Classes had started and the quad was nearly empty except for a few students scurrying from one building to another. "He often said that Odile meant the world to him, and to lose her like this . . ."

By now they had reached Leighton Hall. "This is one of

the older buildings on campus," Maribel said as she used her key card to open the front door. "It's slightly grander than some of the other buildings." She gave a small smile. "It suits Quentin perfectly."

The floor in the lobby was marble and there was a sweeping staircase leading to the upper floor.

"Do you mind the stairs?" Maribel said. She pointed across the lobby. "There's an elevator if you'd rather."

"The stairs are fine."

They climbed the stairs and headed down the short hallway. Maribel paused in front of one of the doors. The low murmur of voices could be heard coming from behind it.

Quentin answered their knock. He'd exchanged his sport coat for an argyle cardigan and a silk ascot and had a cutglass tumbler in his hand.

"Do come in," he said.

The apartment was quite spacious with a high ceiling, tall windows, and walls painted a dark green. A bookcase stuffed with books was along one wall; and the sofa and armchairs were brown leather. One of Odile's paintings hung over a sideboard set with crystal decanters and a silver tray. The scent of pipe smoke hung in the air.

"Let me take your coats," Quentin said, helping Maribel out of hers.

A woman in a black skirt and a white shirt appeared and whisked their things away.

Pen looked around. She recognized Tina Resse along with Adrian Mabry and Layla Evans. Adrian and Layla appeared to be ostentatiously avoiding each other.

"Something to drink?" Quentin said, leading them over to a table set with glasses and various bottles. "There's sherry and white wine and there's whiskey if you'd prefer something stronger."

Pen and Maribel opted for glasses of sherry. Quentin poured them each one and handed them around.

"We should drink to Odile," he said, raising his glass.

"To Odile," Penelope and Maribel said in unison, holding their glasses aloft.

Maribel began to talk to Helen and Pen wandered over to the bookcase and began scanning the volumes. She could never resist checking the titles on someone's shelves. Quentin's was an eclectic collection. There were a lot of history books as Pen would have suspected but also books on art, religion, philosophy, and botany along with a complete set of the Harry Potter novels. Quentin was obviously a well-read man.

Mabry sidled over to Penelope. "Quite the collection, isn't it?" he said, tossing his hair off his forehead. He took a sip of his whiskey and sighed in appreciation.

Penelope froze. She felt uncomfortable knowing that she'd been spying on Mabry and Layla. She'd been told more than once that she didn't possess a poker face and hoped her expression now wasn't giving anything away.

But Mabry didn't seem to notice anything amiss. "Have you seen Quentin's cross?" he said.

"Cross?"

"Quentin acquired a Victoria Cross at auction. They're given for valor in the face of the enemy. They're the most prestigious of the British honors, having been introduced by Queen Victoria during the Crimean War. Quentin's is quite valuable since it dates from the Crimean War."

Mabry took Pen by the elbow and led her over to a glass display case sitting on a small round occasional table.

Pen peered through the glass top. The ornate medal rested on a backdrop of black velvet. It was highly polished and hung from a slightly faded maroon-colored ribbon. On the cross, a lion stood atop a crown with the words *For Valour* inscribed below.

"Checking out my Victoria Cross, I see," Quentin said as he joined them.

The smell of whiskey mixed with the odor of woodsy pipe smoke drifted toward Penelope.

Quentin tapped the case with his finger. "This one is quite valuable. It was given out by Queen Victoria herself." He puffed out his chest. "It's my most prized possession."

"It must have cost a packet," Mabry said, peering through the glass.

Quentin gave a smug smile. "It did, rather. But worth it, if you ask me. I've wanted one of these for ages. I never thought I'd snag one this rare."

"Lovely," Penelope said, to be polite.

Quentin wandered off to refresh his drink and was soon deep in conversation with an older man who was bald save for a ring of frizzy gray hair and had a gold pocket watch hanging from a chain looped across his vest.

The woman in the black skirt and white blouse came out of the kitchen and placed a tray of tea sandwiches on the table, then silently disappeared again. Pen realized she was hungry and wandered over. She picked up a napkin and a small cucumber and cream cheese sandwich and took a bite.

She was reaching for another sandwich when the door opened and Helen Dingley rushed in.

"Sorry to be late," she said to no one in particular as she slipped out of her coat.

Quentin glided over toward her. He took her coat and disappeared in the direction of the bedroom.

Helen looked flustered. She saw Penelope and headed in her direction.

"The sandwiches are lovely," Pen said, pointing to the tray. "Have you gotten something to drink?"

Helen shook her head. "I'm not much of a drinker, I'm afraid, but I do think I'll have one of those egg salad sandwiches. I've always been quite fond of them. Nanny used to make them for our tea."

"Helen." The man with the pocket watch went up to Helen and tapped her on the shoulder. Helen turned around and they began to chat.

Penelope noticed Layla standing off by herself. She appeared to be ill at ease. Penelope went over to her.

Layla smiled shyly. "You're the writer," she said in a soft voice.

"Guilty as charged." Penelope grinned.

Layla fiddled with the gold band on her left ring finger. She looked around the room.

"It was nice of Quentin to host this," she said.

"I gather he and Odile were very much in love. It must be so difficult for him," Penelope said, echoing Maribel's earlier comments.

Layla's eyebrows shot up. "Who told you that?"

"Maribel did. I gather it was common knowledge."

Layla sniffed. "It was also common knowledge that Odile and Quentin fought like cats and dogs more often than not. Odile had a strong ego and so does Quentin. They were like oil and water." She shrugged. "I could never understand why they stayed together."

Penelope looked over at Quentin. He was deep in conversation with a woman in a sapphire blue dress and a jewel-toned scarf.

So things hadn't been so smooth between Quentin and Odile, Penelope thought as she watched him talking and making elaborate gestures with his hands. In books and movies, the boyfriend was always the prime suspect in a murder case. It was a bit of a cliché, but for a reason—it was so often true. Had one of Odile's and Quentin's fights got out of hand? Penelope couldn't imagine what Quentin had to gain by killing her, but that didn't mean there wasn't something.

Layla's cell phone buzzed and Penelope moved away. She found Maribel again and spent a few minutes chatting with her and then decided she'd better get back to the Open Book. She said good-bye to Quentin and assured him she could get her own coat.

She headed down the hallway he had indicated toward the bedroom. She was nearing the open door when she heard voices. A man's voice—she thought it was Mabry. She hesitated. It sounded as if he was talking to Helen.

Pen crept a bit closer and peered around the edge of the door. Helen's face was red and she was playing with the ends of her silk scarf.

Mabry moved closer to Helen and said in a very smooth voice that made Pen think of oil floating on water. "I don't imagine you're exactly mourning poor Odile's death too strenuously."

Helen looked flustered. "What?" Her hands flew to her scarf again. "What do you mean? How can you say that?"

Mabry gave a very nonchalant shrug. "Oh, Helen, I think you know what I mean."

"I don't know what you're talking about," Helen said, trying to sound indignant but sounding more as if she was about to cry.

Pen cleared her throat and stepped into the bedroom. Helen quickly excused herself and scurried from the room.

Coats were piled on the bed, which had a tufted and padded headboard in dark green velvet. A comfortable armchair with a reading light next to it was in the other corner with an end table piled high with books.

Pen dug through the heap of coats, found hers, and slipped it on. She let herself out the door, made her way down the stairs and out the front door. The fresh air felt good—Quentin's apartment had been slightly stuffy with so many bodies in one space. She took a deep breath and began to walk across the quad.

She was mulling over what she had heard as she headed toward the school entrance—what had Mabry meant by saying Helen should be glad that Odile was dead? Did he really mean it? Was it because Odile had been known to order Helen around? Or was it because of something else?

NINE

❧

Penelope was relieved to arrive back at the Open Book in one piece. The taxi driver had been new—it wasn't Mad Max, a driver everyone suspected was at least one hundred years old and drove like it, or Dashing Dennis, who thought he was doing his female passengers a favor by flirting with them or any of the others she'd had before.

The new driver wore a checked newsboy cap, chewed gum a mile a minute, and seemed to think he was driving on the Daytona Speedway and not winding and narrow country lanes.

"You look a bit pale," Mabel said when Penelope walked into the shop. "Is everything okay? How was the memorial service?"

Penelope slipped off her jacket. "I had a new taxi driver. I've never been carsick before, but the way he drove, I thought I was about to be for the first time. Give me Mad Max any day even though I can walk faster than he drives."

"A new shipment of Charlotte Davenport's books have come in," Mabel said, gesturing toward a stack of cartons. Would you mind shelving them for me?"

"Not at all," Pen said. She was glad to avoid her writing room today. She still hadn't figured out how to get Eirene out of her predicament. She feared she was going to have to write the whole scene over.

A couple of customers were browsing the used book section and a woman was seated in one of the armchairs, flipping through a book on photography. It was quiet and Penelope felt that sense of calm that always settled over her when she was at the Open Book.

She slit open one of the cartons and grabbed an armload of books. She had just finished shelving the last one when the door opened and a new customer came in. She stopped at the counter and looked around as if she was searching for something. Penelope didn't recognize her—she wasn't one of their regulars.

She was petite and was wearing skinny jeans, a black turtleneck, a leather moto jacket, and suede booties. Her blond hair was slightly tousled, making it look as if she'd just tumbled out of bed.

Mabel had gone into the stockroom, so Penelope walked over, her mouth stretched into a welcoming smile.

"Welcome to the Open Book. Can I help you find something?"

"Where are your cookbooks?"

"I'll show you. Right this way."

Penelope led her over to the culinary section. "If you need any help, let me know."

Penelope busied herself tidying some shelves and rearranging a display with some new books that had just come in. She was straightening one of the stacks when she noticed the customer approaching the counter with a book in her hand.

Penelope hurried over. "Did you find what you were looking for?"

"Yes, I did." She put the book on the counter.

Penelope glanced at the title—*Dining for Two*.

The woman reached into her handbag, pulled out her wallet, and selected a credit card from a number of others. She put it on the counter.

Penelope glanced at the card. The name on it read *Mrs. Brodie Maguire*.

Her first reaction was to gasp, but she managed to stifle it. Her smile felt plastered on her face as she processed the card, ripped off the receipt, and handed it to Mrs. Maguire. A dozen questions were on the tip of her tongue but she bit down hard and managed to keep her mouth shut.

"Thank you," Pen said, handing the package over to her. Her lips felt numb, the way they did when she got a shot of Novocain at the dentist.

"Good heavens," Mabel said when she came out of the stockroom after the woman had left. "You look like Scrooge being visited by the ghost of Christmas past."

Penelope gulped, but no words came out.

"What you need is a cup of builder's tea," Mabel said, hustling Penelope toward the tea shop.

"Builder's tea?"

"It's a good strong cuppa like workmen drink on their break," Mabel said. "It's very bracing. I'll tell Figgy to put plenty of sugar in it." Mabel led Penelope over to a chair. "Now you sit and I'll be right back. And then you can tell me all about it."

All sorts of thoughts were swirling through Pen's head as she awaited her cup of tea. Was Maguire married? Was it possible there were two Brodie Maguires and this woman was the wife of the other one?

Mabel and Figgy both bustled over with a cup of tea, which Figgy placed on the table in front of Penelope.

"Drink," she said.

Penelope obligingly took a sip. The sweet warmth felt good going down her throat.

Mabel and Figgy sat down. "Now," Mabel said, putting both hands flat on the table. "Tell us what's wrong."

Penelope wet her lips. "A customer came in."

Mabel and Figgy nodded their heads.

"That does happen," Mabel said dryly.

"And she asked where the cookbooks were, so I showed her."

Mabel nodded her head. "Go on."

"She paid with a credit card and the name on the card was Mrs. Brodie Maguire."

Both Mabel and Figgy gasped. Penelope would have found it comical if she hadn't been so upset.

"Maybe there are two Brodie Maguires," Figgy said, putting into words what Penelope had been thinking earlier.

"That doesn't seem very likely, does it?" Pen took another sip of her tea.

"Anything's possible," Figgy said.

"You're definitely a glass-half-full type of person," Mabel said, turning to Figgy. Figgy shrugged.

"The only thing for it is to ask Maguire about it. Maybe there's an explanation."

"Or maybe there's something I need to know," Penelope said glumly, draining the last of her tea.

* * *

Penelope spent the rest of the afternoon trying to work on her book but her heart wasn't in it. Her spirits had sunk to the level of her feet and she now knew why people used the expression *heartbroken*—her heart literally felt as if it were about to crack in two.

She tried to cheer herself up with the thought that there was an innocent explanation for their being a Mrs. Brodie Maguire, but she was failing miserably.

Her poor character Eirene was still tied to the chair in Mr. Bloodworth's laboratory. Penelope hit a few keys on her computer and voilà, Eirene was freed. Not because she'd managed to escape but because Penelope had deleted the part where she had tied Eirene to the chair in the first place. She was going to have to do something else to the poor girl—something that would give her at least a chance of escaping.

Pen chewed on the side of her thumb. Maybe Bloodworth could just lock her in his lab and threaten to come back later? Eirene could climb out the window and get away across the moors.

Pen started typing but then stopped. She wasn't really sure she liked that idea. She thought for a bit and finally powered down her computer and slammed the lid shut in frustration.

Her mind was going around and around in circles and Maguire was at the center of her thoughts. She wasn't going to get anywhere with her manuscript no matter how hard she tried.

She packed up her things and walked out into the salesroom.

"I think I'll go home," she said to Mabel, who was counting out the register.

"Go on. Can you flip the sign to Closed on your way out?"

Penelope put on her coat and pulled on her gloves. She turned the sign over, said good night to Mabel, and left.

The sky was cloudless and sprinkled with stars. They were so much easier to see in Chumley than in New York City, where the lights obscured them, Penelope thought.

She was about to head down the high street toward home when she noticed the lights blink off at the Pig in a Poke across the street. Gladys came out the door, her coat open and her hat still in her hand. Penelope was surprised to see that she was wearing a rather nice dress and had obviously styled her hair.

And she was even more surprised when Gladys headed down the sidewalk, meeting up with a man who had been smoking a cigarette and waiting in the shadows of the doorway of the Knit Wit shop. Gladys put her arm through his and they continued on down the street.

Penelope didn't get a good look at the man—he had his back to her—but the man definitely wasn't Gladys's husband, Bruce, who now used a cane after having had a stroke.

Was Gladys having an affair? Penelope wondered. First Mabry and Layla and now Gladys and some stranger. Penelope thought of Maguire and her own relationship. Was he married and was he cheating on his wife? What did that make her? Penelope wondered.

Penelope watched as Gladys and her companion disappeared into the darkness down the street. She still couldn't believe Gladys would embark on an affair, but then again she was an avid reader of romance novels. And Bruce was hardly the romantic sort.

Perhaps Gladys had decided to live out in real life what she'd been reading about in fiction.

Mrs. Danvers seemed to recognize Penelope's downcast mood when Penelope got home. Normally she was a bit standoffish to let Pen know she didn't appreciate being left alone all day, but tonight she was actually quite affectionate, weaving in and out between Penelope's legs and allowing herself to be petted and scratched under the chin.

Penelope hung up her jacket, dumped her tote bag on the sitting room sofa, and went out to the kitchen. She'd gotten chilled on her walk home and the heat coming from the Aga felt good. She held her hands over it for a minute to warm them, then opened the refrigerator. She still had a bit of chili left and she'd heat that up for her dinner.

She was dumping the chili into a pot when the doorbell rang.

Who could that be? She wasn't expecting anyone. For a horrible, panicked moment, she feared it might be Maguire. She prayed it wasn't. She wasn't ready to face either him or the truth yet—whatever the truth would turn out to be. Penelope braced herself and pulled open the door.

It was Beryl and she was clearly excited. Her face was flushed, and not simply from the brisk weather, and her eyes were shining. She looked happier than Penelope had seen her since she'd found out that Atelier Classique was moving to Paris.

"Come in." Penelope sniffed. "What's that delicious smell?"

Beryl held up a paper bag. "I picked up some dinner for

us from Kebabs and Curries," she said as she slipped out of her coat. "I hope you haven't eaten."

"Not yet," Penelope said as she hung Beryl's coat in the closet and then led her out to the kitchen.

Beryl glanced at the pot on the stove. "Looks like you made chili," she said. "If you'd rather have that . . ."

"It will keep," Penelope said as she spooned the chili back into the container. "I'd much rather have what you've brought. It smells so good."

Beryl put the bag on the counter and opened it. Savory aromas immediately filled the kitchen. She took out several containers and lined them up on the counter.

"You seem to be in good spirits," Pen said.

"I am. I'll tell you why in a minute but first let's get our dinner set up. I'm starved."

She got some serving bowls from the cupboard, emptied the containers into them, and carried them to the table. "Do you have any wine?" she said.

"I have a bottle of plonk," Pen said. "Cheap red wine," she explained when Beryl looked at her blankly.

"I should have brought some champagne," Beryl said as she took a seat at the table and Penelope got wineglasses from the cupboard.

"Champagne? Are we celebrating?"

"Yes." Beryl opened the wine and poured some into each of their glasses. "Cheers," she said, raising her glass in the air.

"So are you going to tell me just what it is we're celebrating?" Pen said after taking a sip. She reached for the bowl of rice and spooned some onto her plate. "What is this?" she said as she reached for the curry.

"Chicken jalfrezi," Beryl said, serving herself some rice. "The fellow behind the counter—Arjun—told me that jalfrezi is now the most popular curry in England. Apparently, it used to be tikka masala, which was actually considered the British national dish because it showcased Britain's multiculturalism. Some people believe it was invented by a chef in Glasgow but that's often disputed."

"You've become quite the expert," Pen said.

"Arjun seems to have taken a fancy to me," Beryl said, adding some chicken jalfrezi to her plate. She pointed to it. "I'm going to regret this later, but it smelled too good to pass up."

"It does smell delicious," Pen said. She took a bite. "It tastes delicious, too. But enough stalling. What is your big news?" She wasn't in the mood to play games with Beryl. "Did you get a job?"

Beryl looked slightly crestfallen. "How did you know?" Her expression perked up again. "But you don't know what it is."

Penelope waited, her fork poised in the air.

"I," Beryl said with great relish, "have been asked to be Charlotte, the Duchess of Upper Chumley-on-Stoke's stylist."

Penelope had to admit she hadn't been expecting that. Her jaw actually dropped a little.

"But that's wonderful," she said, jumping up from her chair to hug Beryl. "You're perfect for it."

Beryl put down her fork and looked at Penelope. "Now tell me what's bothering you because I can tell something is. And don't tell me there isn't. You can't fool me."

Penelope pushed her plate away and put her head in her hands.

"Come on. Out with it. It can't be that bad. What was it Grandma Parish used to say—about a problem just being trouble looking for a solution?"

"I don't think there is a solution for this," Pen said and went on to tell Beryl about the woman who had come into the Open Book with the credit card that read *Mrs. Brodie Maguire*.

Beryl's eyebrows shot up. "So your boyfriend's married?"

"I don't know that he's my boyfriend," Pen said, "and I don't know for sure that he's married but it looks that way, doesn't it?"

Beryl's jaw set. "But the two of you have been going out. Did you get the sense that he was sneaking around?"

Penelope thought back to her dates with Maguire—the times they went to the Book and Bottle, and the local wine bar and the times she'd made dinner for him.

She shook her head. "No, I didn't. He never seemed rushed or stressed or . . . or anything."

"Maybe there's some explanation," Beryl said. "Maybe he's divorced or about to be. You need to ask him. Believe me. If I'd asked Magnus more questions instead of trusting him, I wouldn't be in the situation I'm in now."

"You're right," Penelope said. "I'll ask him the first chance I get."

TEN

❧⟐❧

Mrs. Danvers hovered around Penelope's ankles the next morning while Penelope stood at the kitchen counter, drinking a cup of tea.

"You're going on an adventure today," Pen said as she washed out her mug and put it in the dish drainer to dry.

Mrs. Danvers did not look particularly interested. She sat down and began to groom her back leg.

Penelope retrieved the cat carrier from the foyer closet and took it into the kitchen.

Mrs. Danvers reared at the sight of it and began to slink off toward the sitting room.

"Oh no you don't," Pen said, trying to scoop up the cat. She thought she had a good grip on Mrs. Danvers, but the cat squirmed and broke free.

Penelope started to work up a sweat as she chased the

cat around the sitting room, up the stairs, and into her spare room, where she found Mrs. Danvers hiding in an empty carton.

Penelope grabbed her and managed to keep hold of her long enough to carry her back to the kitchen, where the carrier was waiting.

Getting Mrs. Danvers into the carrier was another struggle—and Penelope ended up with a nasty scratch on her hand—but finally the deed was done and she slammed the door on the carrier shut to the accompaniment of Mrs. Danvers's loud and indignant protestations.

There was a honk outside and Penelope quickly put on her jacket, picked up her tote bag in one hand and the carrier in the other, and went out to where Mabel was waiting, her car humming at the curb.

Penelope wrestled the carrier into the back seat and hopped in beside Mabel. Mrs. Danvers gave a chorus of complaints, which Penelope ignored, as Mabel put the car in gear and began the drive to the Open Book.

They were about halfway there when Penelope heard a scratching noise. She turned around to see Mrs. Danvers reaching a paw out of the carrier and sinking her claws into Mabel's copy of that week's *Chumley Chronicle*.

They parked in front of the Open Book and Penelope carried Mrs. Danvers into the store. She hung up her jacket and flipped the Closed sign to Open.

Mabel went behind the counter, grabbed a piece of paper, selected a bright red marker from the cluster in the jar by the cash register, and wrote in large letters *Please Mind the Cat*. She taped the sign to the front door.

She turned to Penelope. "I'll keep an eye out for Mrs. Danvers so she doesn't try to scoot out the door."

Penelope opened the cat's carrier and Mrs. Danvers streaked out, ran through the bookstore, and disappeared.

"Where did she go?" Mabel said.

Penelope began searching between the stacks. "I don't see her."

"Perhaps she's after the mouse," Mabel said hopefully.

"I hope so," Penelope said, although she had her doubts.

Fortunately the door to the storage room was closed, so Penelope knew the cat couldn't be in there.

"Have you seen Mrs. Danvers?" Pen said to Figgy, who was putting place mats out on the tables.

"Your cat?" She shook her head. "Nope. She hasn't been through here."

"She's bound to come out when she feels comfortable. I think being in the carrier and the ride in the car traumatized her."

A customer came in and walked purposefully toward the section marked *Mysteries*.

He didn't seem to need any help, so Penelope began to set up for her book group. The members had insisted on reading Penelope's own Gothic novel, *Lady of the Moors*. She had been flattered, of course, but also slightly embarrassed by the attention. She had no idea what Gladys, India, Brimble, and the others would make of it.

There was still some time until the group would arrive, so Penelope sought out Mabel, who was opening a carton of books.

"I saw something odd last night," Penelope began.

Mabel stood up with an armful of books she'd pulled from an open carton. "Odder than the usual goings-on in Chum?"

"Sort of. Different," Penelope said. "Of course I may be misinterpreting things."

"Now I'm really curious." Mabel balanced the books on her hip.

"I was leaving the store when I noticed Gladys coming out of the Pig in a Poke. She was dressed rather strangely." Penelope paused. "Maybe not strangely—just different for Gladys. She was in a real dress—a nice one—and not one of the housedresses she usually wears. Half the time she leaves work with her apron still on."

"That's true," Mabel said, "but perhaps she was going somewhere special last night?"

"That's not all," Penelope said. "She met up with a man who was waiting outside the Knit Wit shop."

"Was it Bruce? He's retired now."

"That's the thing," Pen said. "It couldn't have been Bruce. The man didn't have a cane."

"Does Gladys have a brother? An uncle?"

"I don't know. But she went up to him and took his arm. As if they were on a date or something."

"Now that is curious," Mabel said.

"I can't help but wonder what's up," Pen said.

Mabel frowned. "If Gladys is seeing another man, heaven help her if Bruce gets wind of it."

Mabel went back to unpacking the shipment of books and Penelope pulled the last of the miscellaneous collection of chairs scattered around the Open Book into an approximation of a circle.

She was standing back to admire her work, when Mrs. Danvers casually strolled out from under the sagging sofa that was at the center of Penelope's setup. The cat appeared to have a piece of paper in her mouth.

Penelope squatted down and put out her hand. Mrs. Danvers ignored it at first but then finally approached Penelope at a leisurely pace. Pen tried to wrest the piece of paper from Mrs. Danvers's mouth, but the cat resisted and instead dropped the scrap of paper and began to bat at it with her paws.

Penelope waited until Mrs. Danvers was tired of the game and then swooped down and snatched up the scrap. She didn't think Mrs. Danvers would eat it—she turned her nose up at all but one brand of cat food—but she didn't want to take any chances.

She was about to stuff it in her pocket when she noticed there was writing on it. She glanced at it. It read: *Wadsworth and Sons, Book Restorers*. There was also a London address and telephone number.

Someone must have dropped it. Pen stuffed it in her shirt pocket and didn't give it another thought.

Pen's book club wrapped up with a heated discussion as to whether or not Annora, Penelope's protagonist in *Lady of the Moors*, had been reckless in going out onto the moors alone. Brimble declared her foolhardy, while India insisted it showed spunk. Penelope had found it all rather amusing.

As soon as everyone had gone, Penelope headed to her classroom at the Oakwood School for her seminar. The taxi dropped her off at the administration building and she began the walk across the quad toward Corbyn Hall. The sky was blue and there was only a slight breeze that ruffled the hair around her face. She opened her coat as she walked and stopped for a moment to hold her face up to the sun.

Light streamed in the slightly dusty window of Penelope's classroom and she angled the blinds to lessen the glare.

She was checking her trash can—once again there was a bottle tossed in it—this time an empty fifth of vodka—when she heard voices outside her classroom door and caught Nicola's name.

She sidled closer and peeked out. Layla was talking to a woman Penelope hadn't met yet but had seen around the campus.

"I saw her go into the woods," Layla said to the other woman.

"Who? Nicola?"

"Yes. I can't help but wonder what she was doing, wandering around out there," Layla said.

"Perhaps she wanted some fresh air?"

"I don't know." Layla said. She sounded suspicious. "I read that Odile Fontaine was poisoned with deadly nightshade." She lowered her voice. "Grady said there isn't any growing on the campus—he said it's rarely used in gardens and he would have pulled it out if he'd seen any. But the killer had to have found it somewhere. So why not the woods?"

Penelope saw her shrug and then they both moved away from the door and down the hall.

She found it hard to believe that Nicola would poison someone. Nicola was the sort who got into scrapes and caused trouble—but she wasn't a murderer. Pen couldn't bring herself to believe that.

The class went smoothly—Penelope felt as if she was developing her sea legs, so to speak. The students seemed genuinely interested in what she had to say and the nerves she'd felt the first day had eased.

They were discussing the overwrought emotions prevalent in Gothic novels—characters crying and making emotional speeches and experiencing feelings of breathlessness and panic—when the bell rang and the students jumped to their feet. Penelope waited until they had all filed out and then put on her jacket and packed her notes in her tote bag.

A few students were still trickling down the hall. She passed the open door to one of the classrooms, where Greta Danbury, the German teacher, was rearranging some papers on a bulletin board.

The door to the classroom next to that one was open, and at first Pen thought it was empty but then she caught a movement out of the corner of her eye. She paused and peered inside. Nicola was standing next to the wastebasket. She reached into a shopping bag that had *Marks and Spencer* written on it and pulled out what looked like an empty wine bottle. As Pen watched, she dropped it in the bin, where it landed with a dull thud.

So it was Nicola disposing of the empty bottles. Penelope wasn't entirely surprised after what she'd overheard in Maribel's office. The question was who was buying the alcohol for the girls, or had one of them managed to forge an ID?

Penelope headed out the door of Corbyn Hall and began the walk across the quad to the school entrance when her toe caught on an uneven bit of pavement. Before she knew it, she was sprawled on the path. She stumbled to her feet, feeling her face burn with embarrassment.

Her knees were stinging and her leggings were torn. She could feel blood trickling down her legs.

Fortunately her tote bag had landed on the grass. She peered inside and her laptop appeared to be intact.

"That looks nasty," a voice she recognized as Mabry's

said. He took her arm. "Let's get you to the nurse for some sticking plasters."

"Some what?" Pen said.

"Bandages," Mabry explained. "And it looks as if those cuts need cleaning as well."

"I don't want to keep you. I'm sure I can manage on my own if you'll just direct me."

"Nonsense," Mabry said. "I've nothing pressing to do. Come with me."

They began walking, Penelope a bit gingerly since her knees were now hurting in earnest.

"It's Penelope, right?" Mabry said, tossing his hair back from his forehead.

Penelope smiled. "Yes. Penelope Parish."

"I'm giving a concert in the assembly hall tonight if you're interested. It's at seven thirty."

"What instrument do you play?" Penelope winced as her leggings rubbed against her cut knees.

"The violin. I studied under the great Hungarian violinist Béla Nagy." He glanced sideways at Penelope. "Do you know him?"

"I'm afraid I don't," Pen said. Not only did she not play an instrument but in elementary school she had been asked by the music teacher during choir to not actually sing but to just move her lips instead. "Besides, I'm more of a fan of pop and rock music, to be honest with you." Penelope brushed a strand of hair out of her eyes. "Lady Gaga, OneRepublic, oldies like Prince and U2. It's embarrassing, but I also have to admit to having a soft spot for Maroon Five."

Mabry made a snorting sound. "I don't have time for rock music. In my opinion, it's just loud and obnoxious noise."

Penelope was surprised. Mabry wasn't very old—

Penelope thought he must be about her age. She'd never met anyone who didn't like at least some rock music.

"Training with Nagy informed my taste, I'm afraid. It ruined me for lesser music."

Well! Penelope prickled. Obviously Mabry now thought she was totally uncultured. She didn't particularly like the feeling.

They were nearing the administration building when Penelope caught sight of a woman in front of her. She had her back to them, but Pen thought she looked familiar. There was something about her shape and the way she walked that Penelope thought she recognized.

Suddenly the woman turned her head briefly. Penelope could only see her profile but she could have sworn it was Gladys. But what would Gladys be doing at the Oakwood School? She had to be mistaken.

By now they had reached the administration building. Mabry held the door for Penelope and ushered her inside. He gestured toward the end of the hallway.

"The infirmary is right down there."

"Thank you," Pen said.

"My pleasure." Mabry tossed his head. "Maybe I'll see you tonight."

Penelope gave him a noncommittal smile.

The door to the infirmary had a frosted glass window with *Infirmary* written on it in red paint. The sterile smell of antiseptics drifted into the hallway from behind it. Penelope knocked and opened the door.

Layla Evans was seated behind a small metal desk. The door to the room beyond was open and Penelope noticed a rather stark-looking cot, an examination table, and a glass-fronted cabinet filled with supplies.

Layla's eyes were red rimmed, as if she'd been crying,

and her lower lip trembled slightly as she said hello to Penelope.

"I'm afraid I've managed to fall and cut myself," Pen said, pointing to her knees.

Layla jumped up. "Oh, dear. We'd better get that cleaned up." She ushered Penelope into the inner room. "I think you'd best take your leggings off," she said as she motioned toward the examination table.

Penelope slipped out of her leggings as Layla rummaged in the cabinet for what she needed. She put a tube of antiseptic cream, a box of bandages, a bottle of peroxide, and some cotton balls on a cart that was nearby.

Her expression was downcast and Penelope thought her eyes had filled with tears once or twice.

Layla went over to the sink on the wall, washed her hands, and pulled on gloves. She wet a cloth under the running water and used that to clean Penelope's wounds. She wet one of the cotton balls with peroxide and gently dabbed Penelope's knees.

"A little antiseptic cream and some sticking plasters should do it." Layla smiled at Penelope but the smile didn't reach her eyes.

"Is everything okay?" Pen said, wincing slightly as Layla swabbed the antiseptic cream on the cuts.

"Yes. Of course. Why?" Layla kept her head down as she answered.

"You look as if you've been crying."

"I'm fine. It's only allergies." She sniffed. She peeled the backing off the last bandage and carefully placed it over the scrape on Penelope's right knee. "There," she said. "You're all set."

Penelope looked at her leggings—they were a mess but

she could hardly walk out of there in just her jacket. She slipped them on and thanked Layla, who was busy cleaning up the examining room.

She was walking through the outer office when she noticed an envelope on Layla's desk alongside a crumpled piece of paper and an open planner. Had Layla received a letter that had upset her? Pen glanced over her shoulder, but Layla had her back to the door and was wiping down the examination table.

Pen sidled closer to the desk and inched the envelope toward her with the tip of her index finger. There was no return address and it was postmarked six days ago.

Pen carefully teased the crumpled ball of paper toward her. She checked the other room again, but Layla appeared to be rearranging the supplies in the cabinet and still had her back to the open door.

Penelope eased the creases out of the paper and quickly glanced at the contents. She stifled a gasp.

The letter was from Odile Fontaine and she was threatening to tell Grady about Layla and Mabry's affair.

If that didn't give Layla a motive for murder, then Penelope didn't know what did.

Penelope's head was whirling as she sat in the taxi on her way back to the Open Book. Had Layla been the one to murder Odile? She obviously knew about deadly nightshade.

Her thoughts continued to flit from one thing to another, finally alighting on the woman who had been walking ahead of her on the quad earlier. Had that really been Gladys or was Penelope mistaken?

There was one way to find out. She had the taxi drop her off across the street from the Open Book and in front of the Pig in a Poke. If Gladys was behind the counter as usual, then Penelope had been mistaken.

The bell jingled as she pushed open the door to the shop. She would say she was there to pick up something for her dinner.

Gladys wasn't behind the counter, but Ralph, Gladys's brother-in-law, was. He often helped out in the shop now that Gladys's husband had had to retire for health reasons.

"What can I get for you today, young lady?" Ralph said. He had blue eyes under bushy white eyebrows and freckles on his bald scalp.

"I'd like one pork chop, please."

"Your wish is my command," Ralph said, his eyes twinkling. "Boneless or bone-in? I have some nice shoulder chops." He pointed to a display in the counter. "Or, if you really want to splash out, there's your loin chop." He pointed to another row of neatly aligned chops.

Penelope hesitated. Boneless or bone-in? Loin or rib? She had no idea what the differences were.

Ralph leaned over the counter and lowered his voice.

"If you want my opinion, the bone-in chops are much tastier and easier to cook. You don't want to overdo it, though, or you'll end up with shoe leather." He laughed. "For the money, I'd say you'll get plenty of flavor from the rib chops."

"Okay. I'll take one of those, then."

"I'll pick out a nice one for you," Ralph said, reaching into the counter.

While he was wrapping up the chop, Penelope said, "Is Gladys here?"

"I'm afraid not. She's stepped out for a bit. And she was all hush-hush about it, too. Wouldn't say where she was going and I don't know when she'll be back. And that's not the first time." He smiled. "But I expect she deserves a break now and then. She's a hard worker."

So Gladys had *stepped out*, as Ralph had put it. And she had been secretive about it as well. If she'd been going around to the shops or to the post office to mail a letter, surely she wouldn't have hesitated to say.

Maybe that *had* been Gladys she'd seen at the Oakwood School. But what on earth could she have been doing there? And secretly, no less?

Unless . . . unless it had something to do with the man she'd mysteriously gone off with the previous night.

What on earth was Gladys up to? Penelope wondered.

Penelope made a quick trip home to change into a fresh pair of leggings. She put her pork chop in the refrigerator and then headed toward the Open Book. Her knees smarted a bit as she walked and she felt the bandages pulling at her skin. Hopefully her scrapes would heal soon.

Mabel looked up from the book she was reading when Penelope arrived, slightly flushed from her walk and the fresh air.

Mrs. Danvers was curled up in a bit of sunshine that was peeking through the diamond-paned front window of the shop. She was purring contentedly.

"What are you reading?" Pen said as she took off her jacket.

"Charlotte Davenport's latest." Mabel held up the book.

"*The Regency Rogue.*" She rifled through the pages. "Only three hundred more pages to go before the duke and his duchess get together and live happily ever after."

"I wonder how Charlotte feels writing about dukes and duchesses now that she's become an actual duchess herself," Penelope said.

"I imagine it feels a bit otherworldly." Mabel stuck a bookmark in the book and closed it.

"However did Charlotte and Worthington meet?" Penelope said. "I wouldn't think their worlds would overlap."

"It was a blind date, apparently. You were still over in the States at the time and I imagine it wasn't as widely reported there." Mabel smoothed the dust jacket of her book. "It was Cissie Emmott, Arthur's old girlfriend, who introduced them. Charlotte met her when she ordered some dresses from Cissie's Atelier Classique for her book tour. It seems she thought they would hit it off."

"There's your happily ever after," Penelope said. She frowned. "By the way, have you ever heard of a violinist named Béla Nagy?"

"Béla Nagy? I've heard of him but I can't tell you much about him."

"The music teacher at the Oakwood School—Adrian Mabry—studied under him." Penelope sniffed. "He was quite snooty about it, too. He made it clear that rock music was beneath him."

"Maybe it's a generational thing. How old is this Mabry anyway?"

Penelope shrugged. "He's around my age I'd say. Give or take a year or two."

"Your age?" Mabel's eyebrows shot up.

"Yes. Why?"

"Well, Béla Nagy has been dead for fifty years at least.

Unless this Mabry is in his seventies, it would have been impossible for him to have studied under Nagy."

So Mabry had been lying, Penelope thought. What a silly thing to lie about. Was he trying to make himself sound more impressive? Maybe Mabry was just the sort who couldn't help embellishing things.

ELEVEN

❧❦❧

Later that afternoon, when there was a lull in customers, Penelope decided she really ought to put in some time on her book. She'd left poor Eirene hanging long enough. And although her deadline wasn't imminent, she knew how time could speed up until the due date appeared to be coming at her as fast as a freight train.

So Eirene was locked in Bloodworth's laboratory. She'd nixed the idea of tying her to the chair since she had no idea how Eirene would escape, and she didn't like the idea of Eirene getting away out the window. She had to make it a *bit* harder than that or the reader would be disappointed.

Eirene was resourceful, Penelope thought. Sadly, her creator was a lot less so. Penelope was tempted to scratch the scene altogether when she had an idea.

Eirene had grown up with brothers, so it wasn't beyond the realm of possibility she'd know a thing or two about tools and how to use them.

Penelope started to get excited. Eirene would find a screwdriver in one of the drawers in the laboratory. *Note to self*, Pen scribbled on a scrap of paper, *go back and plant the screwdriver earlier in the manuscript.*

Penelope began typing. Eirene has found the screwdriver and she is contemplating the door. It's an ordinary door—nothing special. Eirene decides to unscrew the doorknob and circumvent the lock altogether.

Penelope continued to write, quite pleased with her solution to Eirene's problem. She glanced at the word count at the bottom of the page. Finally, she was making progress.

Her nose began to tickle and then itch. She reached into her shirt pocket, looking for a tissue, but all she found was a slip of paper. She pulled it out.

It was the scrap Mrs. Danvers had unearthed from somewhere in the shop with the London book restorer's name and address on it. Penelope was about to crumple it up and throw it in the trash when she had a thought.

She saved her document, powered down her laptop, and tucked it back into her tote bag.

Mrs. Danvers was strutting up and down in front of the counter when Penelope emerged from her writing room.

"Doesn't she look pleased with herself," Pen said, pointing to the cat.

"As well she should," Mabel said. "Princess here caught the mouse that has been terrorizing us."

Pen gasped. "Good girl, Mrs. Danvers."

Mrs. Danvers blinked at her, clearly unimpressed by the compliment.

"What did you do with the . . . the . . ."

"Carcass?" Mabel said. "I've tossed it in the bin out back. I thought Mrs. Danvers might object, but she didn't appear to mind."

"The mouse isn't the only thing Mrs. Danvers caught." Pen handed the scrap of paper to Mabel. "She found this piece of paper on the floor somewhere."

"Oh, dear. It looks like she dropped it." She handed the paper back to Penelope. "A woman came in asking if I knew of any book restorers. I gave her the name of Wadsworth and Sons. I don't often have a need for them—most used books aren't worth restoring—but occasionally I get my hands on a first edition that might be of interest to a collector."

"Do you happen to remember what the woman's name was or what she looked like?"

Mabel frowned. "I don't believe she told me her name, but she was quite ordinary, I'm afraid." She smiled. "Well, I suppose most of us are, aren't we? Her hair was a light brown—not quite blond—and she was wearing a tartan plaid skirt with a matching twin set." Mabel's eyebrows shot up. "Oh, and she was wearing a silk scarf around her neck. She kept playing with the ends of it. I suspect it was a nervous habit."

Helen Dingley, Penelope thought. It sounded just like her—plain and nondescript.

"Is there something suspicious about this woman looking for a book restorer?" Mabel leaned forward, obviously intrigued.

Penelope explained about the Jane Austen book missing from the Oakwood School.

"Helen was complaining that it wasn't being properly cared for. She said she suspected there was foxing on the pages."

Mabel nodded her head. "Mold. It's the enemy of all old books."

"So you think this Helen Dingley stole the book?"

"I think it's quite possible," Penelope said. "I don't think she means to keep it. Apparently her efforts to have it better taken care of fell on deaf ears, so I think it's possible she decided to take matters into her own hands by bringing it to a restorer herself."

"What are you going to do about it? Go to the headmistress?"

Penelope shook her head. "First I'm going to have a talk with Helen and see if I can persuade her to tell Maribel what's happened to the book. I'm sure Maribel won't press charges and will probably keep it hush-hush. After all, Helen meant well."

"They say the road to hell is paved with good intentions, you know."

"I think in this case, Helen truly did have good intentions. There's only one thing I do wonder about."

"Oh?" Mabel cocked her head to the side. "What's that?"

"Did Odile know Helen was the one who took the book? A number of people have said that Odile treated Helen very poorly—like her own personal dogsbody. And Helen apparently put up with it."

"I don't know why anyone would tolerate being treated like that, but some people are just too timid to stand up for themselves."

"I think Helen put up with it because Odile knew or somehow found out that Helen was the one who had stolen the Jane Austen book. And she was holding that over Helen's head."

"Poor Helen!" Mabel said. "She must have been frightened but also furious. Maybe that was the last straw."

"Not only was Odile treating Helen abominably, but she now had a new weapon—a secret that Helen was desperate to hide."

Mabel shivered. "Odile doesn't sound like a very nice person."

"Still, it's hard to imagine poor, timid Helen resorting to violence," Penelope said, "but perhaps Odile had pushed her to the edge and she snapped. And the only solution was murder?"

Things at the Open Book were slow that afternoon. There were a few customers, but nothing Mabel couldn't handle. All the cartons of books that had recently been delivered were unpacked and all the volumes had been placed on the shelves. Penelope decided it was the perfect time to return to the Oakwood School to see if she could talk to Helen.

The taxi driver was quiet as he maneuvered down the high street, leaving Penelope to her own thoughts. They passed the Book and Bottle and she had a flashback to the many cozy drinks and dinners she'd had there with Maguire. Tears pricked her eyelids and she dashed them away. There had to be some explanation for the other Mrs. Brodie Maguire—maybe his father was Brodie Maguire senior and it was a May–December romance.

Penelope tried to convince herself that that was the case, but what if it wasn't? And if it turned out that Maguire was divorced or in the midst of one, how did she feel about that? She really needed to ask him about it. She knew he was busy dealing with both Odile's murder and the jewel heist, but that wasn't the real reason she was avoiding him—she was afraid of what she was going to find out. But knowing the truth had to be better than torturing herself like this.

She was still feeling glum when the taxi pulled into the

driveway leading to the entrance to the school. She paid the driver and got out.

Penelope opened the front door of the administration building and stepped inside. Class was in session and the hallway was quiet. She headed to Maribel's office and knocked tentatively on the doorjamb. Tina jumped and glanced up from some papers she was sorting on her desk. She looked annoyed.

"You scared me," she said, her mouth clamping shut into a thin line.

"I'm sorry," Pen said. "I didn't mean to. I won't keep you. I just wondered if you knew where Helen Dingley lived. Is she on campus?"

Tina's lips thinned even more. "Yes. She's in Parker House." She clicked a few keys on her computer. "It's number nine, Parker House."

So Helen lived in the same building as Odile had, Pen thought as she thanked Tina and headed out across the quad.

Several students from Penelope's Gothic literature seminar waved as they passed her on the path and Quentin smiled and tipped an imaginary hat to her.

Penelope arrived at Parker House but when she tried the door, it was locked. She'd completely forgotten that the night of Odile's murder, Mabel had used a key card to get in. Tina most likely knew perfectly well that that was the case and was probably sitting in her office right now, laughing at the prospect of Penelope being locked out.

Penelope rang the bell that was alongside the door and waited. Hopefully someone would hear it and let her in. Fortunately she didn't have long to wait before a woman in a black-and-white-checked coat with a red knitted scarf around her neck opened the door and stepped out. She looked at Pen curiously.

"Are you visiting someone?" she said in rather imperial tones.

"Yes," Pen said. "Helen Dingley. I was told she lives here?"

The woman held the door for Pen. "Very well. It's number nine all the way at the back."

Penelope made her way down the hall and rang the bell for Helen's apartment. A moment later, she heard footsteps approaching, the locks rattling, and finally Helen opened the door a crack. It was still on the chain lock.

She peered through the opening. "Yes?"

"Helen, it's me, Penelope Parish. May I come in?"

"I suppose so," Helen said, her voice quivering as she undid the chain and pulled the door wider.

She seemed flustered and kept playing with the ends of her scarf. Penelope smiled at her reassuringly.

"I wasn't expecting anyone," Helen said. "I'm afraid I haven't tidied up."

She picked up a book from the coffee table and clutched it to her chest but not before Penelope got a glimpse of the cover. She was quite certain it was the missing Jane Austen first edition of *Pride and Prejudice*.

Helen disappeared into another room, and when she came out, she was empty-handed.

"Would you like some tea?" she said, clasping her hands together in front of her.

"That would be lovely," Pen said.

Penelope looked around the sitting room while Helen retreated to the kitchen. There was a tiered table displaying figurines of all sorts—from a Picardy peasant to a pair of Staffordshire dogs. A display case on the wall held a collection of souvenir teaspoons Helen must have purchased on her travels around Great Britain.

A few minutes later, Helen came out of the kitchen holding a tea tray. She noticed Penelope looking at her tea-spoon collection.

"I've managed to do a bit of traveling, as you can see," she said as she put the tray on the coffee table.

She sat in a slightly saggy armchair and Pen took a seat on the sofa. The cushions felt lumpy beneath her.

Helen poured the tea. Her hand shook slightly, and a bit of tea dribbled into the saucer. Penelope pretended not to notice.

"You look like a nice young lady," Helen said, her eyes hopeful.

Penelope didn't know what to say to that so she gave a tentative smile.

"I'm in a bit of a pickle, you see. That nice detective was around to see me, but I'm afraid I wasn't able to tell him the whole story."

Penelope cocked her head to the side to show she was listening.

"Some people"—Helen made a face—"told him that Odile and I were at odds with each other—which was par-tially true. Odile could be rather difficult at times. She was an only child of rather . . . bohemian parents who encour-aged her creativity and let her believe that she was entitled to whatever she wanted." Helen fluttered a hand near her face. "Oh, dear. Here I am speaking ill of the dead." She shook her head. "But I do want you to understand. You do, don't you?" She put a hand on Penelope's.

Penelope wasn't sure she did understand, but she nodded her head.

"You've seen the Jane Austen. I could tell by your face. I can't deny that I took it, but I didn't steal it. I have every intention of putting it back. I've had it to the restorer in

London and they've done a marvelous job with it. The lovely woman who owns the Open Book gave me the name and address of someone she recommended. Somehow I managed to lose the slip of paper but fortunately I remembered the name and was able to look up the address."

Helen took a sip of her tea. "Odile knew I had the book. How she found out, I'll never know. It's obvious that it gave me a motive in her murder. She was running me off my feet with all her requests. And if I hesitated, she gave me that look that let me know she wouldn't hesitate to go to the head with the information."

Helen put her teacup down and it clattered slightly in the saucer.

"Anyway," Helen said, "I wasn't able to tell that nice detective where I was the day Odile was murdered. I was in London all day taking the book to the restorer. He promised to make the job a priority. I stayed in town for tea and spent the night at my cousin's flat in Kensington."

"Why didn't you tell Maguire that?" Pen said. She felt a lump rise in her throat at the mention of his name.

"I'd have to tell him the whole story, don't you see? It would mean admitting that I'm the one who took the Austen book."

"You'll have to admit it eventually, won't you?"

Helen shook her head. "I plan to sneak it back into the display case as soon as I can. No one will be the wiser."

TWELVE

꘏

Penelope tried to convince Helen to reveal her alibi to Maguire but Helen was adamant. She didn't think Maguire considered her a serious suspect in Odile's death and until he did, she was going to keep her secret to herself.

Penelope was glad to leave Helen's rather stuffy apartment, where heat was continually blowing out of the ancient radiators. The cool fresh air felt heavenly. She held her face up to the sun as she walked across the quad and didn't see the young man in a long blue and white scarf heading straight toward her.

"Oof," Penelope said, when they collided.

The young man—he was around Penelope's age—looked startled at first but then he broke into a smile.

"So sorry about that. I wasn't looking where I was going." He was slightly breathless.

Pen laughed. "And apparently, neither was I."

"Maybe you can help me," he said, shaking his rather shaggy blond hair out of his eyes. "I'm Edward Grant, by the way." He held out a hand and Penelope shook it. "Do you happen to know where I might find Adrian Mabry?"

"His classroom is in Corbyn Hall." Penelope pointed in the direction of the ivy-covered building. "I believe his office is there, too."

"Brilliant," Edward said. "I haven't seen the scoundrel in yonks—not since he was sent down from Oxford our third year."

"Oh?" Pen's ears perked up. "You mean he left Oxford?"

Edward nodded. "We were in Balliol College together. Mabry got into a spot of bother and had to leave. It was all a bit dodgy, if you ask me."

"Did Mabry finish up somewhere else?" Pen said.

Edward frowned. "I don't know. I should imagine so in order to have landed a position here." He swept an arm encompassing the campus.

Penelope analyzed the conversation as Edward went on his way, his striped scarf fluttering behind him.

If Mabry hadn't graduated from Oxford, maybe he hadn't graduated at all. Had he lied about his credentials when he applied for the job at the Oakwood School? It was possible.

If so, that meant Mabry had two things to hide—his affair with Layla and his lack of a degree. Odile had known about one of these—Mabry's affair with Layla—but since he himself wasn't married, that wasn't likely to be a huge concern to him. But if he had lied about his credentials, that would definitely be something he would want to hide. And if Odile had found out, it would certainly give him a motive for murder.

* * *

As Penelope neared the administration building, she wondered how she could find out what Mabry had put down on his application for the teaching position at the school. She could ask Maribel, but she doubted Maribel would reveal the information. Maribel had confided in Penelope to some extent about certain things, but Penelope doubted she would go that far.

Was there any way she could check Mabry's records herself? She remembered the night she and Maribel had looked up Odile's file. Mabry's was most likely located in the same cabinet. Now, if there was only some way to lure Tina away from her desk.

Penelope glanced at her watch. With any luck, Tina might be on a break, although Penelope strongly suspected she was the sort who never left her desk.

She was still debating what to do when she reached the administration building. As she suspected, Tina was in her office, a small plate with three chocolate digestive biscuits on her desk and a cup of tea by her elbow.

The door to Maribel's office was open. The lights were out and it was clear the room was empty.

How could Penelope possibly get Tina away from her office? A number of ridiculous thoughts like pulling the fire alarm went through her mind, but she quickly rejected them.

The one thing that Penelope knew about Tina was that she was loyal to Maribel and devoted to her job. That gave her an idea.

She pretended to be rushed and breathless as she entered Tina's office.

Tina looked up and put down her teacup when she saw Penelope.

Penelope gave a few fake gasps. "It's Maribel," she said.

Tina furrowed her brow and a look of alarm settled on her face. "What's happened?" She half rose from her chair.

"I don't know. One of the students grabbed me as I was heading over here and asked me to tell you that Maribel needs you right away at the assembly hall."

"The Stewart-Calthorpe Assembly Hall?" Tina said, her look of concern deepening.

"Yes. At least I imagine that's what she meant."

"Did she say it's urgent?" Tina said.

Penelope hesitated. "It sounded as if it might be."

She crossed her fingers behind her back. She felt guilt wash over her as she watched Tina pull on her coat and rush out the door.

Pen waited until the sound of Tina's footsteps had retreated into silence, then tried to look casual as she moved over toward the file cabinets that lined the one wall of the office. She kept looking over her shoulder, but it was quiet and no one passed the open door.

Tina would be furious when she found out that Penelope had sent her on a wild-goose chase, but it was a chance Penelope had to take. Hopefully she would be gone by the time Tina got back.

She felt her stomach rumble and realized she'd forgotten to eat lunch. She glanced longingly at the digestive biscuits on Tina's desk, and was dying to sneak one, but Tina would be sure to notice if one was missing.

Penelope decided to ignore her empty stomach while she faced the row of file cabinets. Suddenly she was no longer sure which was the one Maribel had opened that contained the staff's files. She hesitated and then pulled open one of the drawers. A quick glance at the titles on the folders inside made it clear that it wasn't the correct drawer.

She moved to the next cabinet and quietly eased open a drawer. She saw a file folder labeled *Danbury, Greta,* who was the German instructor. She quickly went through them until she found the manuscript. She skipped through folders labeled *Mabbe, Gerald*; *Mabblestone, Sarah*; and *MacCormack, Elizabeth* but no *Mabry, Adrian.* Had she missed it?

She carefully went through the row of folders again and finally spotted it: *Mabry, Adrian.* She was about to pull the folder out when she heard footsteps in the hall. Two girls in the Oakwood School uniform passed the open door. Pen froze, but they were too busy chatting with each other to notice her.

As soon as the coast was clear, she pulled out Mabry's folder and opened it. She was about to go through the papers when Layla walked into the office. Penelope leaned against the open file drawer, slamming it shut, and tucked the folder under her arm, hoping Layla wouldn't notice it.

Layla gave Penelope an odd look, but Penelope was relieved when she didn't say anything.

"Oh," Layla said when she saw Penelope. "Tina isn't here? I had a question for her."

"I'm afraid she's gone out," Pen said, still clutching the folder.

"Do you know when she'll be back?"

Why didn't Layla leave, for goodness sake? Pen thought.

Penelope shook her head. "No, I don't. She didn't say."

Layla shrugged. "I'll come back later." She smiled. "How are your knees?"

Pen had nearly forgotten about them. Suddenly she realized they were stinging slightly.

"Much better," she said. "Thank you for your help."

"Any time," Layla said as she headed out the door.

Penelope let her breath out in a whoosh. That was a close call. She listened carefully, but there were no footsteps in the hallway or the sound of voices.

Penelope was about to open the folder, when it slipped from her hands and fell, the contents scattering over the floor. She bent down and began to gather them together. She hoped no one would ever notice that they were now probably out of order.

She flipped through the papers as quickly as possible until she located Adrian Mabry's application. She glanced at it and it didn't take long for her to find the information she was after.

Mabry had lied. He'd put down that he had a degree from Oxford when in fact, he'd never graduated.

Pen paid the taxi driver and got out in front of the Open Book. She really had to look into buying another car, she decided.

She still hadn't had any lunch and now it was practically teatime. She loved the British ritual of afternoon tea. It was so . . . civilized.

Mrs. Danvers marched toward Penelope as she opened the door. The cat's eyes were narrowed to slits. Before she reached Penelope, she turned around and marched off, her tail defiantly waving in the air.

"I guess she's still mad at me for putting her in the carrier this morning," Pen said to Mabel, who was behind the counter. "I don't suppose she's going to like it any better on the way home."

"How did it go?" Mabel said, leaning her arms on the counter.

"So-so," Penelope said, gesturing with her hand. "Helen admitted to having the Austen book." Pen hung up her jacket and turned back to Mabel. "Actually I saw the book myself and she was forced to come clean about it."

"What are you going to do?"

Penelope took a deep breath. "I don't know. Helen has promised to put the newly restored volume back in the display case. Does Maribel really have to know that Helen took it?"

Mabel frowned. "That is a tricky question."

Penelope sighed. "I'm going to sleep on it."

"Good idea."

"Meanwhile, I'm going to work on the next Open Book newsletter."

As Penelope was walking to her writing room, her stomach rumbled again. She made a slight detour and headed toward Figgy's tea shop.

"Do you have anything to feed a starving person?" she said to Figgy, who was wiping down a table.

"Of course I do. I just made a fridge cake—a chocolate biscuit cake—or would you like a slice of Madeira cake?"

"I've never had a chocolate biscuit cake," Pen said, her mouth already starting to water.

"It's Prince William's favorite. He had it as his groom's cake at his wedding. The queen is a fan, too. She apparently likes a slice in the afternoon with her tea."

"I'll try it," Pen said.

Moments later Figgy returned with a slice of cake on a plate. It was covered in dark chocolate and looked so yummy Pen thought she would swoon. She took it to her writing room and immediately tucked into it.

She wiped her hands with a tissue and powered up her laptop. She went to work and when she looked at the time, she was surprised to see it was almost six o'clock.

She got her things together, turned out the light, and went out into the salesroom. She retrieved Mrs. Danvers's carrier from behind the counter, where she'd left it, and looked around for the cat.

"This should be fun," Mabel said, her arms folded across her chest.

As soon as Mrs. Danvers got wind of what was going on, she scampered off and sidled under one of the armchairs. Pen grabbed the cat treats she'd brought from her tote bag and tried to lure Mrs. Danvers out. Mrs. Danvers was having none of it.

By the time Penelope did catch Mrs. Danvers and get her in her carrier, she was perspiring and wisps of hair were stuck to her face. She left her jacket open as she and Mabel walked to Mabel's car.

Mrs. Danvers was deposited in the back seat, still protesting loudly, and they headed out.

"I have to go to Tesco," Mabel said. "Do you need anything?"

"Something to go with the pork chop I'm thawing would be a good idea, I suppose." Penelope realized all she'd had to eat since breakfast was a piece of chocolate biscuit cake. She'd make up for it by having a green vegetable with dinner.

They headed down the high street, where shopkeepers were locking their doors and, one by one, the shop lights were winking off.

Mabel pulled into the Tesco parking lot, found a space, and parked the car. They were headed toward the store entrance when another car pulled into the lot. Penelope got a glimpse of the driver as it went by. It was Grady Evans and he had someone with him.

"Wait." Penelope put a hand on Mabel's arm. "That's Grady Evans from the Oakwood School. I think he might be the one buying alcohol for the students."

They scuttled into the shadows at the side of the building and watched as Grady got out of the car. The passenger door opened and he was joined by a young girl who Penelope immediately recognized as Nicola Hyde-White.

They stood by the side of the car as Nicola reached into her pocket and pulled out a wad of cash. Grady gave her the thumbs-up and began to walk toward the store while Nicola waited, leaning against the side of the car. She pulled a cigarette out of her pocket and lit it. Wisps of smoke curled into the air and the tip of the cigarette glowed brightly when she puffed on it.

"Let's go," Penelope said, heading toward the store entrance. "I want to see if Nicola was giving Grady money to buy liquor."

"Well, I doubt it was for a bag of chocolates," Mabel said. "That looked like a significant amount of cash."

They grabbed a cart and headed down the first aisle. Penelope kept one eye out for Grady while she picked up some lettuce, a tomato, and a cucumber and put them in her cart. She grabbed a Tesco roast chicken in a bag and added it, figuring she could have it the following night and several nights after that.

Finally she headed to the section where the liquor was shelved. Grady was at the end of the aisle about to turn the corner.

Penelope followed close behind him as he wheeled his cart over to the checkout counter. There were two people between Penelope and Grady and she couldn't quite see what he was unloading from his cart; but when he picked up the bag the cashier handed him, she heard the unmistakable sound of bottles clinking together.

She didn't need Sherlock Holmes to tell her that Grady was the one buying liquor for the students.

"Looks like you've found your culprit," Mabel said as they carried their grocery bags out to the car.

"I wonder if Odile knew what Grady was up to," Penelope said, putting her groceries in the trunk.

"Possibly," Mabel said. "From what you've told me, she seemed to know a lot of what was going on."

Penelope frowned. "Maribel said she'd warned the staff that the person responsible would be fired immediately. And that she'd make sure they weren't hired anywhere else either. Why would Grady risk it?"

"Well, I have to admit the man was hardly being cagey about what he was doing. But some people are quite arrogant, aren't they—convinced they won't be caught." She laughed. "I remember reading about a thief who was so proud of the burglary he'd just committed that he bragged all about it on social media. And then he was gobsmacked when the police showed up on his doorstep."

"But if Odile had discovered that Grady was the culprit, that might have been enough to get her killed. Maybe Grady came to his senses and realized how serious the consequences would be if he was caught and that was what motivated him to murder her," Penelope said as Mabel started the engine. "And he's become even bolder now that Odile is out of the way."

* * *

Saturday was a busy day at the Open Book, and Penelope always made sure to be there to lend Mabel a hand.

When she arrived, Mabel was going through a shopping bag full of books that someone had dropped off for their used book section.

"Anything good?" Pen said as she shrugged off her coat.

"Quite a few fairly new bestsellers," Mabel said. She held up a copy of Harlan Coben's *The Boy from the Woods.* "She appears to be a fan of thrillers." She ran her hand over the book's dust jacket. "These will all go quickly."

Pen noticed Figgy sitting at a table in the tea shop across from an older woman who was wearing a rather smart tweed suit and had an impressive strand of pearls around her neck. She had dark hair and resembled an older, more toned-down version of Figgy.

"Who's Figgy talking to?" Pen said.

"Her mother." Mabel rolled her eyes.

Pen walked over toward the tea shop.

"Pen," Figgy said in the tone of voice of someone who was drowning and had just been pulled into a lifeboat. "This is my mother, Lady Isobel Innes-Goldthorpe." She turned to Isobel. "Mother, this is Penelope Parrish."

Isobel looked Penelope up and down and raised one eyebrow. "You're the American, aren't you?" she said in a rather tight voice.

"Yes." Pen felt as if she was admitting to being the devil.

Isobel gave a tepid smile.

"I guess I'll go . . . shelve some books," Pen said, glad to escape. Poor Figgy, she thought. Her mother was a real dragon.

Pen had just finished helping a customer find a title she needed for her book group when Figgy came up to her.

"Do you have a minute?" Figgy said. "I need to talk to someone."

"What is it?" Pen said.

Figgy looked quite upset, which wasn't like her. Normally she breezed through life's difficulties with a smile on her face.

Pen joined her in the tearoom and waited while Figgy fetched them cups of tea and a plate of freshly baked Chelsea buns.

"So tell me what's up," Pen said as she stirred sugar into her tea.

Figgy turned her spoon over and over in the saucer. "It's my mother," she said finally, with an enormous sigh that ruffled her short bangs. "She wants me to have a wedding, as she put it, that is befitting the daughter of an earl." She looked at Pen. "Can you imagine me traipsing down the aisle in a white wedding gown and veil holding a bouquet of baby's breath?" She clenched her fists. "That is so not me." She leaned across the table toward Penelope. "And she wanted me to take all my earrings out and cover that tiny tattoo on my ankle." She snorted. "As if anyone would be able to see it under the layers and layers of tulle and organza she expects me to wear."

"I'd have to agree," Pen said, taking a bite of her bun. "That is so not you." Penelope tried to imagine Figgy in a getup like that, but she was completely unable to conjure up the picture.

"Derek and I wanted something less traditional, more relaxed. Although Derek said he will go along with anything I want." She looked down. "It's just that my mother and I don't want the same thing for my wedding."

"Can you talk to her? Maybe come to a compromise?"

Figgy laughed. "And then we'll both be unhappy." She shook her head. "She doesn't do compromises. Her mind is made up. And stopping my mother when she's decided on something is like trying to stop a freight train after it's picked up speed."

Penelope slept late on Sunday. When she got up, Mrs. Danvers was already in the kitchen, sitting next to her half-empty bowl and meowing in protest about how she was being treated.

Pen filled her bowl and put the coffee on. Beryl was coming for brunch, and she hadn't yet adopted the British habit of tea in the morning. She was making an omelet and Beryl was bringing some Chelsea buns and crumpets from the Icing on the Cake.

She was chopping up tomatoes and peppers for the omelet when the doorbell rang.

Beryl breezed in, bringing a whiff of cold air with her. She was carrying a bakery bag with *Icing on the Cake* written on the front in script.

"I'm starved," she said as she took off her coat. "That coffee smells heavenly."

"Let's get you a cup, then," Pen said as they walked out to the kitchen.

Beryl warmed her hands over the Aga while Penelope filled a mug with coffee. She handed it to her sister and Beryl inhaled the fragrant steam drifting from the top.

"How is Charlotte?" Pen said, as she beat some eggs in a bowl. "Doing well, I hope."

"She is," Beryl said, wrapping her hands around her

mug. "She's positively glowing." She took a sip of coffee. "And she's done up the nursery with the most darling wallpaper. Of course it's green—a neutral color—so no hint as to what she's having."

Beryl watched while Penelope poured the eggs into a pan. "I suppose I should make myself useful," she said. She went over to the cupboards, took out a plate, and began arranging the buns and crumpets on it.

"How is your job going?" Pen sprinkled cheese on the eggs in the pan.

"Fantastic," Beryl said. "I can't thank you enough for putting me in touch with the Duchess of Upper Chumley-on-Stoke." She gave a coy smile. "I think Charlotte has been pleased with our partnership. I've been putting her in some of the same designers that the Duchess of Cambridge used when she was expecting and she's been pleased so far."

Beryl frowned. "Although she does seem to prefer her distressed jeans and cozy sweaters when she's alone."

Penelope thought she could hardly blame Charlotte for that.

Beryl's face brightened. "But she has a formal evening event coming up and I can't wait to dress her for it." She picked up the plate of buns and crumpets and carried it over to the table. "And I've been working on her wardrobe for after the baby is born. There are some wonderful Atelier Classique pieces that I'd like to see her in." She frowned. "I do hope she sheds the baby weight quickly."

Penelope thought that would probably be the least of Charlotte's concerns, but she didn't say anything. She cut the omelet in half, placed the halves on two plates, and put them down on the table.

They each took their place and Penelope chose a crumpet from the plate of pastries Beryl had brought.

"I must say, Charlotte has a unique style of her own," Beryl said as she unfurled her napkin and placed it in her lap. "I would call it 'elegantly casual'." She leaned forward and lowered her voice as if she were about to impart some mysterious secret. "She does like to be comfortable." She reached for a Chelsea bun and put it on her plate. "Although when she pulls out all the stops for evening, she really looks spectacular."

They were quiet as they ate their omelets and nibbled on the pastries.

"Has there been any news . . . from home?" Pen said finally. She'd been hesitant to bring up the subject and spoil Beryl's good mood.

Beryl dropped her hands into her lap. "Nothing good. Magnus was found guilty, as you know. He hasn't been sentenced yet, but it doesn't look good." She sighed. "I almost feel sorry for him, but he brought it on himself."

"Are reporters still following the story?"

"If you mean is it splashed all over the front page of every sleazy tabloid in the country, no. There's the occasional mention here and there, but there isn't much to write about. They haven't tracked me here, thank goodness, so they haven't been able to get any juicy photographs of the distraught wife."

Beryl pushed her plate away as if she'd lost her appetite.

"The house and everything in it has been sold, but it's a drop in the bucket compared to what Magnus stole from all those investors." She put her head in her hands. "All I have left is the little I managed to bring with me. God bless Gina, my housekeeper . . . well she *was* my housekeeper . . . who offered to pack up all my personal things—photographs, letters, and the like—and put them in storage for me." A tear ran down Beryl's cheek. "The government has taken everything else to be sold—the house, the furniture, the paintings, the cars, even the jewelry I didn't bring with me."

Penelope was quiet. She didn't know what to say. She couldn't imagine the horror her sister was going through.

Beryl looked up and put on a tremulous smile.

"At least I have you." She reached out and put her hand over Penelope's. "And I have a new job I love. Charlotte is a doll to work for. I'm still pinching myself over my luck."

"You deserve it," Pen said.

Beryl lifted her glass of water. "I'll drink to that."

Pen lifted her glass as well and they clinked them together.

"Who knows?" Beryl said. "Maybe I'll even find myself a new man. I think these British accents are quite dreamy." She frowned and leveled a glance at Penelope. "Speaking of men, what about that man of yours? Maguire. Have you talked to him yet?"

Pen fiddled with her fork, stalling for time. "No, not yet. But I will. I have to find the right moment." She was going to make the excuse that Maguire was too busy—after all, he was dealing with a murder investigation as well as the theft of some very valuable jewelry. But Penelope knew Beryl wouldn't buy that as an explanation.

But the very thought of talking to Maguire made her stomach turn over. She sighed. She knew Beryl was right. She'd have to do it sooner or later.

Penelope's phone dinged on Monday morning as her taxi made its way down the narrow winding road that led to the Oakwood School. She pulled it out of her tote bag and glanced at the screen. She had a text from Tina in

the administration office. For a moment, Penelope feared
Tina might have discovered that Pen had been riffling
through her files, and she breathed a sigh of relief when she
pulled the text up on her screen. It was a reminder that
Maribel was holding an assembly in the Stewart-Calthorpe
Hall that morning.

Pen paid the taxi driver, gathered her things together,
and got out. She looked up. Dark clouds were massed in the
sky and it looked as if rain was imminent. The wind had
picked up as well and whistled around the corners of the
buildings. It lifted the ends of Pen's scarf and tossed them
in her face. She grabbed them and tucked them inside her
jacket.

Fortunately, the wind was at her back as she made her
way across the quad. She was halfway to the assembly hall
when she heard someone call her name. She turned around.
Layla was hurrying to catch up with her.

"Hi," she said, slightly out of breath. "I've been meaning
to talk to you."

"Oh?" Pen couldn't imagine about what.

"I'm not sure if I should tell anyone about this," Layla
said, skipping a bit to catch up with Penelope.

"Tell anyone what?"

Layla bit her lip and hesitated briefly. "I saw Nicola
Hyde-White going into the woods," she blurted out suddenly. "Grady said that's where he's seen that plant
growing—the one that poisoned Odile."

"Deadly nightshade?"

"Yes, that's it," Layla said. "I'm not sure if I should tell
that detective about it or not. I'd feel terrible if I landed
Nicola in it," she said, sounding anything but.

Penelope was of two minds. It was quite possible that
Nicola had simply been taking an innocent walk in the

woods. On the other hand, Maguire needed all the facts he could get in order to conduct a thorough investigation.

"It might be best if you tell him," Penelope said. "Let him sort it out. Nicola's walk in the woods was probably perfectly innocent, and she has nothing to fear."

Penelope wondered if someone like Nicola would even know what deadly nightshade was. But these British girls were surprising—they could arrange an elegant afternoon tea and then turn around, pull on their wellies, and go out and turn over the soil in the flower beds. They were at home in the country in a way Penelope wasn't sure she ever could be. Nicola might very well know about poisons found innocently growing in the garden.

By now they were approaching the assembly hall, where students were streaming through the front doors.

She and Layla went their separate ways and Penelope joined the crowd milling in the lobby.

She wondered if Layla realized what she'd done just now. She'd revealed to Penelope that she saw Nicola go into the woods, of course, but she'd also admitted that her husband, Grady, knew where the deadly nightshade grew.

Penelope found a seat in the assembly hall. Maribel was onstage behind the lectern, going through some papers. She tapped the microphone and a loud screech echoed around the auditorium. She waited until it had died down and then began to speak.

"I know it's tedious," she began, "but there is a bit of business to get through first."

Maribel then went on to make several announcements—the school choir would be giving a concert the following week in the Stewart-Calthorpe Assembly Hall, dinner hours had been extended to avoid overcrowding, and a new stock of uniforms was now available in the school store.

"And now for the reason that I have called you all here today," Maribel said.

Penelope noticed that Maribel's face was glowing and she couldn't contain a broad smile.

"The first edition of Jane Austen's *Pride and Prejudice* has been returned."

A buzz went through the assembled students and teachers. Maribel held up a hand for silence.

"It feels like a miracle, but our librarian, Mrs. Osborne, noticed last night that it was back in its display case, safe and sound."

A cheer went up.

"It is a great relief, as you can imagine. Mrs. Osborne examined it and it's in perfect condition, no damage whatsoever."

"Do you know who took it?" someone called from the audience.

"I'm afraid not," Maribel said. "But whoever took it was very careful with it and for that we have to be grateful." She smiled. "As a matter of fact, the book appears to have been restored—the foxing is gone and it looks almost brand-new."

Maribel closed the assembly by having everyone rise to sing the school song. Chatter broke out as soon as the last note died away and the audience began filing out.

Maribel joined Penelope as they headed out the door.

"I think I can guess exactly what happened to our Jane Austen," Maribel said as they made their way across the quad. "One of our staff was forever making a fuss about the condition of the book and apparently decided to take matters into her own hands. I've suspected that for some time and that's why I didn't want to involve the police."

Penelope glanced over to her right and happened to catch Helen's eye. Helen gave Penelope a timid smile and then turned away.

Maribel said good-bye and went off in another direction and Penelope was headed toward Corbyn Hall when she noticed a familiar figure coming toward her.

It was Maguire.

What was he doing here, Penelope wondered? Her first instinct was to turn and run in the opposite direction. She wasn't ready to learn the truth about Mrs. Brodie Maguire, but the Parishes weren't quitters, as her grandmother used to say. Besides, Maguire had already spotted her. There was nothing for it but to smile and wait for him to catch up with her. She was annoyed with herself when she realized that just the sight of him lifted her spirits.

"Penelope," Maguire called as he got closer.

Penelope froze. Should she ask now about the Mrs. Brodie Maguire who had appeared in the Open Book the other day? Did she really want to know? Was this a good time? *As good a time as any*, a little voice whispered in her ear.

"This is lucky," Maguire said when he'd caught up with her. "I was going to ring you."

Penelope's lips felt stiff as she smiled at him. "Oh?"

"I wondered if you'd like to have dinner tonight?"

"Sure."

"Do you want to meet me at the Book and Bottle? I'll be coming directly from the station."

"Fine."

If Maguire noticed Penelope was speaking in monosyllables, he didn't say anything.

"Brilliant. Seven o'clock?"

Penelope nodded.

"See you then," Maguire called over his shoulder as he walked away.

Penelope felt a wave of relief wash over her. She could wait until tonight to ask Maguire about *the other woman*, as Penelope had come to think of her. And prepare herself for the answer.

THIRTEEN

❧

Dark clouds had gathered in the sky and it began to rain just before Penelope reached Corbyn Hall—big fat drops that splattered as they landed on the paved walkway. She ducked her head, pulled up her collar, and began to walk faster.

There was a couple walking ahead of her, sheltering under a large black umbrella. The man was wearing denim overalls and a short jacket. The wind grabbed the umbrella and momentarily flipped it inside out. As the man struggled to right it, Penelope got a better view of the woman with him. She looked just like . . . Gladys.

Penelope blinked and rubbed her eyes. It couldn't be. This was the second time she thought she saw Gladys at the school. Either it really was Gladys or Gladys had a look-alike.

They were nearing Corbyn Hall now. Pen looked at her

watch. She still had plenty of time before her class began. She decided to follow the couple. Maybe she would find out once and for all if that really was Gladys.

They walked past Corbyn Hall and continued toward the woods where Pen had seen Mabry and Layla. Were they headed there, too? Pen hovered just around the corner of the building and waited.

They didn't enter the stand of trees but continued walking toward an outbuilding Penelope hadn't noticed before. It looked like some sort of storage shed. It was quite large and in good repair—the paint was fresh and the windows were clean.

The man fished a set of keys out of his pocket, chose one, and inserted it into the lock. Penelope was close enough now to see that it was the school maintenance man, Rodney Simpson.

They didn't seem to be aware of Penelope so she moved a bit closer in order to get a better look. The woman suddenly turned her head and Penelope quickly retreated around the corner of Corbyn Hall.

She had seen enough. The woman was definitely Gladys, but what on earth was she doing with Rodney Simpson?

The obvious answer was that they were having some kind of love affair.

Penelope quickly turned away. She didn't know what to think. She knew how difficult Gladys's husband, Bruce, was and felt she could hardly blame Gladys for finding comfort and solace in another man's arms.

Penelope hurried to her classroom and made it just as the bell sounded in the hall. She took off her jacket and shook it out, sending droplets of water spraying across the floor. Her hair was damp and her shoes felt a bit soggy as well.

The students were already assembled except for Nicola, who was late as usual and came rushing in, her jacket wet from the rain.

"Let's talk about omens and curses today," Penelope said when they had all settled down. "Both are typical devices for heightening mystery and suspense in the Gothic novel. For instance, if you've read the *House of the Seven Gables* by Nathanial Hawthorne, you will remember that the family was cursed due to an ancestor having stolen land."

Penelope continued with the lecture and the girls were silent except for the scratching of their pens and pencils across paper. As she was winding up, she realized she was going to miss the students when the seminar was over. She'd enjoyed it more than she had expected.

The closing bell rang and the students immediately jumped to their feet, grabbed their things, and left the room. Penelope had to laugh. Even though she had the impression that the girls were enjoying her class, they always left as if they were deserting a sinking ship.

She was about to pack up her notes and laptop when a loud crash behind her made her jump. What on earth . . . ?

She turned around to see that one of the blinds was lying twisted on the floor. It must have come loose. She hesitated. What should she do? She looked up at the window, which was considerably taller than she could reach. Besides, it looked as if some screws needed to be tightened in the brackets holding the blinds up.

"Need some help?" A male voice startled Penelope. She spun around.

Grady stood slouched in the doorway.

"I'm not sure who I should call to get this fixed. I don't want to just leave it for someone else to find."

Grady squinted up at the window. "No need to call any-one. I can take care of it. I'll need a ladder, though."

His phone beeped and he pulled it out of his pocket. He glanced at the screen, scowled, and tossed the phone onto the sofa. "I'll be back in a tick."

Pen glanced at Grady's cell phone. She was itching to scroll through Grady's texts to see what she could find. But she also didn't want to get caught doing it. She inched closer to the sofa and listened carefully but there were no footsteps in the hall.

She had to act fast before the phone locked. She snaked out a hand and grabbed it. She realized she was panting slightly and her heart was sending the blood racing through her veins and making her dizzy.

She found Grady's list of texts and scrolled through them. As she had suspected, there was one from Odile. Pen looked over her shoulder and listened carefully before tap-ping on the text. She scanned it quickly.

It read:

I know you've been buying liquor for the girls at
Tesco. This must stop. I don't want to be forced to tell
Maribel. The school's reputation must be preserved.

Pen heard a scraping noise in the hallway. Was that Grady dragging the ladder? She quickly put the phone back on the sofa where he'd tossed it and walked over toward the window, hoping the frantic beating of her heart wasn't au-dible.

Grady appeared, holding a tall wooden ladder, which he angled to fit through the doorway. He grunted when it mo-mentarily became stuck.

"This is really nice of you to do this," Pen said. "Isn't there a maintenance man?"

"Rodney?" Grady said slightly breathlessly as he struggled to position the ladder. "Sure, but I like to help out when I can." He opened the ladder and stood it next to the window. He broke into a broad grin. "I'm going to be a father." He pointed at his chest. "Layla's got a bun in the oven. She's three months along and I plan to ask for a raise." He frowned. "I don't want us to end up skint because she has to take some time off work."

"Congratulations," Pen said. "So that's why you're making yourself indispensable?"

"I guess you could call it that," Grady said over his shoulder as he began to climb the ladder.

"I'll leave you to it." Pen began gathering her belongings together, slipped on her jacket, said good-bye to Grady, and left.

That was interesting, she thought as she headed across the quad. The rain had stopped, but threatening clouds still lingered and puddles were scattered along the walkway.

So Layla was pregnant. Was it Grady's baby or could it be Mabry's? There was no way of telling. And Grady was worried about keeping his job. That would have made it doubly important to prevent Odile from going to the head.

And killing her was certainly one way to do it.

Penelope was nearing the administration building when she heard someone call her name. She turned around to see Maribel walking briskly toward her.

"I've heard wonderful things about your Gothic literature seminar," Maribel said as they fell into step together. "The girls are all talking about it."

Penelope flushed with pleasure.

A young girl was approaching them. She looked excited. Penelope recognized her as Cecily, a rather earnest student in her seminar. She was one of the youngest girls in the class.

"Are you going to the exhibition?" she said when she reached Penelope. "I'd love for you to see my paintings. Please do say you'll come."

"Yes," Pen said, looking at Maribel and raising her eyebrows.

"Brilliant," the girl said. "Goodness, I'm going to be late." And she took off running, her long braids flapping against her back as she trotted away.

Maribel gave an indulgent smile. "I believe she's quite taken with you."

Penelope was startled. "I don't think—"

"Girls at this age are apt to develop crushes on their teachers. It's quite harmless." She paused. "Actually, I think it's rather beneficial. Not all of them have strong role models to look up to at home."

Penelope was flattered, but she wasn't sure what sort of role model she could conceivably be. Despite her success as an author—she had one bestseller under her belt, didn't she?—neither her mother nor her sister seemed to take her seriously, although Beryl did appear to be coming around.

"We have a few girls here who are on scholarships," Maribel said as they approached Stewart-Calthorpe Assembly Hall. "They come from modest backgrounds obviously, and their parents don't always understand the value of an education for girls or even encourage it, for that matter. Many of them had teachers in primary school who were the ones who supported them."

Maribel sighed. "And our students who come from wealthier or even aristocratic families aren't spared either. There's often something amiss in their home life—an alcoholic father or a mother who is what used to be called "a bolter," like in Nancy Mitford's novels. I'll never forget the poor girl whose mother took off with the scullery maid, causing great mental anguish to the rest of the family, not to mention quite a scandal."

They had reached the assembly hall by now. Penelope pulled open the door and motioned for Maribel to go ahead of her.

"It's this way." Maribel led Penelope down the hall to the art studio.

The sun had come out in earnest and was streaming in the windows and skylights, flooding the studio with light and highlighting the students' paintings, which were displayed on easels set up around the room.

"I so wish Odile had lived to see this," Maribel said, clasping her hands together. "She was a fabulous teacher and knew just how to encourage the girls."

Penelope glanced around the room quickly. The paintings varied in level of skill but all were copies of famous masterpieces. It was an eclectic mix. She recognized what looked like a Modigliani painting of a young girl, a Cézanne still life, and a wildly colorful Matisse nude, which was a rather daring choice for a high school student.

Maribel must have noticed her looking at it. She smiled.

"Odile liked to push boundaries. It was so like her not to censure the students' choices."

"These are amazing," Penelope said, strolling between the easels. "Some of them are actually quite good."

"Odile planned field trips to London to the Tate for the girls. They'd take the train and spend the afternoon at the museum sketching their choices. Back at school, they would begin work on the paintings." She reached out and straightened one of the easels that was slightly out of line with the others. "It's a classical technique for teaching art that has fallen out of favor in recent years, but Odile felt it to be very valuable."

"I'm sure the students enjoyed it."

Maribel smiled. "I suspect they did. Odile would take them all to tea at Fortnum and Mason afterward."

Odile had certainly had a strong influence on her students, Pen thought as she left the assembly hall and began to walk toward the school entrance. No wonder the students liked her—taking them to museums and tea in London. It must have made a nice break from their classes.

Penelope was still marveling at the skill of Odile's students when a thought struck her. If the students copied famous masterpieces, could Odile have done the same thing?

Was it possible that the Matisse painting Odile owned was merely a copy she'd made herself and the whole story about her great-grandmother posing for Matisse was one that she'd made up? And had someone tried to steal it?

Penelope shook her head. That didn't make sense. If Odile had surprised someone breaking into her apartment to snatch the painting, surely they would have hit her over the head or stabbed her if they had been carrying a knife?

Odile had to have been murdered by someone she knew—most likely someone from the school—and their intention had been to keep her from revealing something they didn't want known.

Fifteen minutes later, a taxi picked Penelope up outside the administration building at the entrance to the school. The driver was new—it wasn't Mad Max or Dashing Dennis or anyone she'd ever seen before.

"Are you new?" Pen said as the driver braked for a slow-moving vehicle.

"Just started today." He glanced over his shoulder at Penelope. "I used to drive a cab in London but the missus wanted to get out of the city. Said the noise was getting to her and the pollution wasn't doing her asthma any good. The noise never bothered me and we had a bit of a barney over it." He slapped the steering wheel and chuckled. "I should know better than to argue with the missus. She always wins." He glanced in the rearview mirror. "But it's a nice place—Chumley. We could have done worse."

He turned and looked over his shoulder again. "You're not from here. I can tell. You're American."

Penelope groaned silently.

"The funny thing is," the driver continued, "the missus was always worried about the crime rate in London. She was sure she was going to be mugged any day. So here we come out to Chumley and what's the first thing she reads in the paper? That a teacher out at that school where I picked you up was murdered. It gave her a real fright."

By now they were heading down the high street and Penelope suddenly realized she hadn't had any lunch. Actually, she hadn't had much of anything to eat that day at all.

Pen had the driver drop her off in front of the Pig in a Poke. With any luck they would have some of Gladys's Cornish pasties left.

Gladys was handing a customer his change when Penelope walked in. Penelope had a flashback to Gladys at the Oakwood School, sneaking off with the handyman, and suddenly felt awkward.

She felt her face getting red and Gladys gave her a strange look but didn't say anything. Pen had to clear her throat twice before speaking.

"I was wondering if there are any pasties left?"

"How many will you be wanting? There's only the one."

"That's fine."

Gladys reached behind her, picked up the last pasty with a sheet of glassine, and placed it in a paper bag. She put it down on the counter.

"Is something wrong?" Gladys said. "You're acting all peculiar."

Pen was dying to ask Gladys what she'd been doing at the school, meeting with Rodney, but she was afraid she already knew what the answer was.

"No, no, nothing," Pen said. She grabbed the paper bag. "I'm just in a bit of a rush, that's all."

The cool breeze outside felt good against her flushed face as she left the Pig in a Poke. She walked briskly down the street, not stopping to look in any of the windows. Pen heard someone across the street shout and turned to look. It was a young boy with a backpack slung over his shoulder hurrying to catch up with his friends.

A man passing the boy looked familiar. His hair had fallen onto his forehead and he tossed his head with an impatient gesture.

He looked like Adrian Mabry, Pen thought. He must have come into town to do some shopping.

The wind, which had seemed so refreshing when she left the Pig in a Poke, now felt cold and she was glad when her cottage came into view. She couldn't wait to make a hot cup of tea, light the fire, and curl up on the sofa under a throw.

She heard Mrs. Danvers meow as she put her key in the lock, opened the front door, and walked inside. She stepped on a piece of paper on the floor and slipped, briefly losing her footing. The paper went flying and Mrs. Danvers went after it, batting at it with her paw, sending it skittering across the floor.

Pen chased after it and picked it up. It appeared to be a note of some sort. Someone must have slipped it under her door. It was typewritten on ordinary copy paper in large type. There was a quote at the top of the page from Shakespeare's *Hamlet*.

Revenge should have no bounds.

The rest of the note went on to threaten her with dire consequences if she continued to poke her nose into Odile's murder.

Pen was so startled, she dropped the paper. Mrs. Danvers went after it, batting at it again with her paws, and sending it whirling under the sofa.

FOURTEEN

❧

Penelope was so shaken by the note that she lost her appetite. She put the Cornish pasty in the refrigerator and made a cup of tea instead. Her hand shook as she brought the mug to her mouth.

Who would do such a thing? Who would leave a note like that?

The murderer, that's who, a little voice sounded in her ear. Penelope shivered even though she had gotten a roaring fire going and was sitting on the sofa under a knitted throw.

She remembered seeing Adrian Mabry in town. Or at least she had seen someone who looked like him. Had he been the one to slip the note under her door?

She'd been dreading her dinner with Maguire that evening but now she couldn't wait to see him. She'd show him the note and see what he thought. And she'd swear off any more investigating and leave it all to the police. At least that's what she told herself.

Perhaps the note was just a nasty prank? Maybe some kids thought it was funny? Something told her that wasn't the case.

Pen spent the rest of the afternoon under the throw trying to take her mind off the threatening letter. Every noise outside made her jump and Mrs. Danvers had become so annoyed that she fled from the sofa and went to sit in the corner where she stared balefully at Penelope.

She started to feel a bit shaky and decided it wouldn't be wise to put off eating until dinner that night. She poked around in the refrigerator and found a small lump of Stilton, which she ate on some crackers.

Then, with a feeling of dread, she went upstairs to get ready.

Pen paced her sitting room with one eye on the clock. She ought to be heading to the Book and Bottle now or she'd be late, but she couldn't bring herself to leave the cottage. Mrs. Danvers watched her, her tail swishing back and forth in time to Pen's footsteps.

Finally, she could put it off no longer. Pen grabbed her jacket, slipped into it, and headed out the door.

The temperature had dropped, and her breath made puffs of condensation in the air. The moon was partially covered by clouds and a haze hovered over the streetlights.

It didn't take Pen long to get to the Book and Bottle, where she was meeting Maguire. She was tempted to drag her feet, but she'd forgotten her gloves and her hands were cold.

The rush of warm air when she pulled open the door to the pub felt heavenly. The noise—glasses clinking, people shouting, laughing, and chattering—washed over her as she scanned the crowd for Maguire.

He'd secured them a table at the back of the pub. He

waved at Penelope and she began to make her way through the group of people gathered around the bar. A man with a large drooping mustache accidentally elbowed her as he raised his tankard to his lips.

"Sorry, love," he said, foam dripping from his mustache.

Maguire stood up when Pen reached him. He kissed her on the cheek, helped her out of her jacket, and draped it over the back of her chair.

"I took the liberty of getting you a cider," he said, motioning to a glass on the table. "And I got us some pork scratchings to start."

"Perfect," Pen said, although she had no idea what pork scratchings were and it didn't sound too appetizing. She peered into the thick stoneware crock.

Aha, Penelope thought. Pork scratchings were what they called pork rinds back home.

"Shall I put in our orders or do you want to have your drink first?"

Truth be told, Pen actually felt rather queasy, so she was more than happy to wait.

"Let's have our drinks." She took a sip of her cider. She was tempted to gulp it in hopes that it would relax her, but she forced herself to put the glass down after one swallow.

She watched as Maguire picked up his glass of lager. He was casually dressed, as usual, in jeans and a cable-knit sweater that looked handmade. Pen wondered if his wife had knit it for him.

Pen, who had always felt so relaxed around Maguire, suddenly felt awkward and tongue-tied.

"Lovely sweater," she said to break the silence that had fallen between them.

"You like it?" Maguire beamed. "My sister Kathleen made it for me."

"She's very talented," Pen said.

"That she is. She makes sweaters and other knitted things for a local shop where they're very popular. Poor Kathleen."

Pen raised her eyebrows.

Maguire set down his glass. "She was in an accident when she was sixteen—her horse threw her as she approached a jump. It left her partially paralyzed and she's been in a wheelchair ever since. She took up knitting to pass the time and has managed to turn it into a business. She designs her own patterns, and many of them have appeared in women's magazines around the world."

So, his wife hadn't knitted the sweater. Pen was relieved although she was sad to hear about his sister.

Maguire looked at Pen over the rim of his glass. "Is something wrong? You don't seem yourself tonight."

Was something wrong? Pen had to stifle a laugh. Yes, she'd received a note threatening her life and she'd discovered that the man she was dating was possibly married. Which should she bring up first?

Pen took a deep breath and pulled the note out of her bag. "This was slipped under my door today," she said, handing it to Maguire. It would give her some time to figure out how to bring up the subject of Mrs. Brodie Maguire.

The change in Maguire's expression was almost comical, Pen thought. Unfortunately, she didn't feel much like laughing.

"I don't like this," Maguire said, waving the note in the air. "You've touched a nerve. What have you been doing?" He leveled a stern gaze at Penelope.

She squirmed a bit in her chair. "Nothing really." Surely no one had found out she'd been searching the school records for Mabry's application. Or that she had discovered that

Helen had been the one to take the valuable Jane Austen book. Or that she'd stolen a look at Grady's phone. Or that she'd followed Layla when she met up with Mabry.

Maguire didn't look convinced. "We can talk about that later." He looked at her and tilted his head. "That's not the only thing that's bothering you. I can tell. There's something else."

She tried to think of a subtle way to put her suspicions into words but in the end just blurted it out.

"Are you married?"

A look of astonishment crossed Maguire's face.

"A Mrs. Brodie Maguire came into the bookstore the other day. And don't tell me she's your mother. She doesn't look old enough."

"She's not my mother. She's my stepmother. She comes to Chumley occasionally to see her cousin who lives here."

Maguire was now looking rather amused. "My father is Brodie Maguire senior. My mother passed away ten years ago, and in a fit of loneliness he decided to get married again. Besides, the poor man can't so much as boil water and had been subsisting on microwave dinners, takeout, and bangers and mash at his local pub."

Pen felt terrible for almost believing the worst. She could tell her face was getting red.

"What?" Maguire laughed. "You didn't think she was my wife?" He looked incredulous. "You did!"

Pen began shredding her napkin. She couldn't look at him. "I did wonder . . ."

"Is that what's been bothering you? Why you seem to have been avoiding me?"

Pen didn't say anything. She just nodded.

"Well!" Maguire said. "Now that that's out of the way, what do you want to eat?"

Pen glanced at the chalkboard hanging by the bar. She had planned to have something light like Welsh rarebit, but now that her stomach was no longer in knots, she realized she was starving.

"I'll have the shepherd's pie."

Maguire nodded, grabbed their empty glasses, and started to get up. "I'll be right back."

Penelope watched him walk over to the bar. She was so relieved that he wasn't married after all. She'd been silly to think he would be. He didn't seem like the sort who would cheat on his wife.

Maguire muscled his way back to the table with shepherd's pie for Penelope, a steak and ale pie for himself, and refills on their drinks.

"Have you made any progress on that robbery out at Birnam Woods?" Pen said, dishing up a bite of her shepherd's pie.

Maguire scowled. "None of our leads has panned out and I'm getting a lot of pressure from my governor to solve the case. It's as if the jewels vanished into thin air. None of them have even been pawned yet as far as we know."

Maguire looked at Penelope and grinned. "I still can't believe you thought I was married." His expression turned serious and he reached across the table for her hand. "I would never do something like that, believe me." He cocked an eyebrow. "You do believe me, don't you?"

"Yes," Penelope said in a rather small voice.

They finished their meal and held hands as Maguire walked Penelope home. The clouds had parted and moonlight lit their way.

"Would you like to come in for a cup of tea?" Pen said, when they reached her cottage and Maguire had escorted her in.

Maguire made a face. "I'd love to but I have a really early morning meeting tomorrow and I need to be on top of my game."

He reached out and pulled Penelope toward him.

Pen closed her eyes as he leaned toward her for a kiss.

Afterward, as Penelope got ready for bed, she realized she hadn't told him about what she'd uncovered—how Mabry had lied on his employment application, Layla was having an affair, and Odile had discovered that Grady was buying liquor for the students. But perhaps he already knew all those things?

She decided that none of what she'd uncovered probably even meant anything and would only muddy the waters. She could always tell Maguire about it the next time she saw him.

FIFTEEN

◦⟐◦

Penelope felt prickles of apprehension as she walked to
the Open Book the next morning. Was the killer following her? Was he lurking in the shadows of one of the doorways? He knew where she lived. Did he know where she
worked as well?

Was it a coincidence that she'd spotted Mabry in town
right before finding the note? Was he the one threatening her?

Penelope was relieved when she got to the Open Book
and she stood in the entrance for a moment to relish the
warmth and light of the shop.

The shop wasn't busy, so she headed to her writing room
first thing. She powered up her laptop and read the last few
pages of her manuscript to see where she'd left poor Eirene
hanging.

Eirene had managed to undo the doorknob of the laboratory where Mr. Bloodworth was keeping her prisoner and escape. What now? Pen chewed on the side of her thumb.

Eirene had to get out of the house but where to go? It was surrounded by moors with no other houses in sight. She'd worry about that later, Pen thought. First, she had to get Eirene out safely.

Penelope felt chills up and down her spine as she led Eirene through the darkened hallway and down the stairs. She knew how Eirene felt—her skin prickling, her breathing rapid, her heart beating hard. She'd felt that way herself walking to work this morning.

Penelope was exhausted when she finished the scene even though all she'd done was sit at her computer and hit the keys. Emotionally she felt drained.

She decided to call it quits for the moment and go see if Figgy could scare up a Chelsea bun or a scone for her and maybe a hot cup of tea.

When Penelope emerged from her writing room, Mabel was bending over, shelving some books.

"I had dinner with Maguire last night."

"Oh?" Mabel straightened up.

"The Mrs. Brodie Maguire who came into the shop is his stepmother."

Mabel laughed. "So there was a perfectly innocent explanation after all. But surely there's quite an age difference? What do they call them? May–December romances."

"Or a middle-age crisis maybe?" Pen said.

"Yes," Mabel said, slotting a book into position on the shelf. "But Maguire's father must be well past middle age. He's going to have trouble keeping up."

Penelope hesitated. Should she tell Mabel about the

threatening note that she'd found slipped under her door? Ultimately she decided against it. She knew that Mabel felt quite motherly toward her and Pen didn't want her worried or making a fuss.

She headed toward the tea shop, where Figgy was serving tea and crumpets to two ladies in waxed jackets. She tucked the empty tray under her arm and walked over to Penelope.

"We've suddenly gotten busy," Figgy said, blowing a lock of her short spiky hair off her forehead. She smiled at Pen. "By the looks of you, I'd guess you were after something to eat."

Pen laughed. "Am I that transparent? What gave it away?"

"That hungry look in your eyes." Figgy shifted the tray under her arm. "Wait here and I'll be right back with something delicious."

Pen sat at one of the tables while she waited. It didn't take long. Moments later Figgy returned with a tray laden with a cup of hot tea, a plate of shortbread cookies, and a plate of crumpets.

"This should do you," she said as she put the plates down on the table.

"You're a lifesaver," Pen said, picking up a crumpet.

She finished her tea, brushed some crumbs off her sweater, and went to work on a display by the front counter of dystopian novels—worlds that seemed far away from quaint and peaceful Upper Chumley-on-Stoke. Suddenly the door to the shop opened and Gladys rushed in. She had dashed across the street without a coat and still had a bloodstained apron tied around her waist.

Penelope had often heard the expression *her eyes bugged*

out but she'd never seen anyone's eyes actually do that. Until now. Gladys's blue eyes were wide-open and nearly popping out of her head.

Mabel put down the catalogue she was thumbing through. "What is it, Gladys? Is something the matter? You look as if you've seen the ghost of Banquo from Shakespeare's Scottish play."

Gladys gave a mournful cry. "I don't know what to do. I shouldn't have done it."

"Done what?" Pen said, thinking maybe she ought to fetch Gladys a cup of tea laced with plenty of sugar. It was the standard British offering no matter whether the person was overcome with grief, fear, or joy.

"I shouldn't have done it," Gladys repeated. "It was wrong of me. If I hadn't, I never would have found them."

"Found what?" Mabel said. "Maybe you should start at the beginning."

Penelope admired Mabel's patience. Personally, she felt like throttling Gladys herself.

"Catch your breath," Mabel said to Gladys, who had begun to pant slightly and was wringing her hands in agitation. "And start at the beginning," she said again.

Figgy had obviously heard the commotion and had run over with a strong cup of tea. She handed it to Gladys.

"I've put plenty of sugar in it."

Gladys blew on it and then took a sip. She inhaled deeply.

"It's like this," she said. "It's all because I was stepping out on my Bruce. I knew it was wrong and I shouldn't have done it. And now it's come to this."

Gladys was taking so long to tell her story that Penelope could see that even Mabel's patience was wearing thin.

"Did Bruce find out?" Pen said.

Gladys shook her head vigorously. "No. And I hope he never does."

"So what's happened to put you in such a state?" Mabel said.

"It's Rodney Simpson. He's the handyman at the school where Penelope is teaching that class. We've been stepping out together."

"How did you meet him?" Pen said.

"He came into the shop, looking for some gammon for his tea."

Pen raised her eyebrows and looked from Gladys to Mabel.

"It's a sort of bacon," Mabel explained.

"And the next time it was rump roasts," Gladys said. "After that he began to come in regularly—every Friday at three o'clock on the dot—for a steak or a couple of lamb chops or a bit of pork loin. He was ever so polite, too. He gave me compliments—said I had lovely skin and beautiful eyes." Gladys's face flushed. She raised her chin defiantly. "He made me feel pretty and like I was young again and where's the harm in that?"

Pen and Mabel were silent.

"Anyway," Gladys continued, "one day he asked if I'd like to go for a walk. And then the next time it was out for a pub lunch. No crime in that, so I said okay. We didn't go to the Book and Bottle because someone might have spotted us. He took me to the Wolf and Whistle in Lower Chumley." Gladys gave a loud sniff. "He called me his little crumpet."

Gladys broke down in tears and they waited while she collected herself.

"Next thing you know, I'm agreeing to go with him over to the Oakwood School, where he had a shed for his tools.

He'd fixed it up real nice with all his hammers and wrenches and such, all neat and proper." Gladys hesitated. "He had a small desk and a cot where he said he liked to have a bit of a kip in the afternoons if he wasn't busy."

Gladys was blushing in earnest now.

"I think we can guess what comes next," Mabel said dryly. "But what has you so upset if it wasn't Bruce finding out?"

"There was a robbery out at Birnam Woods—those big fancy houses with cars that cost the earth parked out front. Just asking to be broken into, if you want my opinion." Gladys took a deep breath. "I read all about it in the *Chumley Chronicle,* how the thieves nicked a whole lot of jewelry and that the police still haven't found it.

"Anyway, Rodney asked me to meet him there—at the shed—one day. He said he didn't have time to come into town to get me. I wasn't too keen on it, but I wanted to see him so I went."

Gladys drained the last of her tea and put the empty cup down on the counter.

"Rodney wasn't there when I got to the shed so I had a bit of a look around. And now I wish I hadn't."

"What did you find?" Mabel said. "I assume you found something."

"Something to do with the robbery?" Penelope said.

Gladys nodded mutely.

"Well, what was it?" Mabel said in exasperated tones.

"The sun had come in through the window and something in the corner of the shed was sparkling—like it was lit up or something. I went over to have a look and . . ."

By now Mabel and Penelope were both leaning forward.

"It was a diamond necklace. It was partially stuffed into a sort of velvet pouch. I opened the pouch and there were

more jewels inside—ruby rings, sapphire earrings, the lot."
She looked at Mabel and Penelope, her eyes round and staring. "I didn't know what to think at first, but then I realized
that Rodney must be the thief who stole those jewels from
the house in Birnam Woods."

SIXTEEN

꘎

I think you could do with another cup of nice hot tea," Figgy said. She and Penelope each put an arm around Gladys and led her to the tea shop.

"Frankly, I wouldn't mind a cup of tea myself," Mabel said, pointing to the only customer in the shop—an older man asleep in a chair, his head tipped back and a pile of books in his lap. "I don't think I'll be needed at the front counter unless a new customer comes in."

"Tea all around, then," Figgy said.

"I could do with a little something to eat," Gladys said. "I'm feeling a bit wobbly."

Mabel and Penelope exchanged a look, while Figgy hastened off to the kitchen. When she returned, she had a tray laden with cups and saucers, a squat round teapot covered with a red-and-white-gingham-checked cozy, and a plate with slices of lemon drizzle cake fanned out on it.

While Figgy poured the tea and passed the cups around,

Gladys reached out a trembling hand and helped herself to a slice of cake.

"There's something else," Gladys blurted out. Penelope and Mabel turned toward her. Gladys looked down at her plate and broke off bits of her cake and rolled them between her fingers. "I think it was Rodney's wife that broke the window of our shop. She must have found out about me and Rodney." She began to sniffle. "I've caused so much trouble."

"You'll have to go to the police," Mabel said, as she stirred milk into her tea.

Gladys drew back, her eyes round and staring like a spooked horse's.

"I could never . . ."

"But you have to. The jewels must be returned to the rightful owner," Mabel said.

"Couldn't I give them . . . what do they call it . . . one of those anonymous tips?"

"That might work," Penelope said, looking at Mabel. "Don't you think?"

Mabel shook her head. "The police get so many of those they might put the caller down as being a bit barmy and simply ignore it."

"But if I give them my name, won't the police wonder what I was doing in the toolshed at the Oakwood School?" Gladys said, reaching for another slice of cake, her appetite apparently undiminished by the morning's events.

"I should imagine so," Penelope said. "It's not as if you happened to just wander there. You had to have a reason."

"I could make something up," Gladys said, her face brightening.

"It would be much simpler to tell the police the truth.

They're not going to pass any judgment about your having an affair."

Gladys looked slightly affronted at Mabel's use of the word *affair.* "That makes it sound so sordid," she huffed.

"What would you prefer? *Dalliance*? *Rendezvous*?"

"That last sounds too Continental."

"Whatever you call it," Mabel said, "the police are hardly going to advertise it in the *Chumley Chronicle*. I think you can rest assured that they will be discreet."

Gladys didn't look entirely convinced.

"Maybe I could ask to speak to that detective Maguire," Gladys said hopefully. "I wouldn't mind so much if I could tell him about it. He's ever so nice."

"I don't see why not," Penelope said. "I know he's going to be so relieved to have the case solved."

"So, me finding the jewels is a good thing," Gladys said, her face reddening slightly. "Maybe I won't even have to tell him what I was doing in the toolshed."

Penelope, Mabel, and Figgy looked at each other.

"Maybe," Penelope said.

That was one mystery solved, Penelope thought as she set up for a signing for a London businessman who had penned a book titled *How to Prepare for the Coming Recession*, which Penelope found to be awfully doom and gloom and for a fleeting moment she considered adding it to her display of dystopian fiction.

Maguire would be pleased to have the Birnam Woods robbery solved and off his plate. She doubted he would press Gladys to reveal what she was doing in the toolshed at the Oakwood School in the first place. At least she hoped not.

Penelope dragged out the folding table they used for book signings and positioned it at the front of the store where customers would see it as soon as they walked in. She covered it with a white cloth and set a stack of the author's books off to one side and a brand-new pen in the center. Some authors brought their own favorite pen but one would be there just in case.

The book signing wouldn't start for an hour yet, but Penelope wanted to be prepared. She was setting out a bowl of Norfolk Manor Wine Gums—anything to lure potential buyers to the table—when the author, Leo Fox, arrived. He was all silk suspenders, monogrammed gold cuff links, and crisp aftershave. He reminded Penelope of a shark.

Fox slapped his briefcase down on the table and popped open the locks.

"I'm going to do a spot of work until we're ready to start," he said, whisking out several folders.

"Would you like to sit at a table in the back?" Pen said.

"That would be brilliant." Leo grinned, baring his professionally whitened teeth.

Pen showed him to a secluded spot and was heading toward her writing room when Laurence Brimble popped out from behind one of the shelves, a book tucked under his arm.

"Cheerio," he said, smoothing an index finger over his mustache. "It's quite bracing out, but there's some sun. Have to enjoy it while we can, right?"

Penelope nodded. "Are you here for Leo Fox's book signing?"

Brimble fingered his mustache again. "No, my dear. I have all my money safely tucked away." He cleared his throat. "Now, if you had Archibald Stewart in—he's written that book on military history that I've been looking forward to—I'd definitely want a signed copy."

He held out the book he'd been carrying. "I'm chuffed to have found this in your used book collection." He tapped the cover. "*Victoria Crosses on the Western Front—Battle of Amiens*. It's the latest in Oldfield's series." He smiled. "Looks like someone else in Upper Chumley-on-Stoke is as interested in military history as I am."

Victoria Crosses. That rang a bell. Pen searched her memory and suddenly recalled Quentin's prized Victoria Cross.

She put a hand on Brimble's arm. "You must know a lot about the Victoria Cross."

"A bit." Brimble preened slightly.

"Are they very valuable?" Quentin had said he'd paid a lot for the medal but 'a lot' was subjective. If it was terribly expensive, how could he have afforded it on a teacher's salary?

Brimble fingered his mustache again. "That would depend. Do you know what year it was given?"

"Apparently during the Crimean War."

Brimble's eyebrows shot up. "That would be quite valuable indeed. I can't put an exact figure on it. You might ask one of the auction houses that specializes in such things. There's one in London on King Street. It's called Taylor's."

"Thanks," Pen said.

Where on earth had Quentin gotten the money to purchase something so valuable? Pen wondered.

The book signing finished up by early afternoon. There'd been quite a crush with people coming from Lower Chumley and even quite a few from London. Mabel had been very pleased and so had Leo Fox, who had packed up his briefcase and left for the 2:17 train back to the city.

Penelope breathed a sigh of relief as she watched the door close behind him.

Mabel was talking to someone on the telephone when she removed the receiver from her ear, held it against her chest, and motioned for Penelope.

Penelope raised her eyebrows as she walked over to the counter.

"Could you possibly do me a huge favor?" Mabel said, her voice quiet.

"Sure. What?"

"I have a woman on the phone who wants to sell a first edition of *A History of British Birds* by Morris. I don't usually dabble in first editions but I promised Worthington I'd keep a look out for that volume. He's been wanting to add it to his collection." Mabel lowered her voice even more. "The problem is, the owner, Mrs. Rutledge, is quite elderly and can't manage a trip to Chumley and she doesn't want to trust it to the mail. Would you mind running up to London to pick it up? I've got her address and phone number." She handed Pen a scrap of paper.

"Now? I'd be happy to."

"Brilliant. I'll let Mrs. Rutledge know you're coming."

Penelope gathered her things together and on an impulse phoned Beryl to see if she wanted to go along. Beryl was delighted at the prospect and agreed to meet Penelope at the train station.

Penelope phoned for a taxi and was relieved when Mad Max pulled up to the curb. Their trip to the station was dignified and sedate and Pen arrived at the station blessedly feeling neither shaken nor stirred.

Beryl had her ticket and was already waiting on the platform for Penelope. She was wearing a new coat—Penelope hadn't seen it before—it was a light wool in royal blue with a funnel neck.

"Your coat is very chic," Penelope said.

"Thank you. Charlotte gave it to me. She didn't want it anymore. She said she'd already been photographed in it too many times."

"Maybe you'll be mistaken for a duchess," Pen said.

Beryl made a face. "I doubt it."

"What are you planning to do in London?" Pen glanced down the tracks to see if she could spot the train. It was two minutes late by her watch.

"I'm scouting out some clothes for Charlotte to wear post-baby. She'll need some transition pieces while she works to get her figure back. I thought I'd pop into Atelier Classique if they haven't already packed up for their move to Paris."

A loud whistle echoed down the tracks and the train chugged into Upper Chumley-on-Stoke's Victorian-era station. The cars weren't crowded and Penelope and Beryl quickly found seats.

The train slowly picked up speed, and soon the landscape was speeding by the slightly dusty window. Beryl was reading a magazine and Penelope was lost in thought.

"How did he manage to afford it?" Penelope suddenly blurted out, not realizing she'd spoken out loud.

Beryl lowered her magazine. "Who? Afford what?"

"Sorry," Penelope said. "I guess I was thinking out loud."

"Literally," Beryl said dryly. "Do you want to tell me about it?"

Penelope explained about Quentin and the Victoria Cross.

"Laurence Brimble said a Victoria Cross can be very valuable. Where did Quentin get the money?" Pen turned to Beryl. "It's not like teaching pays a lot."

"Does his wife work? Perhaps she's one of those high-powered investment banker types who's making seven figures in the City?"

Penelope shook her head. "He's not married."

Beryl swiveled in her seat to face Penelope. "What about his parents? Perhaps he inherited a fortune?"

"I don't know. I wonder if Maribel knows. I'll have to ask her."

Beryl gave her a stern look. "I thought you were finished with all your snooping."

"Investigating," Penelope corrected. "And I am. I'm just doing a bit of research. There can't be any harm in that."

Beryl reached over and patted Penelope's hand. "I'd feel a lot better if you left the investigating—I mean research—to that handsome detective of yours."

Penelope and Beryl parted ways at King's Cross Station, where sunlight came through the thousands of panels in the fluted roof, warming the interior of the station.

Penelope strolled along the Western Concourse, peering into the shop windows. She paused for a moment to admire the display at the Harry Potter store and to get a coffee at Caffè Nero.

It didn't take her long to reach the home of the elderly woman who was selling the first edition of *A History of British Birds.* She invited Penelope in for a cup of tea, but Penelope declined. An idea had struck her while she was walking and she saw no harm in following up on it.

She paused outside the woman's white stucco home and pulled out her phone. She entered Taylor's Auction House into a search engine and their website popped up. She checked the address and then headed back down the street.

She wasn't *snooping*, as Beryl put it. She wasn't even investigating. She was merely doing research. At least that's what she told herself as she walked along King's Road. She found the Taylor's Auction House easily enough. It was a magnificent limestone building with a red flag hanging out front and the entrance flanked by two elaborate topiary trees in ceramic pots. A gray-uniformed doorman smiled and held open the door.

The spacious, hushed interior was painted a rich dark green with recessed lighting that gave the room a soft glow.

A man in a black suit immediately glided across the marble floor toward Penelope.

"May I help you, madam?" he said, tilting his head slightly like a bird.

He was wearing round tortoiseshell glasses and had an egg-shaped bald head. He barely came to Penelope's chin. She glanced at his gold name tag, which read *Reginald Kenworthy.*

"I understand you specialize in collectible medals."

"That we do, madam. Among other things."

"I have a question about a Victoria Cross."

"Then you've come to the right place," Reginald said. "Are you looking to buy one or to sell one?"

"Neither, actually. I just need some information about them. I hope you can help me."

Reginald gave a self-satisfied smile. "I'm sure I can."

"Would a Victoria Cross from the Crimean War be especially valuable?"

Reginald drew in his breath and straightened up. "One

from that era would be highly collectible. The highest price paid for a Victoria Cross was for the one given to Vice Admiral Gordon Campbell. He steered his ship, the HMS *Farnborough,* directly into the path of a German torpedo," Reginald said with relish. "He then released the ship's hidden guns and quickly dispatched the U-boat. The medal sold for over eight hundred thousand pounds. A record."

Penelope nearly took a step backward. Eight hundred thousand pounds? Where would Quentin have gotten money like that?

"We auctioned off a Victoria Cross quite recently ourselves," Reginald said, putting up a hand to adjust his glasses. "If you don't mind waiting a minute, I will go get the catalogue."

Penelope nodded. "Of course."

"Back in a tick," Reginald said as he scampered away and disappeared through a door off to the side.

Penelope looked around while she waited. The walls were hung with ornately framed paintings—dark landscapes, portraits of brooding and bearded men and fair-skinned voluptuous nudes.

She jumped when Reginald suddenly reappeared at her side. He was holding an auction catalogue folded back to display an inside page.

"Here it is," he said in reverent tones. "Our Victoria Cross." He handed the catalogue to Penelope and tapped the page with a well-manicured index finger. "We sold it two months ago."

This Victoria Cross wasn't valued as highly as the one Reginald had told her about but the estimate was between one hundred and two hundred thousand pounds—certainly a considerable sum and more than most schoolteachers could afford.

"You don't happen to know who bought it, do you?" Penelope handed the catalogue back to Reginald.

Reginald looked sad. "We have records, of course, but we are not allowed to release that information. As you can imagine, the buyers demand confidentiality."

Penelope had thought that would be the case but had figured there was no harm in asking.

She thanked Reginald for his trouble and left. Her mind was busy analyzing the facts as she walked along, occasionally stopping to look in a window.

Reginald's Victoria Cross had been auctioned off two months ago. Could Quentin have been the buyer? If so, he had to have spent between one hundred and two hundred thousand pounds to procure it. Perhaps it had been bid up even higher than that.

Where on earth had he gotten money like that? As soon as she got home, she would see if she could find any information on Quentin's parents. For all she knew, his family owned a castle in Scotland and were distantly related to the royal family. Maybe teaching was simply an avocation for him—something he did to make a difference and not necessarily to earn money.

Somehow that didn't jive with the little Penelope had gleaned about Quentin Barnes.

B eryl was buzzing with excitement when she met Penelope at King's Cross Station. Penelope had spent her time walking around the Tate and perusing the shelves at Hatchards, a bookstore said to be the queen's favorite.

Beryl had been to Atelier Classique, which hadn't yet moved.

"I saw sketches of some things that would be wonderful for Charlotte," she said, as she and Penelope waited for the train. "Yvette was very kind to let me in. They're in the midst of packing up for their relocation to Paris. Fortunately, she knows what Charlotte likes so all I have to do is phone her with Charlotte's measurements."

Beryl pulled several sketches from her handbag and showed them to Penelope.

"I'm thinking this outfit for the baby's christening," she said, pointing to a cream-colored dress with three-quarter length sleeves and a lace overlay. "Rosie Olivia will be making a bespoke hat to complement the outfit."

"It's lovely," Penelope said, trying to picture herself in a dress like that. She failed miserably.

"How was your day?" Beryl said as she pulled a notebook and a pen from her handbag. "Is that the book?" She pointed to the padded envelope in Penelope's hands. "I can see by your lack of shopping bags that you didn't do any shopping."

Penelope laughed. "Very clever, Sherlock." She told Beryl about her visit to the auction house.

"It's true that a Victoria Cross from the Crimean War can be very valuable. As valuable as two hundred thousand pounds."

Beryl gasped.

"There's no way Quentin could have afforded that without a rich relative or friend leaving him money. I'm going to do some research on his family as soon as I can."

"What about that note you told me about?" Beryl put the sketches in her lap and turned toward Penelope. "Didn't you say you saw one of the teachers in town the same day it appeared under your door? Was it this Quentin?"

"No. It was Adrian Mabry, the music teacher. It could

have been a coincidence." Penelope didn't sound convincing, even to herself.

Penelope was flummoxed. There were too many people with too many motives—Mabry, Quentin, Grady, Layla, even Nicola. And so far, she'd only managed to eliminate one—Helen Dingley.

Beryl was still going through her sketches and making notes and Penelope was nearly dozing when they pulled into the Upper Chumley-on-Stoke train station.

Penelope shook herself awake. They gathered their things together and followed the other passengers off the train.

"I'm starved," Beryl said as they walked through the station and out to a taxi. "Let's get some dinner."

"We could stop at the Book and Bottle," Pen said, waving to the cabdriver sitting outside the station, his motor idling. He'd rolled down the window and was puffing on a cigarette, blowing the smoke out into the air where it drifted upward until it disappeared.

"Good idea," Beryl said, pulling on her gloves. "I could do with some of their wonderful shepherd's pie."

The taxi driver this time was the one with the checkered cap. He was quiet as he drove, occasionally reaching forward to change the radio station.

"Here you are," he said, pulling up in front of the Book and Bottle.

Noise assaulted them as Pen pulled open the door—raucous laughter and the pinging of the fruit machine—and she saw Beryl flinch slightly. She was surprised her sister had been willing to eat at the pub in the first place.

They found a table in the corner where it wasn't exactly quiet, but they were as far away as they could get from the Upper Chumley rugby team that was celebrating at the bar after a win over Lower Chumley-on-Stoke, with whom they had a long-standing rivalry.

"What would you like to drink?" Pen said, beginning to get up from her chair.

"A glass of chardonnay. Nothing too oaky, please."

Penelope raised her eyebrows but didn't say anything. The pub was not likely to offer a huge selection of white wines. She could imagine the bartender's reaction if she asked for a chardonnay that wasn't *too oaky*. Beryl would have to make do with whatever they had on hand.

Penelope waited patiently until there was an open slot at the bar and she was able to sidle up. After pulling pints for two other customers, the bartender finally noticed her. Penelope knew it didn't do to wave or attempt to get his attention. She had learned that much about pub etiquette during her time in Chumley. It wasn't like some of the bars in New York City, where waving a ten dollar bill got you faster service.

She ordered a cider for herself and a glass of wine for Beryl, hoping it wouldn't be too oaky—whatever that meant.

She managed to get the glasses back to the table without being jostled and without spilling any. She put the wineglass in front of Beryl. She noticed Beryl had a piece of creased yellow paper in her hand.

"What's that?" Pen said as she took a sip of her cider. She was thirsty and tried not to gulp it.

Beryl waved the paper at Penelope. "I found it under the salt shaker. It was all folded up. I was curious, but it's nothing much." She handed it to Penelope.

Penelope looked at it. It was obviously a flyer for music night at the Book and Bottle. Sunday was the quietest night of the week at the pub and the owner had started hiring local bands to play in hopes of luring in more customers.

Ten days ago it had been a rock band called the Allegros. Pen scanned the names of the members of the band. One of them in particular jumped out at her. Adrian Mabry, guitarist.

So Mabry had been lying about his distaste for rock music, Pen thought. Was he embarrassed to be playing the guitar in a band instead of his violin in a string quartet?

Penelope checked the date on the flyer. It was the Sunday that Odile had been killed. If Mabry had been playing at the Book and Bottle on that Sunday night, he couldn't have killed Odile.

It must have been someone else who put that note under her door and who had dropped the poisonous deadly nightshade juice into Odile's wineglass.

SEVENTEEN

❧

She was now down two suspects at least, Penelope thought as she popped some bread into the toaster the next morning. Helen Dingley had an alibi and, as it turned out, so did Adrian Mabry. But there was still Grady, Quentin, Layla, and Nicola.

Layla had said she had seen Nicola walking in the woods where the deadly nightshade grew. Was she trying to cast suspicion on someone else so no one would look too closely at her?

Penelope added some food to Mrs. Danvers's dish as Mrs. Danvers looked on in approval. She gave the cat a scratch under the chin, which Mrs. Danvers endured for a couple of seconds before moving away.

Pen slid her laptop into her tote bag and reached for her jacket. She glanced out the window. The sun was shining and large puffy clouds drifted lazily across the sky. She noticed Mr. Patel pass by with his dog, a newspaper tucked under his arm. At least she didn't need her umbrella, she thought as she closed and locked the door to her cottage.

The walk to the Open Book was pleasant and Penelope stopped to look in several shop windows along the way. Delicious aromas drifted out of Pierre's Restaurant, where the front door was propped open while delivery men walked in and out carrying large cartons with *Frozen Seafood— This Side Up* and an arrow printed on the sides.

When Pen opened the door to the Open Book, Mabel was standing on a ladder that she had leaned against the wall. She had a feather duster in her hand.

"What are you doing?" Pen said as she took off her jacket.

"I'm clearing away some cobwebs that I've been meaning to take care of for several weeks now. Suddenly I couldn't stand them anymore."

"Do be careful," Pen said as she headed toward her writing room.

Penelope got settled at her desk and powered up her laptop. She was itching to see what she could find online about Quentin Barnes. She brought up her favorite search engine and was about to type in his name when she heard a scream and a crash coming from the shop.

She nearly bumped into Figgy, who had heard it as well and was running out of the tea shop to see what was going on. They both stopped short when they saw Mabel lying on the ground with the ladder on top of her. Her expression was dazed and her normally rosy complexion was a pasty white.

"Are you okay?" Penelope and Figgy said in unison.

Mabel winced. "I'm alive but I fear I've done something to my leg."

Penelope glanced at Mabel's leg and was alarmed to see that it was at an odd angle.

"Help me shift the ladder," Figgy said, grabbing hold of one end.

Penelope took the other end and they laid it on the floor next to Mabel.

"Can you move?" Penelope said.

Mabel grunted. "No. It's my leg. I think it's broken." She winced again.

"We need to get you to hospital," Figgy said.

"I have my cell phone." Pen pulled it out of her pocket and dialed nine nine nine, which she'd learned was Britain's version of nine one one.

"They'll be along in a tick," Figgy said while Penelope talked to the dispatcher.

"Can you help me sit up?" Mabel said.

"I think you'd better stay where you are," Penelope said. "If something is broken, it's better not to move," she said, glancing at Mabel's leg again.

The bell over the front door tinkled and Mabel groaned. "How am I going to manage?"

They were all relieved when they saw that it was Laurence Brimble.

"My sainted aunt," he exclaimed as he rushed over to Mabel. "What's happened?"

"She fell off the ladder," Penelope said. "We've already called for an ambulance. They should be here any minute now."

Brimble tutted under his breath. "Dear, dear," he said as he took off his coat. He folded it up and slipped it under Mabel's head.

"Thank you." She turned to look at Penelope. "Now I need to call Kip."

Kip Farrington was a twenty something young man who occasionally helped Mabel out in the store. He was going to design school at night and was grateful for any odd jobs he could do during the day.

"I'll call him," Penelope said.

"There's a list of phone numbers by the telephone on the counter. His should be on it."

Mabel's voice was getting weaker. Penelope hoped the ambulance would be along soon. She'd no sooner had the thought than she heard a siren in the distance.

"They're almost here," Brimble said. He knelt down next to Mabel and held her hand.

The siren got louder and Penelope ran to open the front door. The ambulance pulled up to the curb and a man and a woman jumped out. They ran around to the back and pulled out a gurney that they wheeled into the Open Book.

Their movements were swift and sure and in no time at all, they had Mabel's leg splinted and she was strapped to the gurney. Brimble quickly shrugged on his coat.

"I'll go to hospital with you," he said, standing by Mabel's side, his hand resting lightly on her arm. Before Mabel could protest, she was wheeled out the door and into the back of the ambulance and Brimble was headed for his car.

Pen and Figgy stood together by the window and watched as it disappeared down the high street.

Pen was manning the front desk when Kip Farrington dashed in, his scarf flying behind him. He was tall and thin and was wearing black stovepipe pants that emphasized his skinny legs. He had large brown eyes and dark brown hair with a clump in the front dyed bright orange.

"I came tout de suite," he said rather breathlessly as he

threw his jacket on the coat-tree. "Not to worry, dears, Kip is here." He turned and smiled at Penelope and Figgy.

"We're glad to see you," Pen said. "I have to get over to the school for my seminar. Are you sure you'll be okay?"

"Of course, dear," Kip said, getting comfortable behind the counter. "Just leave everything to me."

After Mabel left for the hospital, Penelope called for a taxi, which dropped her off in front of the Oakwood School administration building. She tipped the driver and began to head toward the quad. Several of the students in her class had decided to try their hands at writing their own Gothic novels and had begged Penelope for help.

As Penelope walked swiftly toward Corbyn Hall, a girl with her long hair gathered into a ponytail skirted around her and ran down the path.

Penelope glanced at her watch, but she still had ten minutes before the time she'd agreed to meet the girls. She reached Corbyn Hall and headed down the corridor, looking for the lounge the girls had reserved. As she was rounding the corner, she noticed a movement ahead of her and looked up to see Nicola grab Grady by the arm and pull him into what looked like a utility closet.

Penelope crept closer, trying to make as little noise as possible. Why were they, being so secretive? She thought she could guess. The door to the closet had a vent at the top and Nicola's and Grady's voices carried into the hall. Grady kept shushing Nicola but she only got louder and more strident.

It was obvious they were arguing about something. Pen

looked up and down the hall but it was empty. Nonetheless, she bent down and pretended to be fussing with the laces on her boots. If someone did come along, they wouldn't realize she was eavesdropping.

"Why?" she heard Nicola say, her voice rising plaintively.

"It's become too dangerous," Grady said. "I can't risk it."

"It's not any more dangerous now than it was before." Nicola's tone was adamant. "No one knows. You won't get into trouble."

"You read that memo the head sent out the other day. Your father is threatening to pull his funding from the school if the person buying alcohol for the students isn't stopped."

Nicola grumbled something Penelope didn't quite catch.

"Look"—Grady's tone was pleading—"I can't afford to lose my job. I'm going to be a father." There was a note of pride in his voice. "Layla's pregnant. And she wants to quit work after the baby is born."

There was a moment's silence.

"I'm sure you don't want the head to find out that you're the culprit," Nicola said in a voice that was both smooth and menacing. "But that's what will happen if you don't give me what I want."

There was the sound of rustling behind the door and Penelope quickly scooted down the hall. She was walking into the lounge when she heard the door to the utility closet squeak open and Grady's and Nicola's footsteps echoing down the hall.

Nicola had sounded furious. But not in a hot, boiling over sort of way. She had been as cold as an Arctic wind. And somehow that had been even more frightening than red-hot rage.

Penelope had had her doubts before but now thought it

was quite possible that Nicola was the sort of person who would resort to murder to get what she wanted.

A s soon as Penelope's writing group ended, she pulled out her cell phone and dialed Figgy. There might be some news about Mabel—good news, hopefully.

Figgy answered on the third ring. Mabel was still in hospital. The doctors had taken X-rays and she had a simple fracture. As soon as they put a cast on her leg, she would be discharged. Brimble was still with her and planned to bring her home. According to Figgy, that had taken some persuasion—Mabel had been determined to head back to the Open Book instead.

Penelope clicked off the call and headed across the quad toward the administration building. She wanted to check the mailbox that had been assigned to her on her first day. Maribel was a bit old-school at times and preferred to distribute hard copies of important memos. She said she'd heard the bogus excuse that her e-mail hadn't been received too many times to rely on that means of communication.

Penelope checked the cubbyhole that was her mailbox and pulled out two sheets of paper. One was a flyer announcing a concert in the Stewart-Calthorpe Assembly Hall on Saturday evening and the other was a notice that there would be a staff meeting on Friday afternoon.

Penelope stuffed the papers into her tote bag, headed down the hall, and ducked into the ladies' room. As the door swung shut behind her, she heard crying coming from one of the stalls. The door opened and Layla came out.

Her eyes and nose were red and she had a crumpled tissue in her hand.

"Is everything okay?" Pen said.

Layla sniffed loudly. "Not really, no."

"Do you want to talk about it?" Penelope tried to keep her tone neutral.

Layla leaned on the sink and stared into the mirror. "I look a positive fright." She turned around to face Penelope. "It's that detective. I think his name is Maguire. He was around asking questions again."

Layla paused and Penelope was quiet, waiting for her to continue.

"He wanted to know where I was the night Odile was killed. I told him the last time he asked me. I was home watching the telly."

Layla turned on the cold tap and splashed some water on her face.

"He asked me if anyone saw me. I told him no. I was on my own. Grady was meeting some mates at the pub in Lower Chumley for a couple of pints. They get together every week to have a drink and to play darts."

She grabbed a couple of towels from the dispenser and dabbed at her face.

"He asked if anyone saw me and I said of course not. I was alone in my own home. The only way anyone could have seen me would have been by peeping through the window."

"Didn't he believe you?"

Layla's face crumpled. She shook her head. "The thing is, I didn't kill Odile, but I can't tell him where I really was."

"Why not?" Pen put a hand on Layla's arm. "No matter what it is, he'll understand."

She had visions of Layla and her friends visiting some male strip club or gambling away money in a casino. While that might be embarrassing, it certainly wasn't criminal.

"I just can't," Layla said, lifting her chin. "It would only get me in trouble." She pushed past Penelope and reached for the door handle. "Excuse me. I have a meeting with the head and I'm already late."

That was certainly curious, Penelope thought. She knew Layla couldn't have been with Mabry. She'd already discovered that he had been playing at the Book and Bottle the night Odile was killed. And Layla would have no reason to keep her visit to the pub a secret, especially if it would clear her of murder.

Where could she have been that she was afraid to say?

Penelope finished in the ladies' room and walked out into the hall. She remembered that the one time she'd been in Layla's office, she had noticed an open planner on her desk. Obviously, Maribel wasn't the only one who was old-school. Penelope wondered if Layla might have made some note about whatever it was she was doing on that Sunday night.

Curiosity overcame her and she headed down the corridor toward the infirmary. It took a certain amount of mental gymnastics to convince herself she wasn't snooping or investigating. She peered through the frosted glass window, but there were no shadows moving about. The room appeared to be empty.

The door gave a loud squeak as she opened it and she cringed, but fortunately no one was around to hear it.

Layla's office was empty and Pen quickly glanced into the examining room, but it was empty as well. If anyone came in, she'd say she had a headache and was hoping to get something for it.

Just as she remembered, Layla's diary was open on her desk. Today's appointment with Maribel was noted along with several others. Penelope crossed her fingers that she'd been as diligent about recording where she'd been on the night Odile died.

She flipped through the pages, trying to make as little noise as possible even though she doubted the sound would carry into the hallway. On one of the pages, Layla had drawn a little sketch of a man's face. Mabry's? Penelope wondered.

She turned a few more pages and found the one she was looking for.

She didn't know the exact time Odile had downed the poisoned wine, but according to Maguire, it couldn't have been much more than an hour or two before she succumbed to the deadly nightshade.

Odile had arrived at the Open Book a little before seven o'clock, so she had to have met with her killer shortly before leaving her apartment.

There was a note scribbled in the diary in the five-thirty spot. It was an address but not one that Penelope recognized. She pulled a notebook from her tote bag and quickly wrote it down.

She froze when she heard footsteps coming down the hall, but they stopped short of the infirmary. She opened the door a crack and peered out. The corridor was empty. She slipped out the door and closed it softly behind her.

EIGHTEEN

❧

Penelope stood outside the administration building, waiting for her taxi. She was about to ring them again when she saw the cab making its way down the drive.

The cabbie was one of the new ones who had recently started—the one who had moved to Chumley from London to please his wife.

"I remember you," he said, as he put the car in gear. "You're the American, right?"

Penelope admitted as much, wondering when she would cease to be a novelty in this small English town.

The driver put on his blinker to turn right as they left the school grounds.

Penelope leaned forward and tapped him on the shoulder.

"Excuse me. I'm not going into town this time. Can you take me to number six Station Road?"

"Catching the train, are you?"

"No. It's an address."

"Must be near the station, then." He pulled out of the drive and headed down the lane.

"How are you liking Chumley?" Pen said as they got under way.

"It's fine enough, I suppose. Although now the missus is all up in arms over that robbery out at Birnam Woods. The thieves made off with a lot of jewelry, I gather." He glanced in his rearview mirror. "She wants me to install one of those doorbells. She said they're the new smart technology, although for the life of me I don't know what makes them smart." He pulled a handkerchief from his pocket and blew his nose.

"She said with one of those doorbells you can see who's at the door before you open it. So you don't accidentally let in a thief." He chuckled. "She's also after me to get one of those alarm systems that you have to turn on and off every time you come home or leave the house." He sighed. "Sounds like a lot of work to me. Besides, my memory isn't so good. I know I'll forget the code and end up stuck outside my own home."

They were nearing the station now. Penelope heard the faint sound of a train whistle in the distance. Up ahead she could see a cluster of run-down cottages with the train tracks threading through their backyards.

"Here we go," the driver said. "It's number six you're wanting, isn't it?"

Pen glanced at the paper in her hand and checked the address again. "Yes. Number six."

The driver turned around in his seat. His expression was doubtful. "Do you want me to wait for you? This place looks a bit rough." He pointed to one of the cottages, where a rusted chain saw had been abandoned in the scrubby grass.

"That might be a good idea," Penelope said. She realized her heart was pounding. This neighborhood was quite unsavory looking and she had no idea who was going to answer the door of number six. It would probably turn out to be the home of someone who used to work with Layla or went to school with her or some such. But if that was the case, why didn't Layla simply tell Maguire where she'd been that night?

Weeds pushed up through the cracks in the slate path leading to the house, which was as dilapidated as the others clustered around it. A shutter had come loose and was hanging askew, and the paint was peeling off in long strips. A chipped ceramic pot with a dried-up plant in it sat beside the door.

Penelope hesitated and then rang the doorbell.

She heard footsteps and someone grumbling, and then the door was flung open. A man stood there. His chin was pocked with gray and black stubble and his blue eyes were bloodshot. He was wearing an undershirt that was stained yellow under the arms and worn jeans that were a bit too short. He smelled of cigarettes and beer.

Penelope took a step backward.

"You're not Layla," he said, turning his head and giving a phlegmy cough. "I thought Layla was coming. I got it all arranged with this bloke in London, like I told her I would when she stopped by last Sunday night. He wants a twenty percent cut for his troubles and she said that was okay." When Penelope didn't say anything, his eyes narrowed and he gave her a suspicious look. "You're not one of those Jehovah's Witnesses come to pray for my salvation, are you?"

He gave a cackling laugh. "Because it would be a waste of your time."

"No," Pen said, shaking her head vigorously. "I'm not. I'm a friend of Layla's," she hazarded.

He looked relieved. "So Layla sent you. I thought she was going to come herself." He glanced at Pen's tote bag. "Do you have them with you now?"

"Have what?" Penelope said.

"The jewels," he said, enunciating carefully as if he was speaking to a child or a foreigner. "We arranged that I would get them to my bloke in London."

Penelope clamped her jaw shut and tried to contain her look of surprise, although she knew her eyes had flown open wide. So this man was a fence? And Layla had been in on that robbery at Birnam Woods along with Rodney? No wonder she didn't want to tell Maguire where she'd been the night Odile was murdered.

It would land her in jail for sure.

But it also meant she couldn't have been the killer. She had an alibi even if she couldn't admit to it.

"So?" the man said, tapping his foot impatiently. "You do have them, don't you? My bloke has already got some things lined up."

"I . . . I'm doing a survey," Penelope said. It was the first thing that popped into her mind. "Would you mind answering some questions?"

The man glowered at her. "Hey, wait a minute," he said as he lunged toward Penelope.

Penelope bolted for the taxi, got in, and slammed the door shut. "Go!" she shouted.

As the driver peeled away from the curb, Penelope realized she was trembling.

She looked out the window, but without really noticing

the scenery. She had to admit she was shaken by her encounter. The man had looked rough and mean enough to kill. If the taxi hadn't been waiting for her, who knows what might have happened. She had taken a foolish chance.

It was odd that he was still expecting Layla to bring the jewels, when the police must have already swept in and recovered them after Gladys told them where to look. No doubt Rodney was in jail by now as well.

It was equally odd, Penelope thought, that Maribel hadn't mentioned anything about it. No doubt she would have been quite distraught at Rodney being arrested and worried about what it meant for the school's reputation. But not if . . . A thought flashed through Penelope's mind. She yanked her phone from her tote bag and rang the number of the Pig in a Poke.

Gladys sounded a bit testy when she answered. Pen glanced at her watch—it was nearly closing time and she was probably getting ready to lock up.

"What did Maguire say when you told him that you'd found those stolen jewels in Rodney's toolshed?" Penelope said after Gladys said hello. "You did tell him, didn't you?"

There was a long silence on the other end of the line.

"You did tell him, right?" Penelope said again. She chewed on the edge of her thumb.

"Not exactly," Gladys said.

Penelope dropped her head back against the seat. "What does 'not exactly' mean?" she said as she glanced out the window.

Gladys heaved a big sigh. "I meant to, didn't I? I really did. But I couldn't bring myself to do it. What if word got out and my Bruce found out? I wouldn't know what to do, would I?"

Now it was Penelope's turn to sigh. She reassured

Gladys that everything was going to be okay and ended the call.

She tapped the driver on the shoulder. "Can you take me to the police station, please?"

The station was quiet when Penelope got there. A woman was complaining to a bored-looking constable about her neighbor who insisted on playing the television too loudly at night. He was scribbling notes on a pad and nodding occasionally.

The constable behind the desk was shuffling through a stack of papers. He looked up when Penelope cleared her throat and broke into a smile.

"You'll be wanting Detective Maguire, I should imagine."

"Yes, if he's here."

He jumped up from his chair and escorted Penelope down the hall.

Maguire's door was open and he was behind his desk. There was a sandwich sitting on a bit of plastic wrap in front of him.

He shoved his chair back and stood up when he saw Penelope.

"I'm sorry to interrupt your meal," Penelope said as she took a seat in the chair opposite him.

Maguire shook his head and gave a sheepish grin. "I thought I'd grab a chip butty before things got busy." He pushed the sandwich away from him. "I had to endure a lecture on nutrition from PC Buttrick about how a sandwich of chips on white bread with butter was going to clog my arteries."

Penelope couldn't argue with that.

"So." Maguire frowned and leaned forward in his chair. "I hope nothing is wrong?"

Penelope didn't know what to say. Something was very wrong indeed.

She told Maguire about Gladys finding the jewels in Rodney's toolshed and how she was supposed to call Maguire but never did.

Maguire's eyebrows shot up. "Gladys? Do you mean the woman who runs the Pig in a Poke?"

Penelope nodded.

"She was having an affair?"

Penelope nodded again.

Maguire shook his head. "I guess you never know about people." He reached for the telephone. "I'll have my sergeant arrange for a couple of constables to bring this Rodney in and retrieve the stolen items. Let's hope they haven't been moved." He held up his crossed fingers. "Too bad Gladys never made that phone call to alert us to this."

Penelope waited until he had completed the call. "That's not all," she said when he'd hung up.

She told Maguire about Layla having an appointment with a fence.

Maguire's expression turned grim. "You went to see the fence?" His voice rose in astonishment.

Penelope looked at her lap and nodded. "I had the taxi wait for me."

Maguire let out a breath that sounded like a steam engine warming up. He stared at his hands as if looking for an answer.

Finally, he said, "We'll have to bring Layla Evans in as well. I thought something was up when I interviewed her. She was . . . evasive . . . and insisted she was tucked up at home the night Odile Fontaine was killed. She said she was watching the telly but couldn't remember what program it was." He held his hands out, palms up. "In my experience, people are usually faithful watchers of a certain group of shows and tend to know exactly what days and times they're on. *Coronation Street* on Mondays, Wednesdays and Fridays, *EastEnders* on Mondays, Tuesdays, and so forth." He frowned. "It seemed fishy to me that she couldn't remember what she'd watched." He shrugged. "It wasn't proof, of course, but now I know where she really was—arranging to fence stolen goods."

He suddenly grinned. "At least that's one case wrapped up." His expression turned somber. "Now to find out who murdered Odile Fontaine."

Penelope called for another taxi. With all the money she'd been spending on cabs lately, she could have bought herself a new car by now.

The driver pulled up and Penelope gave him Mabel's address, which was outside of town and down a narrow country lane.

The cottage was bigger than Penelope's with half-timbering, a steeply pitched thatched roof, and diamond-paned windows. A winding brick path led to the robin's egg blue front door with a trellis arched over it covered now with the remains of the summer roses.

Penelope picked up the door knocker and let it fall. It was opened moments later by Laurence Brimble. He had a frilly apron tied around his waist, which was at odds with his tweed suit.

"Come in, Penelope." He held the door wider.

The interior of Mabel's cottage was as charming as the

exterior. A cozy fire crackled in the hearth and the large sitting room was furnished with a slipcovered sofa and two armchairs. The sofa was flanked by matching tables and two blue-and-white floral porcelain lamps.

Mabel was sitting in one of the armchairs. Her leg was in a cast and propped up on an ottoman. She had a tray table in front of her with a cup of tea and a serving of beans on toast.

Brimble smoothed his mustache and cleared his throat. "I'm afraid my culinary skills are somewhat limited," he said, pointing to the plate.

"It's comfort food," Mabel said, smiling up at Brimble. "Just what the doctor ordered."

Brimble turned to Penelope. "Would you care for a cup of tea? I can put the kettle on."

"That would be lovely," Penelope said.

Brimble disappeared into the kitchen and Penelope sat down on the sofa near Mabel.

"I came to see how you are. Brimble seems to be taking good care of you."

Mabel sighed. "He certainly is." She leaned forward a bit in her chair. "I've learned something from all of this, believe it or not." She swept a hand toward her leg.

Penelope raised her eyebrows.

Mabel sighed and her eyes took on a faraway look. "I've always prided myself on my independence. I've convinced myself that I don't need anyone, that I can do it all myself." She shifted in her chair. "All along, in the back of my mind, I was waiting for Oliver. A man who was never going to return." She pulled a tissue from her pocket and dabbed her eyes.

"But you thought Oliver might be alive," Pen said. "And that note . . ."

Mabel shook her head. "I was fooling myself. That note was from years ago. If Oliver was alive, he'd have found me by now. Maybe he went back to his wife. Or"—her voice caught in her throat—"he no longer cares for me and chose to disappear."

She looked down at her hands for a moment, then lifted her chin.

"Either way, it's time for me to move on and put the past where it belongs—in the past."

Brimble walked in carrying a tray with a cup of tea on it. He put it down on the coffee table in front of Penelope.

Mabel smiled up at him. Her eyes sparkled in a way that Penelope had never seen before.

Penelope heard Mrs. Danvers scratching at the door when she got home. She was in an affectionate mood and wound back and forth between Penelope's legs. Penelope breathed a sigh of relief as she took off her jacket. It was good to be home. It had been a long day.

Mrs. Danvers was trying to urge Penelope toward the kitchen. Perhaps her food or water bowl wasn't filled to her satisfaction? Penelope decided she'd better check.

As soon as she stepped into the kitchen, she stopped dead in her tracks. Lying in the middle of the floor, with Mrs. Danvers looking at it with a proud expression, was a dead mouse.

Mrs. Danvers gave a long, drawn-out meow as if to say *Well, aren't you impressed with this gift I've brought you?*

Penelope doled out ample praise while she fetched a paper towel and scooped up the mouse's corpse. She wasn't sure what to do with it. Put it in the garbage can? She had the absurd impulse to take it outside in the back garden and bury it.

In the end, she settled for leaving it at the end of the garden. Nature would take care of the rest.

Odile's murder was a bit like a game of cat and mouse, Penelope thought as she shut the back door. Was the cat going to win or was the mouse going to get away?

She made a cup of tea and carried it out to the sitting room. She retrieved her laptop from her tote bag and set it up on the coffee table. It was high time she checked her e-mail. She cringed at the thought that there might be one from her editor, Bettina, asking if the current manuscript was on track to meet the deadline. Penelope was quite sure it was, but she wasn't prepared to swear to it.

Penelope's laptop sprang to life, the screen displaying a picture she'd taken of Mrs. Danvers. She was about to open her e-mail when she remembered that she had planned to do some research on Quentin Barnes. The tumultuous events of the day had put the thought right out of her head.

She typed Quentin's name into the search engine. Several entries popped up and Penelope scanned through them quickly. Most were links to papers Quentin had written or articles mentioning a talk he had given.

She scrolled down some more and found an obituary for an Elizabeth Barnes née Campbell. Penelope read through the article. Quentin was listed as a surviving son, along with Peter Barnes, his father. The obituary also mentioned that Elizabeth Barnes was noted for her research on Solanales.

What on earth was that? Penelope wondered. She'd have to look it up later.

She scrolled some more and came upon a Wikipedia entry for a Quentin Barnes. She was surprised but, apparently, he was not only a teacher but a noted historian who had written several scholarly books on Britain's participation in World War I.

The entry detailed Quentin's early education and his acceptance to Balliol College at the University of Oxford on a scholarship.

Penelope nibbled on the side of her thumb. If Quentin had been a scholarship student, it stood to reason then that he didn't come from money.

The entry also mentioned that he was teaching history at the Oakwood School for Girls. So it was definitely the right Quentin Barnes.

If Quentin didn't inherit money, where did he get the wherewithal to purchase that Victoria Cross?

Penelope was about to close her laptop when she remembered she'd meant to look up that odd term in Elizabeth Barnes's obituary—Solanales.

She typed the word into her search engine and after having to correct her spelling twice, the results came up. According to the online dictionary, Solanales was an order of flowering plants.

Penelope closed her laptop. That was one word she wasn't ever likely to use in a conversation.

She went out to the kitchen and was about to see what she had on hand for dinner when there was a knock on the door. She headed through the sitting room into the foyer and reached for the door handle. It was funny but back in her apartment in New York City, she would have first peered through the peephole to see who it was. But in Upper Chumley-on-Stoke, half the people never even locked their doors.

She pulled open the door and Figgy breezed in along

with a gust of cold air. Her nose and the tips of her ears were red, making her look more like an elf than ever.

"Have you eaten yet?" Figgy said as she unwound her brightly colored paisley scarf.

"No. I was about to see what I could scrounge up."

"There's an opening tonight at this newish gallery in Lower Chumley-on-Stoke. I thought you might like to go with me. There's bound to be plenty of wine and cheese to nibble on and if we're still hungry afterward, we can go for some fish and chips."

Penelope had been envisioning a quiet evening at home but Figgy's suggestion sounded like a lot more fun.

"Should we invite Beryl?" Pen said.

"Sure. Why not?" Figgy bent down to pet Mrs. Danvers's head. Mrs. Danvers's good mood had clearly persisted, because she allowed it without protest.

Pen found her cell phone and dialed Beryl, who said she would be delighted to go with them—it would save her from a sad and lonely evening eating leftover doner kebab from the doggie bag she'd brought home from her lunch at Peri Peri in London.

Pen clicked off the call and slipped her phone into her pocket. She touched a hand to her hair.

"I'd better go freshen up, I suppose."

Figgy looked at her critically. "I came prepared. You don't need freshening up. I have just what you need." She reached into her tote bag and pulled out a handful of baubles. "Here, put this on." She handed Pen a multistrand necklace of brightly colored wooden beads. It reminded Pen of the necklace Odile had worn to the wine and paint party at the Open Book.

"And these," Figgy said after Pen had slipped the necklace over her head, where the many strands nestled against her black sweater like a bib. She handed Penelope a pair of earrings with gold discs dangling from a French wire. Figgy frowned. "Your ears are pierced, aren't they?"

Penelope nodded. She took out the tiny gold studs she was wearing and substituted the ones Figgy had given her.

"And now, for the pièce de résistance," Figgy said triumphantly as she dug in her tote bag again and whipped out a very long African print scarf with fringe on the ends. She motioned Penelope toward her and wrapped the scarf around her neck several times.

"Doesn't this all . . . clash?" Penelope said, fingering the beads. "Wasn't it Coco Chanel who said that before going out you should look in the mirror and remove one thing?"

"Oh, bah," Figgy said. "It's perfect. Just right for a trendy gallery opening."

Penelope had her doubts about how trendy a gallery in Lower Chumley-on-Stoke was likely to be, given that the town was every bit as charmingly provincial as Upper Chumley-on-Stoke.

Penelope said good-bye to Mrs. Danvers, who didn't seem in the least interested in Pen's departure, and they headed out to Figgy's car.

"I told Beryl we'd pick her up," Penelope said as she closed the door and fastened her seat belt.

Figgy pulled away from the curb so abruptly that it jolted Penelope in her seat and the long, dangling earrings Figgy had insisted she wear slapped against her neck.

As they pulled up in front of the Icing on the Cake, the light glowing from the window of the apartment above went out and moments later the door opened and Beryl appeared. There was a wave of expensive scent as she climbed into the back seat.

Penelope swiveled around and looked at her.

Beryl was wearing a black moto jacket, black turtleneck, black pants, black boots and had some sort of product in her hair that made it look like what the magazines and fashion pundits had taken to calling *bed head*.

"What is that you're wearing?" Penelope said. She had never seen her sister dressed in such a getup before. She had expected Beryl to appear in a cashmere sweater, wool pants, high-heeled pumps and with an Hermès scarf tied around her neck.

Beryl looked offended. "I can hardly go to a trendy gallery opening looking like a housewife from Connecticut, can I?" She ran a hand through her blond hair, leaving it even messier than before. "There will be men there who can afford expensive art. Who knows what might happen?"

Pen didn't think the men who could afford expensive art would be dressed like refugees from 1950s Greenwich Village. They'd be more likely to be sporting bespoke suits from Savile Row, shirts from Turnbull & Asser or one of the other shops on Jermyn Street, and highly polished shoes from Church's.

But far be it for her to rain on Beryl's parade.

Penelope wished she'd had a nip of the Jameson that Mabel kept under the counter at the Open Book to give her some Dutch courage in the face of Figgy's driving. She was beyond relieved when they saw the sign for Lower Chumley-on-Stoke and even more relieved when the car was safely parked at the curb.

Most of the storefronts along the high street were shuttered and dark, but light spilled out from the large plate glass window of the Winston Gallery, where a piece of twisted metal—Penelope supposed it was a sculpture—held pride of place under a spotlight.

As soon as they walked in, a young woman in a tight-fitting black pantsuit directed them to a rack where a variety of coats were hung, including several furs, which Penelope had assumed were no longer in vogue.

She glanced at Beryl and saw that her face was flushed with excitement. There were a number of people dressed in funky outfits like Figgy's or all in black like Beryl, but plenty of other women were in silk dresses and pearls. They looked slightly out of place amid the bold modern art hanging on the walls.

A waiter in black pants, a pleated white shirt, and a black bow tie was circulating with a tray of champagne flutes. They helped themselves to one as he passed by and Penelope took a big gulp. The bubbles went up her nose and she began to cough.

Beryl, who was clearly embarrassed, gave her an annoyed look and started to edge away, quickly disappearing into the crowd. When Penelope caught sight of her again, she was deep in conversation with a man who had a deep tan and was wearing a Rolex watch.

Penelope and Figgy made their way around the gallery, occasionally plucking an hors d'oeuvre or another flute of champagne from the circulating waiters. The exhibition was an interesting mix of drawings and paintings by established artists as well as works by what the gallery catalogue described as *up-and-comers*.

Some of it looked to Penelope like the scrawls of a group of hyperactive toddlers let loose with a box of crayons, but other pieces she actually found intriguing. Figgy had been an art student at one time and was very helpful in explaining the theory behind some of the more unusual works.

There was a small Lucian Freud drawing that Penelope was quite taken with, as well as a sculpture by Annie Field that she found very intriguing. But she knew there was no point in looking at the price tags—they were certainly well beyond her reach.

They turned the corner into another smaller gallery off the main room where a brightly colored painting held pride of place, a spotlight aimed at it and adjusted just so.

Penelope stopped in her tracks when she saw it.

"That's—that's," she stammered, pointing at it. "That's the painting that was missing from Odile Fontaine's apartment. Her Matisse. I'm almost sure of it." She reached for her phone. "I'm going to take a picture of it."

Figgy put a hand on Penelope's arm and pointed to a small sign on the wall. It read *No Photographs Allowed*.

"It must be in the catalogue," Figgy said, taking her copy out from under her arm and riffling through it. She folded it open to a page and held it up for Penelope to see. "Here it is."

"I'm going to go to the school tomorrow and check this against the photograph, but I'm almost certain it's the same painting."

Figgy frowned. "If it belonged to Odile, how did it wind up here?"

"I don't know. Maybe she sold it to the gallery?"

One of the gallery staff appeared behind them and Penelope nearly jumped when he suddenly spoke.

"Do you like it?" he said, pointing to the painting. "Those colors . . ." He sighed deeply.

"It's beautiful," Penelope and Figgy said in unison.

He clasped his hands to his chest. "It's quite the jewel of our collection. Frankly, we've never been asked to take something so valuable on consignment before—us, a little-known gallery in Lower Chumley-on-Stoke. He could have taken it anywhere—the great auction houses in London or one of the well-known galleries like the Gagosian Gallery in Westminster."

Penelope and Figgy looked at each other.

"He?" Penelope said. "It was a man? Do you remember his name?"

His hand flew to his mouth and he gave a look of mock horror. "That was terribly indiscreet of me. We don't give out information like that, I'm afraid."

"Of course," Penelope said.

The man silently glided away and Penelope turned to Figgy.

"So Odile didn't bring the painting in for consignment herself. It was a man." She looked at the Matisse again. "Maybe it really was stolen after all."

NINETEEN

꒦꒷

Despite sampling copious amounts of hors d'oeuvres at the gallery opening—endive with goat cheese, bacon-wrapped dates, and potted shrimp on crackers—Penelope, Figgy, and Beryl were still hungry enough to make a stop at the Chumley Chippie for some fish and chips.

It was late by the time they finished their meal and Penelope got back to the cottage. Mrs. Danvers was meowing by the back door, so she let her out into the back garden and made herself a cup of tea.

She carried her tea out to the sitting room, kicked off her shoes, and settled down on the sofa with her laptop.

She checked her e-mail—it was still early enough in New York for a message from her editor—but there was nothing more interesting than solicitations for donations to various charities, book suggestions from an online book retailer, and ads for walk-in bathtubs. Penelope shook her head at that one and was about to close out of her e-mail program when one last one popped into her in-box.

She recognized the e-mail address and, curious, she clicked on it. It was from her former boyfriend Miles, who she had left behind in New York. He was announcing his upcoming wedding to Sloan, who he'd met while Penelope was off in England. At the time she'd been about to break up with him, but he beat her to the punch and announced that he had found someone new. Penelope had been surprised that the rejection had stung as much as it had.

She examined her feelings now and realized that she no longer cared a whit for Miles and that she was actually happy for him. Based on what she had heard, Miles and Sloan deserved each other.

Pen yawned and stretched her arms over her head. She glanced at her watch. She really ought to get to bed. She was about to power down her computer when she remembered that odd word in Quentin Barnes's mother's obituary. It had had something to do with plants.

Deadly nightshade was a plant. An idea was forming in Penelope's mind, and she knew it would niggle at her all night and keep her awake unless she researched it further.

She grabbed her tote bag and dug around for the piece of paper she'd written the word on. She pulled out the receipt from the Chippie Chumley, one from Tesco, an old grocery list, and finally found the scrap she was looking for.

The word was *Solanales*. Pen typed it into the search engine. The entry in the online dictionary popped up at the top, but there were other entries as well—most of them more in-depth articles on the subject. She clicked on one of them and began to read.

Apparently under the order Solanales was the family

known as Solanaceae. It included vegetables like potatoes, eggplants, tomatoes, and peppers, which were commonly known as . . . nightshades.

By now, Penelope was no longer sleepy and her curiosity was aroused. She continued to read. Also within the family Solanaceae was *Atropa belladonna*, commonly known as . . . deadly nightshade.

Penelope bolted upright on the sofa. Odile had been poisoned with deadly nightshade. Quentin's mother was an expert on plants that happened to include deadly nightshade. Was it simply a coincidence? Or was there some connection between the two?

She rubbed her forehead. She was getting a headache. Perhaps it would be best to go to bed and think about it some more in the morning.

She opened the back door and called for Mrs. Danvers, who strolled in and swept past Penelope with a swish of her tail.

Penelope closed the door, turned out the lights, and headed up the stairs to bed.

As Penelope boiled an egg for breakfast the next morning, she thought of her plans for the day, which definitely included a visit to Maribel to compare the painting in the Winston Gallery catalogue with the one missing from Odile's apartment. She was quite sure they were one and the same, but she wanted to be certain.

But first she grabbed her cell phone and called the Open Book. With Mabel out of commission, Kip was having to cope all on his own, but he assured her he was fine.

Penelope breathed a sigh of relief and called for a

cab. She checked Mrs. Danvers's food and water bowls, shrugged on her jacket, and went outside to wait for the taxi.

It was a pleasant day with only a slight breeze. Mrs. Clark, who lived across the street from Penelope, was dead-heading the mums in the planter next to her front door; and her next-door neighbor was outside, taking advantage of the fine weather to wash her windows.

Penelope could tell by the way the taxi pulled up to the curb outside her cottage that Mad Max was the driver. The ride to the Oakwood School would be safe, if not exactly swift.

Penelope was half right. She swore she could walk faster than Max was driving, but it was less hair-raising than taking the twists and turns in the country lane at high speed.

Everything was going well until they encountered a bright red truck loaded with lumber coming from the opposite direction. Mad Max had no choice but to back up and try to get the car as far over to the side of the road as he could.

He went a little too far and they ended up with the wheels on the left side of the car stuck in a ditch.

"Looks like we're properly stuck," Max said laconically as if he didn't have a care in the world.

Fortunately, they were within sight of the drive leading to the school. Penelope didn't have the patience to wait until a tow truck came to pull the taxi out. She thanked Max, paid him, and got out of the car.

By the time she reached the administration building, she was quite warm and had unbuttoned her jacket and taken off her gloves. She headed toward Maribel's office.

Tina was riffling through some folders in the file cabinet but turned around quickly when she heard Penelope. She gave Penelope a tight smile.

"Is Maribel in?" Pen said as she waited in the doorway.

"She is in, but I'm afraid she doesn't want to be disturbed at the moment."

"Do you know when I might speak to her?"

Tina frowned. "I'm not sure. All she said was that she didn't want to be disturbed this morning."

Suddenly the door to Maribel's office flew open. "Penelope, I am so glad you're here." She motioned with her hand toward the open door. "Please. Come in."

"I wish it wasn't so early," Maribel said as she closed the door. "I could certainly do with a glass of sherry right now."

Maribel did look somewhat distraught. Her shirt was rumpled and her hair was pushed behind her ears and looked as if she'd barely combed it. It wasn't like her. Normally her appearance was pristine.

"I don't know what I'm going to do," Maribel said, motioning toward the sofa at one end of her office. "Layla and Rodney have both been arrested. Can you imagine? What are the parents going to think?"

She fiddled with the top button of her blouse. "And what am I going to tell the girls? Layla was quite well liked and will definitely be missed by them." She was silent for a moment, staring into space. "I will have to hire another nurse immediately. Fortunately, Dr. Varma, in town, said he would be willing to come out if needed." She turned toward Penelope. "And Grady is beside himself. Of course, that's to be expected. It's all so . . . shocking."

Penelope nodded.

"Imagine! Two Oakwood School employees embroiled in a robbery in Birnam Woods." She wrung her hands. "I do hope the papers don't get hold of this."

Penelope didn't know what to say. There was little enough news in Chumley—she was quite certain the

Chumley Chronicle was going to jump on this story, and she was afraid that it would be front-page news in the bigger tabloids as well.

Maribel made an attempt at a smile. "I imagine you've come to see me for a reason, and here I've been nattering away all this time."

"I did, actually. Do you still have the photograph of the painting that was missing from Odile's apartment? The one we think is a Matisse."

"I do, why?"

Penelope explained her visit to the gallery and seeing a painting that looked just like it.

"Let me get the photograph," Maribel said. She got up and went over to her desk, where she opened a drawer and pulled out the picture.

"Here it is." She handed it to Penelope.

Penelope pulled the catalogue from the Winston Gallery out of her tote bag and opened it to the page with the Matisse painting. She took the photo from Maribel and placed them side by side on the table in front of the sofa.

Maribel gasped. "It's the same painting. Odile must have sold it."

"I'm afraid not," Pen said, closing the catalogue and returning it to her tote bag. "The gallery owner said it was a man who brought the painting in. He wanted to put it on consignment."

"That is most odd," Maribel said, tapping her chin with her index finger. "I suppose that means someone did steal it." Her eyes opened wider. "I wish we knew who the man was who consigned it."

"I've been thinking about that and I've come up with an idea that just might possibly work."

She explained it to Maribel and Maribel's face lit up.

"That sounds splendid. Perhaps we'll get to the bottom of this affair after all."

K ip was at the counter, talking to a customer, when Penelope arrived at the Open Book later that morning, and she was quite surprised to see Mabel there as well, sitting in one of the armchairs with her leg up on a stool.

"Aren't you supposed to be at home resting?" Penelope said.

"I'm supervising." Mabel laughed. "Isn't this what supervisors are supposed to do?"

Penelope laughed.

Figgy, who was bringing Mabel a cup of tea, also laughed.

"I'd say your imitation of a supervisor is spot-on. They sit around and criticize while everyone else does the work."

"And I'd best get busy," Penelope said. "There are some cartons that need to be unpacked."

A new delivery of books had arrived and the cartons were stacked in the storage room. Penelope planned to spend the morning shelving them so that Kip could stay at the counter to help with customers.

She slit open the first carton, grabbed an armful of books, and headed toward the shelves. She was putting the last one into the appropriate slot when an older woman approached her. She was in a coat that smelled of mothballs and was wearing stout walking shoes.

"Can you help me?" she said to Penelope in a tremulous voice. She handed Penelope a book. "I've forgotten my glasses and I wonder if you can read the first few paragraphs for me so I can see if I like it."

Penelope had to hide a smile. She was used to odd requests from customers by now—asking for a book with a blue cover and no clue as to the title, or the wrong name for the author or the wrong title—but this was a new one.

She was happy to oblige and the woman gave a big smile when Penelope had finished the first page.

"That's lovely. I think I'll take it. Do I pay you?"

Pen pointed toward the counter. "Kip is at the front counter and he can take care of it."

The woman was about to turn away when she touched Penelope's arm.

"You have a lovely voice."

"Thank you."

She walked away and Penelope headed to the storage room for another armload of books.

She finished emptying the cartons a bit before lunch. Things seemed to be going smoothly, and once her seminar was over, she planned to take the rest of the afternoon off, but she had to see if Beryl was free because she was going to play an important role in the plan Penelope had hatched.

TWENTY

Penelope phoned Beryl and Beryl was not only willing to take part in Penelope's plan, she was eager. They arranged to meet at Beryl's apartment.

The heady scent of sugar and butter wafted from Icing on the Cake and the pastries in the window made Penelope drool when she reached the door.

The scent led her to Beryl's apartment, and she nearly gave in and headed back to the bakery to buy a slice of the Bakewell tart that she'd seen in the window.

But just then the door to Beryl's apartment opened and she called down the stairs.

"Is that you, Penelope?"

"Yes, coming." Penelope reluctantly abandoned the idea of visiting the bakery and made her way upstairs instead.

Beryl's apartment was barely more than a bedsit, but she'd added her own unique touches—colorful throws and pillows, a collection of framed black-and-white drawings she'd found at Oxfam, and a vase of fresh flowers on the table.

"You look . . ." Pen said when she saw her sister.

"Rich?" Beryl said. "That's the look I'm going for. Rich enough to be able to afford a Matisse painting."

Today, Beryl's hair was in a silky-smooth bob and she was wearing a knitted cashmere dress and knee-high black suede boots. She had diamond studs in her ears and a heavy gold bracelet on her wrist.

"I think you've nailed it," Pen said.

"Do you think they'll recognize me from our first visit?"

"I doubt it. You look completely different. And there was such a crush that night."

Penelope had called a cab and it was waiting when they got downstairs. "Let's go over our plan again," she said as they got into the taxi.

Beryl pursed her lips. "I'm to look around the gallery but show a special interest in the Matisse painting. Chat up the gallery director and claim I'm thinking of buying it but I need to know more about it—like the provenance of the work."

"Yes," Pen said. "That's what we need to know—the previous owners of the painting and where it came from originally."

"Got it," Beryl said as the taxi driver pulled up in front of the Winston Gallery.

"I'll lurk around and pretend to look at the exhibition," Penelope said as they got out of the cab. "But let's not walk in together. I don't look as if I belong with you," she said, indicating her utilitarian jacket and scuffed boots.

Penelope pretended to look in the window of the Magical Moon, a new age shop next to the gallery. Obviously Lower Chumley-on-Stoke was more progressive than Upper Chumley-on-Stoke. She could just imagine Gladys's or India's or Brimble's reaction if a shop like that opened up on Chumley's high street.

After five minutes had elapsed, Penelope noticed that the pedestrians passing by were beginning to look at her curiously. Did they suspect her of loitering for some nefarious reason? She'd better go into the gallery—she'd waited long enough.

She noticed right away that Beryl was having an intense conversation with the gallery director. Hopefully she was worming the information they needed out of him.

Several people were wandering idly around the gallery. There was a girl in a short skirt and Doc Martens scribbling on a notepad and a man in a black coat with a velvet collar who had his back to Penelope and was staring intensely at one of the drawings.

Penelope made her way around the room. The faint smell of oil paint was coming from a curtained-off area of the gallery. She looked around but no one was paying any attention to her. She carefully eased the curtain back slightly.

Beyond it was a storage room with cartons of catalogues, a water cooler, a rather beat-up table, a roll of kraft wrapping paper, and a sink.

The smell of oil paint was stronger now. Penelope eased behind the curtain after checking again to be sure that no one was watching.

Several paintings were set out on the table. Penelope glanced at them. She recognized a Miró, a Picasso, and another Matisse. She bent closer to them and sniffed. The smell of oil paint was very strong now. She reached out a finger and very carefully touched the corner of the Miró. The paint was tacky and her finger came away with a spot of red on it. Penelope looked at it in dismay. She tried to rub it off but only managed to smear it.

Penelope looked at the paintings again. All of these artists had been dead for years. If the paintings were real, the paint certainly would have thoroughly dried by now.

She sensed, rather than heard, footsteps coming her way. She quickly scooted out from behind the curtain and pretended to be admiring the Lucian Freud drawing that she'd noticed on her first visit to the gallery.

The receptionist, in an uncompromising black pantsuit and suede stilettos, gave Penelope an odd look as she swept past, leaving behind the faint scent of Acqua di Giò. Penelope quickly balled her hand into a fist to hide the red paint on her index finger. She hoped the woman hadn't seen it or the pulse beating frantically in her neck.

Penelope was wondering how much longer Beryl was going to be, when Beryl breezed past her in a cloud of Miss Dior perfume.

Penelope waited a discreet amount of time and then followed her out the door. By now she was nearly bursting with curiosity.

"Well?" she said when she joined her sister on the sidewalk.

"No luck," Beryl said. "He wouldn't tell me the name of the owner of the Matisse even though I gave him my telephone number and promised I'd have dinner with him one night when he was free. He did say that the painting had been in the collection of someone in South America." Beryl waved a hand. "I've already forgotten the name."

Penelope pulled out her phone and was about to call a taxi when she noticed the door to the gallery opening. A man walked out and Penelope's jaw nearly dropped.

It was Quentin Barnes.

He gave her a strange look, turned, and walked down the street toward a black BMW parked at the curb.

Penelope felt a chill that had nothing to do with the mild breeze that was blowing. She had the feeling that Quentin knew what she was up to. And that he was involved somehow.

If he was Odile's killer, that could be a dangerous position to be in.

L et's have lunch," Beryl said, hooking her arm through Penelope's. "I don't have to be back in Chumley until later this afternoon. I'm dressing Charlotte for a very important occasion tonight—dinner with the prime minister. I've chosen a lovely dress for her from Atelier Classique that takes the little black dress to a whole new level. I know she's going to look wonderful in it."

For the life of her, Penelope couldn't imagine what it meant to take a little black dress to a new level, but Beryl had impeccable taste, so it was undoubtedly perfect for Charlotte and the occasion.

They continued walking down Lower Chumley's high street, looking in the shop windows. They had just passed the chemist's when Penelope stopped and sniffed.

"What's that delicious smell?"

"It's coming from down the street," Beryl said. "There must be a restaurant of some sort."

They continued walking and soon came to the Swan, a respectable-looking pub.

"I'm starved," Beryl said as they opened the door and walked inside.

The Swan was a bit more upscale than the Book and

Bottle in Upper Chumley. It was more bistro than pub, with white tablecloths and a waitress, balancing a huge tray on her shoulder, bustling between the tables.

Penelope and Beryl were shown to a table by a hostess in a long paisley dress that Penelope thought looked like something Figgy would have worn. The waitress glided by and slapped down two menus. Beryl picked one up immediately and opened it.

"I'll have the coronation chicken salad." Beryl snapped her menu closed. "What about you?"

Penelope scanned the menu. Everything sounded good. She frowned as she went over the selection one more time.

"I'm going with the hamburger. No, I think I'll get the cheeseburger. It's topped with English cheddar, which is delicious."

Beryl sighed. "You're so lucky—you never gain weight. I so much as look at a piece of cake and I put on a pound."

The waitress appeared and plunked a basket of bread and a crock of butter on the table. She took down their order and then scurried away.

Beryl leaned her arms on the table. "How do we know if that Matisse painting is real or not? A gallery in Lower Chumley-on-Stoke seems like a strange place to sell something so valuable. You'd think the owner would choose a gallery in London or one of the big auction houses instead."

"That's what made me suspicious," Penelope said. She explained about Odile's copying famous paintings to practice technique.

"So you think she painted the Matisse?" Beryl said, reaching for a piece of bread, then changing her mind.

"Yes," Pen said, pulling the bread basket toward her. She selected a slice and put it on her plate. "I managed to sneak into the gallery's back room and they had several paintings by notable artists—all long dead—out on a table. I touched one of them and it was still tacky." She held up her finger with the dot of red paint on it.

"How long does it take for oil paint to dry?" Beryl said, drumming her fingers on her water glass.

"Quite a long time. Figgy said it can take several weeks. She worked with oils when she was in art school."

"But surely the gallery checked the provenance of the paintings," Beryl said, eyeing the bread basket again.

"Not if the gallery owner is in on the scam." Penelope broke off a piece of bread and began to butter it.

Beryl frowned. "But who in this backwater town would have enough money to buy paintings like that?"

"Chumley is growing," Pen said, taking a bite of her bread. "There are any number of big fancy developments going up in both Upper and Lower Chumley. I imagine these paintings are well priced—certainly a lot less expensive than the real ones would be—and too tempting to pass up."

"So you think Odile had some sort of racket going on?" Beryl said. "She makes copies of paintings and brings them to the gallery to sell?"

"Sort of," Pen said. "Only I think someone else was in on it and they were the ones arranging to sell what Odile produced."

Beryl raised her eyebrows. "Who?"

"I have a strong suspicion that person was Quentin Barnes."

"But would he have killed Odile?" Beryl finally snatched a piece of bread and began to butter it. "That would be like killing the golden goose, wouldn't it? The more she churned out, the more money they'd make."

Penelope sighed. She felt slightly crestfallen. "You could

be right. Maybe Quentin didn't kill Odile. I sure wish I could figure out who did."

The taxi dropped Penelope and Beryl off in front of Beryl's apartment after they'd finished their lunch. They said good-bye and Penelope began the short walk to the police station. She wanted to talk to Maguire about what she'd discovered. Her mind was whirling furiously as she tried to put the pieces of the puzzle together. Every time she thought she had things figured out, something new popped up that threw a monkey wrench into her theory.

If Odile really had been a part of a scheme with Quentin, were there more copies of paintings stashed somewhere? Somewhere on the school grounds where Maribel wouldn't find them?

Penelope was still pondering it when she reached the police station. She was so engrossed, she nearly collided with Constable Cuthbert, who was coming out the door.

Maguire was at the coffee machine when the officer at the desk showed Penelope down the hall. He'd been frowning at the machine, but when he turned around and saw her, he smiled.

"Would you like a cup of coffee? Fair warning, it's absolutely terrible."

Penelope laughed. "No, thanks."

"Smart move," Maguire said as hot brown liquid splashed into his cup, steam rising from the top.

"Do you have some more news for me?" Maguire said, a small smile playing around his lips.

"I do," Penelope admitted as she followed him into his office.

A drop of hot coffee sloshed over the edge of his cup as he was putting it down on his desk and he grimaced.

Penelope told him about the painting in the gallery and how she was quite certain that it was a forgery. Maguire pulled a pad of paper toward him and began taking notes. His head shot up when she mentioned that she had seen Quentin Barnes at the gallery.

"I think Quentin is involved in the art scam," Penelope said. "But I don't know if he's the one who murdered Odile."

"Well, that *is* my job," Maguire said with a smile. "This is all very interesting." He leaned back in his chair and it squeaked loudly. "I think I'll have another chat with Mr. Quentin Barnes."

TWENTY-ONE

❧

Mabel was gone when Penelope got back to the Open Book later that afternoon. According to Kip, Brimble had come by to take her home to rest.

Mabel was lucky to have Brimble, Penelope thought as she hung up her jacket. He might not be the love of her life, but he obviously cared for her deeply.

She went around the store and collected the books that had been abandoned on tables or stuck in display racks where they didn't belong. The front door opened and Penelope paused briefly and looked up to see if Kip needed help.

A delivery woman stood just inside the door, holding a large bunch of paper-wrapped flowers.

"Delivery," she called to Kip.

Kip clapped his hands together. "How lovely. Who are they for?"

The woman glanced at the ticket stapled to the paper.

"A Penelope Parish. Is she here?"

"Penelope," Kip called. "Delivery for you. Someone has sent you flowers," he said in a singsong voice.

Penelope put down the books she was holding and walked up to the counter. She signed for the bouquet and pulled out a small white card with the florist's logo embossed on it. Her name was written on the front in black ink.

"Well, open it," Kip said impatiently. "Maybe you have a secret admirer?"

Penelope felt her face flush as she read the words on the card. It said *Thinking of you. Love, Brodie.*

"Don't keep me in suspense, dear," Kip said, leaning over the counter in an attempt to see the card.

"They're from Maguire."

"The DCI?" Kip said. He batted his eyelashes at Penelope. "So what is going on between you two?"

Penelope was too embarrassed to answer. "Nothing," she said and scurried away with the excuse that she needed to get the flowers in some water.

She took them into the storage room and looked around for something to put them in. High up on a shelf she spied a lone vase covered in dust. She got it down, washed it off, and filled it with water.

She was arranging the flowers in it when she had a thought. She slapped her forehead with her palm. How could she have been so dense?

Flowers. Botany. She remembered the gathering at Quentin's after Odile's memorial and scanning the titles on his bookshelves. There had been a book on botany. She could see it in her mind's eye.

And his mother was a noted scholar of the Solanales order of flowering plants that included Solanaceae, or nightshades. As in deadly nightshade.

Surely Quentin had picked up some knowledge himself along the way?

But what would his motive have been?

Maybe he was stealing those paintings from Odile in order to sell them and she found out? She might have threatened to go to the police and Quentin had had to stop her. Or, if she had been in on the whole scam, maybe she'd decided to cut Quentin out.

Either way, that would have made him mad enough to kill.

There was a faculty tea at the school late that afternoon and Maribel had urged Penelope to join them. By now, it was only an hour until closing and Kip reassured her that he would be just fine without her.

Penelope called for a taxi and soon arrived at the Oakwood School without incident. She had just gotten out of the taxi when she noticed two men standing by a black Mercedes that was idling in a parking spot in front of the administration building. She nearly did a double take when she recognized the gallery owner from Lower Chumley-on-Stoke. He had a parcel under his arm wrapped in brown paper that was the size and shape of a painting. The other man had his back to Penelope, but she was certain it was Quentin Barnes.

The gallery owner wasn't looking in her direction, so she quickly crouched down and made her way between the parked cars until she was as close as she could get to the two men without being seen.

She was thankful for the quiet of the school's country

location, the only sound being the occasional chirp of a bird. The men's voices carried to her quite clearly.

"I still have a few more of Odile's paintings left," Quentin said. "But I think we should wait until the Matisse sells." He cleared his throat. "We need to have patience. We don't want to arouse suspicion."

"Quite right," the other man said. He paused. "Too bad Odile won't be copying any more paintings."

Quentin made a sound like a snort. "She was getting greedy." He shook his head. "She wanted more money. She was demanding a bigger share of the profits and wanted to make an arrangement with one of the less reputable galleries in London, where we might get a better price. I told her it was too risky. Besides, you and I had a deal." He put his hands in his pockets and jiggled the change. He ran a hand through his hair. "She threatened to go to the police and tell them I'd stolen the paintings from her."

"Still, it's a shame," the gallery owner said.

Quentin shook his head. "She had to go. There was no alternative."

The other man nodded, popped open the trunk of the Mercedes, and put the paper-wrapped bundle inside.

Penelope took advantage of the moment to quickly scurry away, her head down and her collar pulled up around her face.

She felt triumphant. She'd been right: Quentin, the gallery owner, and Odile had all been in on the scam. Until Odile had gotten greedy, as Quentin had put it, and he'd made the decision that she had to go.

Penelope hurried into the administration building and down the hall to the Jane Austen Room. The room was already buzzing with chatter when she arrived. A table covered in a white cloth was set up along one wall with a silver urn for hot water and a selection of tea bags and platters of cakes, cookies, and tiny crustless sandwiches.

Helen came up to Penelope as she was at the buffet, helping herself to a cup of tea and a shortbread cookie.

"So nice to see you," Helen said, ducking her head shyly and fingering the silk scarf around her neck. "I fear I haven't thanked you enough for . . ." She waved a hand in the air. "Everything."

Penelope smiled and patted Helen on the arm.

Penelope noticed Maribel beckoning to her over the heads of the guests. She made an excuse to Helen and wove her way through the crowd toward Maribel.

"I'm so glad you could come," Maribel said when Penelope reached her. "I see you've gotten yourself some tea and you must try the Victoria sponge. It's excellent." She looked around her and then leaned closer to Penelope. "How did you make out at that gallery in Lower Chumley?" she said in a low voice.

Penelope described her visit and Beryl's performance. "Beryl did a wonderful job of playing the rich collector, and the gallery director didn't suspect a thing, but unfortunately he still wouldn't tell her who the current owner of the painting is."

Penelope took a sip of her tea. She put a hand on Maribel's arm. "I'm sure you'll be glad to know the Matisse painting is a copy." She explained about the wet paint on some of the works in the gallery's storage room and the conversation she'd just overheard.

Maribel pursed her lips. "So Odile painted it herself." She frowned. "And there was no great-grandmother posing for Matisse. She made it all up." She shook her head. "You think you know someone but then you find out you're wrong. Totally wrong."

Penelope was about to mention that Odile had been part of Quentin's art scam but then she thought better of it. Maribel had enough on her plate as it was.

Penelope spent an hour at the tea, then retrieved her coat and left. She was still thinking about Quentin as she headed down the hall.

According to him, there were still some of Odile's paintings left, but where were they? They could be stacked in a closet in Quentin's apartment, but that seemed terribly risky. What if his cleaning lady stumbled upon them? Or a nosy visitor?

No, she was positive they had to be stashed somewhere else. Of course, they could be literally anywhere—in a storage unit or possibly even in another city. But where would Quentin keep them if he wanted to have them close at hand? Penelope was positive they had to be on the Oakwood School campus somewhere.

Penelope pulled her cell phone from her tote bag and was about to call for a taxi when a thought struck her. She remembered seeing a hunting blind in the woods the day she'd followed Layla and Mabry.

She stuffed her phone into her jacket pocket. It wouldn't take her long to see if that was where Quentin had hidden the paintings.

She skirted the administration building and headed toward the quad. Classes were over and it was fairly quiet, although occasionally she could hear shouts and cheers coming from the hockey field.

No one seemed to notice her as she went around Corbyn Hall and headed into the small woods beyond.

Leaves crackled and branches snapped under Penelope's feet as she made her way to where she thought she remembered seeing the hunting blind. The exterior of the blind was made to blend with the surroundings and it wasn't easy to spot. For a minute she wondered if it had been moved or taken down, but she thought she spied it in the distance.

The branch from a shoot of a larger tree snagged on her leggings. Penelope bent down and freed herself and brushed off some dried leaves that were clinging to her ankles.

She thrashed her way through the trees, fending off low-hanging branches and skirting around damp muddy spots until she got closer to the blind. She paused briefly and looked behind her. The coast appeared to be clear.

She nearly ran the rest of the way, her excitement building with every step. When she reached the blind, she took a moment to scan the area again, but there was still no one in sight.

The blind was well hidden, set against a backdrop of trees and with several large branches draped over the top to camouflage it. Penelope circled the canvas structure twice before finding the zippered flap that led to the interior.

She undid it, pushed the flap aside, and stepped in. It was dark, with only a bit of light filtering through the narrow windows. Penelope waited till her eyes adjusted and then began to look around. It didn't take long. The interior was barely six feet by six feet.

It looked as if her hunch had been right—raised up off the ground on a pallet made of pieces of wood placed on top of bricks was a tidy stack of canvases carefully wrapped in a waterproof tarp.

Penelope slipped her tote bag off her shoulder and set it down. She removed the tarp, crouched next to the paintings, and began flipping through them.

She recognized most of the artists—a brightly colored Miró, a distorted Picasso portrait, a Twombly abstract, and several others. They were good copies, Penelope thought as she stood up, her knees giving a loud crack in the process.

Suddenly there was a noise—a twig snapping, perhaps—and she froze, her ears attuned to any further sounds. Her heart felt as if it was straining against her chest and her mouth was dry.

Was someone out there?

She waited several seconds, then, as quietly as possible, picked up her tote bag and slung it over her shoulder. She listened again and then bent down low, pulled the flap to the blind open, and stepped outside.

She looked up and stifled a scream.

"Well, well, well." Quentin was standing in front of the hunting blind, his arms crossed over his chest. "Who do we have here?"

TWENTY-TWO

❧⋅❧

Penelope felt the way she had the time she'd been caught trying to sneak into the house after her curfew. Her parents had been waiting by the door, their expressions grim. Only this was worse. Much worse.

Then it had only been a matter of being grounded; but judging by the expression on Quentin's face, this was more a matter of life and death.

She had to do something. Should she attempt to push past him and run? It wasn't far to the campus, where people would be strolling along the paths crisscrossing the quad or going in and out of the buildings. Quentin wouldn't dare try anything with everyone watching.

Penelope stood frozen to the spot. Her heart was galloping faster than a horse on the home stretch at Ascot and her mouth was so dry her tongue was sticking to her teeth.

What to do? Suddenly adrenaline surged through her, and her legs began to move almost of their own accord. She pushed past Quentin, shoving him hard enough to put him momentarily off-balance, and began to run.

She'd never been much of a runner—she was always the last one around the track in gym class—but having a killer chasing you was an incredible motivator. The woods presented a bit of an obstacle course and she had to dodge low-hanging branches and small sucker trees as well as being mindful of uneven ground.

She was nearly out of the woods—she could see the back of Corbyn Hall in the distance—when she tripped over a tree root and plummeted forward, landing flat on her face. She barely had time to register the pain before Quentin reached her.

He grabbed her arm and yanked her roughly to her feet. Penelope saw a flash of metal as he produced a wicked-looking knife with a long, thin blade.

"Start walking," he said, still clutching her arm tightly.

He forced Penelope forward and she had no choice but to obey.

It wasn't long before they were out of the shadow of the woods. Penelope was amazed that life was going on as if nothing was happening—students were clustered in groups chatting, people were going in and out of buildings—all unaware of Penelope's plight. It felt surreal. She thought of screaming for help but she could feel the sharp point of Quentin's knife through the fabric of her jacket and she didn't dare.

Penelope could see Grady in the distance, shovel in hand, digging a hole for the burlap-wrapped bush in his wheelbarrow. It made Penelope think of a grave and she shivered. Hopefully that wasn't a harbinger of things to come.

Quentin led Penelope around the back of Corbyn Hall

where the building blocked out the sun and cast shadows on the path. Her teeth were chattering even though she could feel sweat trickling down her sides.

They finally came to a small parking lot. The only vehicles were a black BMW and the Oakwood School van. Penelope recognized the BMW as Quentin's.

As they approached it, he retrieved a key fob from his pocket. He pressed a button and the lid of the trunk popped open. Penelope feared she knew what was going to happen next.

And she was right. She remembered reading that you should never let a killer take you to another location, but with a couple of prods with his knife, Quentin persuaded her to get into the trunk. She hit her head on the lid, and the sudden pain brought tears to her eyes, but she refused to allow herself the luxury of crying.

She tried to still her breathing to conserve energy, but when Quentin slammed the lid shut and darkness descended, she abandoned the attempt and began to pant.

Penelope pulled her cell phone from her pocket and unlocked it. It glowed brightly in the darkened trunk. She checked the signal and wanted to cry. There was none. Zero. Zilch. She stuffed the phone back into her pocket.

She felt the vibrations as the car started up and began to move. Where was he taking her? She tried to think. She had to be ready to bolt the second he opened the trunk, but it was going to be difficult. The trunk wasn't large and she was curled up, sharing the space with an emergency car kit in a blue plastic case and a large cardboard box. Her legs were going to be stiff and cramped when she got out of there, but she had to try.

The drive was smooth at first, but then they must have left the paved road because they were suddenly bouncing over rough ground. Penelope had to put her hands up to keep from hitting the roof of the trunk.

She found herself having absurd thoughts—like, what would her character Eirene do in a situation like this? Unfortunately, this was one scene Penelope couldn't rewrite.

She was beginning to feel sick to her stomach when the car finally came to a stop. She heard a door slam and assumed that Quentin had gotten out. She braced herself but was still surprised when the lid popped open. The sudden brightness of the light blinded her, and she instinctively closed her eyes.

So much for bolting, Penelope thought as Quentin yanked her out of the trunk by the arm. Her leg grazed the rim and she felt the sharp sting as it scraped her skin through her leggings.

"Where are we going?" she said, annoyed by the shaky sound of her voice.

Quentin exhaled loudly through his nose. "You'll know soon enough. But first we're going to take a little walk." He grabbed her arm and gave her a shove. "You had to go snooping, didn't you? You never would have found those paintings if I hadn't had to move them. The police were getting a little too close for comfort so I removed them from my storage unit as a precaution. The duck blind wasn't ideal, but it was only temporary. I planned to return the paintings to storage again as soon as the coast was clear."

Penelope looked around her as they walked. They were in the countryside but she had no idea where. The terrain was gently hilly, with scrubby grass and patches of tall weeds that waved in the breeze. A section of an old rusting fence, fallen down in parts, trailed along the field for fifty yards or so before ending abruptly.

Penelope was tempted to run, but the grip of Quentin's

hand on her arm and the promise of the knife in her back kept her moving along obediently. Several times she stepped in a rut and nearly lost her footing, but each time Quentin dragged her to her feet again.

Her arm was sore from his viselike grip and her ankle hurt from twisting it, but Penelope barely noticed. She was consumed by fear. Quentin was ruthless. He had killed Odile and had no reason not to kill her, too.

Trees now dotted the landscape, gradually getting closer and closer together. Quentin pointed to a plant with gray green leaves roughly the shape of an arrowhead.

"That's *Digitalis purpurea*, also known as common foxglove. It's a short-lived herbaceous perennial of the plantain family. It contains digitalis and other glycosides that affect the heart." He gave a chilling smile. "Like *Atropa belladonna*, or deadly nightshade, it can be poisonous. However, deadly nightshade is by far the more toxic of the two." He cleared his throat. "And while foxglove has a bitter taste, the berries of deadly nightshade are sweet."

"You studied botany?" Penelope said, trying to put the thought of poisonous plants out of her head.

"Both of my parents were experts in the field, although they each had different areas of concentration. I picked up a lot from dinner table conversations."

"So you knew how to identify deadly nightshade?" Penelope said.

"Of course. It's quite distinctive. And, as I said, the berries are sweet." He smiled as if at a memory. "I tested that out when I was in primary school."

"You ate some?" Penelope stared at him. "But you said they were poisonous."

"They are." Quentin laughed. "But Percy didn't know that. He was a willing guinea pig. He found them quite delicious."

"What happened to him?"

"He died, of course. His parents were quite distraught."

"So you put juice from the berries in Odile's wineglass," Pen said.

"Yes. She did say she thought the wine tasted a bit . . . off. But she drank it anyway."

"And then you washed her glass," Penelope said.

Quentin's head spun around and he stared at her. "Yes. I went back after Odile had left for your bookstore. She'd given me a key, you see. I washed her glass, left it on the kitchen drainboard along with several other dishes she hadn't gotten around to putting away."

"Very clever," Pen said. "But the police have figured that out, you know."

Quentin shrugged. "That won't help them find who did it."

"Did Odile know you took her copy of the Matisse painting?"

Quentin stopped for a moment and the sudden move caused Penelope to stumble.

"Of course. We were partners in the scheme."

Quentin sighed deeply. "Odile had a real talent for creating works in the style of well-known artists."

"Forging them, you mean," Penelope said.

Quentin's lip curled. "That's such a crass word. I prefer *creating*. But no matter—they were good enough to fool collectors and gallery owners. When I discovered her unique skill, I came up with a plan to take advantage of it and she was happy to go along."

"So what happened?"

"What do you think? We'd agreed that I would get fifty percent for flogging the works. I was taking the bulk of the risk, after all. But then Odile decided she wanted to keep more of the money for herself. I couldn't have that."

They walked a bit farther and Quentin sighed. "We were sitting on a gold mine. No one had gotten even a whiff of the fact that the paintings weren't real and that's because we stayed away from auction houses and the bigger galleries, where they were more sophisticated, and stuck with the ones who were greedy enough to go along with our scam. Odile wanted to branch out and try some of the London galleries. That would have ruined everything."

They were approaching a small river now and it gurgled and babbled in the distance.

"I offered the paintings to them at a price that had them salivating. They were more than happy to sell them for us. And both Odile and I walked away with a tidy profit."

By now they had reached the banks of the river. It wasn't large but the water flowed swiftly, eddying around rocks and clumps of grass.

Penelope stared at the water. Surely Quentin wasn't going to . . . She couldn't even finish the thought. The water didn't look too deep, but people had drowned in their bathtubs, hadn't they?

Quentin pointed to the river. "The current is swift. It will carry you downstream, where it collects in a deep pool before going over a small waterfall." He gave a wicked grin. "It should be a fun ride. I do hope you'll enjoy it."

He pulled a length of rope from his pocket.

"Hold out your hands."

Quentin had no choice but to put the knife down in order to tie Penelope's hands. As he bent to lay it on the ground, Penelope saw her chance.

She kicked him hard, catching him under the chin. The

blow sent his head snapping back. He let out a strangled cry, momentarily stunned.

Penelope began to run. The field was pockmarked with holes and ruts and it would be so easy to step into one and lose her balance or to get her foot caught in the thick vines that dotted the field here and there. But she couldn't think about that now. She had to get away.

She had no idea where she was. Nothing looked familiar. She had to make it back to the road that Quentin had turned off of. Surely there would be cars and perhaps even people.

She didn't dare turn around to look, but she thought she heard Quentin's footsteps thudding close behind her. She was nearing a group of trees and that gave her an idea.

Penelope didn't think she could run any faster—her chest was already burning and her heart felt as if it was about to explode—but she managed to pick up her speed just enough to reach the nearest tree.

One of the branches wasn't far from the ground and, thanks to her height, Penelope was able to jump up and reach it. She pulled herself onto the branch. She grabbed another branch slightly above it and hoisted herself up. She paused for a moment, her throat dry from panting.

As she expected, Quentin came to stand under the tree, looking up, a furious scowl on his face. He made Penelope think of her childhood dog, Reg, who would chase a squirrel up a tree and then stand there barking, frustrated at not being able to get at it.

Penelope was sitting on the branch, and it creaked as she pulled herself to her feet. She looked down at Quentin. The drop wasn't any farther than the one from the roof outside her bedroom window to the ground and she'd done it many times that month she'd been grounded. It had been years since she'd attempted it, and she'd been quite a bit younger then. But it was her only hope.

She held her breath for a moment, counted to ten, and jumped. She landed smack on top of Quentin as she'd planned. The impact not only knocked him to the ground but apparently knocked the wind out of him as well because he didn't immediately get up to follow Penelope when she began to run.

If someone had been there with a stopwatch, Penelope was quite certain she would have beat Florence Griffith Joyner's time in the two-hundred-meter sprint. She flew over the ground, fortunately missing any obstacles that might have tripped her up and cost her time.

She didn't dare turn around to see if Quentin was behind her for fear of losing precious seconds. She had to reach his car before he reached her.

Quentin's BMW was finally in sight. Penelope used the last bit of her energy to reach it.

She grabbed the door handle and mercifully it wasn't locked. Quentin was right behind her as she got in, slammed the door, and locked it with a satisfying click.

Penelope looked around and discovered Quentin had left his key fob in one of the cup holders. She pressed the ignition button and the BMW purred to life. Quentin was pounding on the windows now, his face contorted with fury. Before she pulled away, she reached into her jacket pocket, pulled out her cell phone, and tossed it onto the seat beside her.

Quentin chased the car and, as Penelope began to ease onto the road, he flung himself at it, landing sprawled on the hood of the car.

Penelope had to suppress a laugh as she drove sedately along the country lane.

She kept her speed down but it was still fast enough to rustle Quentin's hair and send it falling into his eyes. His knuckles were white as he held on. He looked like a strange sort of hood ornament.

Penelope had no idea where she was going, since she'd been in the trunk of Quentin's car on the journey out. She prayed they would come to a town soon. She imagined Quentin felt the same way and the thought gave her a brief moment of satisfaction.

A car passed her going in the opposite direction. The look on the driver's face was priceless and, in spite of the situation, Penelope laughed out loud.

Finally, she spotted a wooden sign by the side of the road with the words *Nether Thrompton* carved on it. Penelope prayed there would be a high street and a police station or at least a cluster of shops.

She groped for her cell phone on the passenger seat next to her. She'd call Maguire and let him know that Quentin was the killer and she had him trapped, so to speak.

She asked Siri to dial Maguire's number and to put the call on speakerphone.

The phone rang once, twice, three times. Penelope was praying Maguire would pick up and felt relief wash over her when he finally did.

She explained that Quentin had kidnapped her and planned to kill her but that she currently had him captured on the hood of the car.

"You have him *where*?" Maguire's voice rose an octave in disbelief.

"He's clutching the hood of my car. Actually, it's his car," Pen explained. "A black BMW." She could imagine Maguire shaking his head.

"Where are you?" Maguire sounded frantic.

"A place called Nether Thrompton. I think I'm approaching the high street."

"I'll be right there," Maguire said, and ended the call.

She had nearly reached the town proper when a police car overtook her. It stopped, the car doors flew open, and two police officers jumped out, their expressions grim. As Penelope put on the brakes and brought the car to a halt, Quentin lost his purchase on the hood and slowly slid off.

The two police officers were scratching their heads. Penelope couldn't blame them. It wasn't every day you saw a woman driving a BMW down the street with a man clinging to the hood. At least she didn't think it was a particularly common occurrence.

One of the officers—the one with bright red hair peeking out from under his cap—helped Quentin to his feet. Penelope expected Quentin to flee, but he didn't even try. His face was white and his knees appeared to be buckling. He had to lean on the car for support.

The other officer—an older man with an awkward gait—approached Penelope. She buzzed down her window as he approached and attempted to smile. It felt slightly lopsided but it was the best she could do. Reaction had set in and she was having to clench her teeth to keep them from chattering.

"I suppose you have an explanation for this," he said when he reached Penelope. "Lover's tiff? A bit of a barny with the partner maybe?"

Penelope took a deep breath. Where to begin? She decided that simple was best.

"He tried to kill me."

"Did he now?" The officer smiled condescendingly, showing tobacco-stained teeth. "It looks as if you were on track to kill him."

Penelope barely had the strength to explain but she did the best she could. She told the officer about being forced into Quentin's trunk, how he planned to tie her hands and throw her into the river.

The skeptical look never left his face. Penelope felt like crying but she refused to give in. She was telling the truth and wasn't there some saying about the truth always winning out in the end?

She wondered what made-up story Quentin was telling the red-haired officer. She glanced out the front window. The tale appeared to involve a lot of hand gestures on Quentin's part, and far from looking skeptical, the officer's expression was grave and he kept darting stern glances at Penelope.

Penelope had the sinking feeling she was going to end up in jail again. Hopefully Maguire would arrive soon. Where was he anyway? She'd been in jail once before—a mix-up when she'd foiled a killer—but Maguire had quickly set things straight. She prayed he was on his way now. She didn't relish the thought of spending even an hour locked up.

And what if they believed Quentin and let him go? Penelope had no doubt that he had the wherewithal to disappear abroad before anyone could catch him.

She kept her eyes on the road ahead, imagining that every car in the distance was Maguire's, only to be disappointed again and again. She started to panic when the police officer opened the car door and asked her to step out.

Penelope groaned as she got to her feet. She hurt in places she didn't even know she had. She brushed at the dead leaves clinging to her sweater and stared in dismay at her torn leggings.

Suddenly there was the screech of tires as a car slammed

to a stop in front of the Nether Thrompton police car and Maguire got out.

Penelope had never been so glad to see anyone in her life. At the sight of him, Quentin slipped past the police officer who had been talking to him and headed down the high street at a gallop.

Maguire and both officers were immediately in pursuit; and Quentin hadn't made it very far before the two Nether Thrompton officers had him in their grip and were marching him back down the street, one on either side of him.

Maguire joined Penelope, who was slumped against Quentin's car. His face was creased with concern.

"Are you okay?" He put a hand on her arm.

"Sort of," Penelope said, attempting a smile. "A bit sore and, frankly, a bit traumatized."

"Once again, you've captured the killer. You've got to leave something for me to do, you know, or I'll end up sweeping the floors at the station."

Penelope laughed. "I can't picture that."

"How did you know it was Quentin?"

Penelope explained about the Victoria Cross, his mother's profession, and the conversation she'd overheard.

Maguire shook his head. "We were beginning to look at him because one of the teachers said she saw him leaving Odile's apartment the evening she died, but we were still a long way from uncovering the motive."

"Maybe you'll get an award for solving the case."

Maguire laughed. "I'd have to give it to you." He put his arm around Penelope's shoulders. "The most I can hope for is that they spell my name right in the *Chumley Chronicle*."

TWENTY-THREE

꒰ঌ◆໒꒱

Penelope woke up the next morning feeling excited but also slightly nervous. Her second book had just come out and Mabel was holding a book signing for her.

She threw back the covers and shivered when her feet hit the cold floor. She started to stretch but stopped abruptly. She was still quite sore from the previous day's adventures—being thrown in a car trunk, climbing a tree, and then jumping out of said tree added up to a number of aches and pains.

She had the usual roller coaster of feelings as she took a little more care dressing that morning—donning the gray pencil skirt she'd bought for Charlotte and Worthington's prewedding dinner and the new baby blue cashmere sweater Beryl had insisted she buy from Francesca and Annabelle's boutique.

Her stomach felt unsettled as she thought about her book—what would the reviews be like? Would anyone show up for her book signing other than her sister? Would it sell as well as the first book? The sale of an author's second book could often be disappointing even though the first one had been a bestseller.

Penelope made herself a cup of tea but didn't have anything to eat. She was too nervous. Mrs. Danvers rubbed up against her leg, as if sensing her distress, and Penelope bent down to pet her. Petting an animal was always soothing and it did help to calm her nerves somewhat.

She retrieved her cell phone from the counter, where it was charging, and pulled up her e-mails. As she'd expected, there was one from her editor, Bettina. She almost didn't want to read it and at first only glanced at it with her eyes half shut.

Slowly she opened her eyes fully and the text came into focus.

Pen darling, good luck today with your book signing. Some early reviews are in and they're good! Brava! It looks as if we might have another bestseller on our hands. Now tell me, how is the third book coming along? I don't mean to sound pushy but we are all very excited about it and I can't wait to read the manuscript! Do keep me posted. XXX, Bettina

Sometimes Penelope wondered why she had gotten on this treadmill in the first place, but she had to admit she loved it even with all the pressure and worry.

She was ready to leave but first she put food in Mrs. Danvers's bowls, turned out the lights in the kitchen, and went to get her jacket.

The sun was out and Pen gloried in it as she walked to the Open Book. She relished being alive, realizing just how close she had come to being murdered by Quentin. The thought made her shiver, and she pulled her jacket closed around her.

Mabel was at the bookstore when Penelope got there, ensconced in a comfortable armchair that had been pulled to the front of the store for her. Her leg was resting on a stool and Brimble appeared to be waiting on her hand and foot, fetching cups of tea and tempting pastries from the tea shop.

Kip had stayed on to help and was putting the finished touches on his hand-lettered tented sign that read *Bestselling Author Penelope Parish*. Underneath it was written *The Woman in the Fog*, the title of Pen's book.

"We're going to set the table up right here," Kip said, gesturing with his hands. "That way people will see you as soon as they walk in."

Penelope crossed her fingers. Hopefully a few people would show up. Mabel had advertised in the *Chumley Chronicle* and some of the shopkeepers had even agreed to have small signs in their windows.

Bettina had argued that Penelope should have her first book signing at a large bookstore in London—Foyles had agreed to host one, as had Hatchards—but Penelope had insisted that she wanted to give Mabel and the Open Book first dibs.

Kip retrieved the folding table from the storeroom and dragged it to the front of the store. Penelope spread out the white tablecloth and arranged a stack of books on one side. She hoped she wasn't being too optimistic in setting out so many.

She glanced at the cover of one of them. It had turned out extremely well after multiple e-mails going back and forth between her, her editor, and her agent.

She found the glass bowl they used for candy and brought
it out. She retrieved the bag of Matlow's fruit-flavored hard
candies she'd bought, ripped it open, and emptied it into the
bowl, which she placed in the center of the table.

"Very festive," Kip said. "Mind if I nick one?"

"Go ahead," Pen said as he reached his hand into the
bowl.

Penelope stood back to look at the table. Stack of
books—check. Bowl of candy—check. Pen—check. Kip's
sign—check. Everything seemed to be in order.

There was half an hour to go yet, so Penelope headed to
the tea shop. Maybe a nice soothing hot cuppa would calm
her nerves.

Figgy brought each of them a cup of tea and sat down
opposite Penelope.

"I have some good news," she said, cradling the teacup
in her hands.

"Oh?" Penelope reached for a packet of sugar.

"My mother has relented about the wedding." Figgy
frowned. "Maybe not relented exactly, but we've compro-
mised." She put down her cup. "She's agreed to have the
wedding here in Chumley at St. Andrews instead of at the
cathedral where all the members of the Innes-Goldthorpe
family have been married."

"That's wonderful," Pen said.

"And . . ." Figgy paused. "She's agreed to trim the guest
list down to friends and family and not all of my father's
business associates and half the county's so-called landed
gentry."

"That is good news," Pen said. "Are you still going to
wear the *lehnga* your future mother-in-law gave you?"

Figgy had insisted that she wanted to wear the brightly

colored and richly embroidered Pakistani wedding garb instead of a traditional white gown and veil.

Figgy frowned and fiddled with her teacup. "That's still under negotiation but I'm confident she'll come around."

"You can always wear it for the reception."

Figgy smiled. "Great idea. It's perfect for a party." She shrugged. "I still hope to persuade her, though."

Penelope glanced at her watch. "Ten minutes till showtime. I'd better get up front."

"Good luck," Figgy called after her.

I was just about to come and find you," Kip said as he fluttered around the table, straightening the pile of books and the sign he'd made.

The first person through the door was Gladys. She picked up a copy of *The Woman in the Fog* and handed it to Penelope to sign.

"This is so exciting," she said. She leaned over to see what Penelope was doing. "Can you make it out to Gladys, please?"

"Certainly." Penelope penned a short note on the title page and then signed her name with a flourish. She'd been practicing in her spare time so that it wouldn't come out as her usual scrawl. She handed Gladys the book.

"I'll just go pay," Gladys said. "Ralph is minding the store and he has to leave soon for a dental appointment." Gladys pointed to her jaw. "He thinks he's got a cavity in one of his molars."

India was next in line after Gladys. Penelope knew that India lived on a small income and was quite touched that she was spending some of her money on Penelope's book. She hoped India would find the story enjoyable.

"It's an honor to know you, dear," India said as Pen handed her the book. "I will treasure this."

Pen felt herself tear up and she sniffed loudly.

More people arrived and were milling about the bookstore, when Figgy wheeled out a tea cart laden with plates of sliced lemon drizzle cake, Battenberg cake, and Victoria sponge. She had set up a separate station with an urn of hot water, disposable cups, and a selection of teas.

Suddenly a buzz went through the assembled crowd and Penelope looked up to see that Charlotte, the Duchess of Upper Chumley-on-Stoke, had arrived. The whispers intensified as she approached Penelope's table.

"How is the signing going?" she said to Penelope. "I know these things can be nerve-racking."

"I had a dream last night that no one showed up," Penelope admitted.

"That certainly doesn't seem to be the case." Charlotte looked around and smiled. "But I know what you mean."

Penelope signed a book for her.

"Thank you. I'm going to check out that tea cart. I seem to be hungry all the time." She patted her stomach. "Any day now."

There were more customers in line behind Charlotte; and Penelope spent a busy hour talking to people and signing books. Even her neighbor Mr. Patel bought a copy, asking rather shyly that she inscribe it to his wife, Anika.

Penelope was chatting with the owner of Jolly Good Grub, the gourmet shop at the other end of the high street, when she heard someone cry out.

She turned to see Charlotte holding her stomach, her eyes wide with surprise.

"I think I'm in labor," she said, her voice ringing with excitement and also an edge of panic.

Brimble, who had been tending to Mabel, stepped into the breach.

"We must get you to hospital, then."

Charlotte gave a smile that quickly changed to a grimace. "I think it's too early yet," she said after a pause. "My driver is outside. He can take me home."

Brimble helped her with her coat and rushed for the door. Penelope noticed Charlotte's driver standing at attention beside the open back door of her car.

Brimble guided Charlotte outside with a hand resting gently on her elbow and waited while she got comfortable in the back seat and the driver had closed the door.

The women in the store had by now all clustered together and were whispering excitedly. Penelope could imagine what they were saying. *I was there when the duchess went into labor.* The news would be all over Chumley by nightfall.

A gust of fresh air swept into the shop when the front door opened again.

"I'm not late, am I?" Beryl rushed up to Penelope. "I had an early appointment in London and the return train was late getting in. Something about a car stuck on the tracks somewhere." She reached out a hand and touched the few books that were left on the table. "I can't tell you how impressed I am," she said. "I know I gave you endless grief about your choice of career and how you were wasting your time, but you knew better. I'm so proud." She reached across the table and hugged Penelope.

The door opened again. This time it was Maguire. He was smiling.

"I'm sorry I couldn't get here sooner. I was dealing with

all the paperwork regarding the Fontaine murder." He picked up a copy of *The Woman in the Fog* and shook his head. "The Irish greatly revere writers and poets, you know." He tapped the book with his index finger. "This is very impressive." He grinned. "And I think it calls for a celebration. How about dinner tonight at Pierre's?"

"I'd love to."

Penelope breathed a sigh of relief as she reflected on the past few weeks. Odile's murder had been solved and the killer caught. She herself had escaped being killed. Her book had come out and seemed to be doing well.

And tonight, she'd be having dinner with Maguire at Pierre's. All was right with the world.

ONE

◦§◦

If Penelope "Pen" Parish had known how useless a master's degree in Gothic literature would turn out to be, she would have opted for something more practical instead—like accounting or mortuary science. After keeping herself somewhat afloat for several years with a hodgepodge of temporary jobs like waitressing and data entry, she'd hit upon a solution.

Instead of studying other authors' Gothic novels, she would write one of her own.

She'd subsequently spent every bit of her spare time in her attic garret—okay, a fifth-floor walk-up with drafty windows—with her fingers on the keys of her used laptop, surrounded by empty takeout containers, channeling her favorite Gothic authors—Mary Shelley, the Brontës, and Ann Radcliffe. By adding a touch of horror à la Stephen King, she had managed to produce a book the critics called a "unique, fresh twist on the classic Gothic novel."

You could have knocked her over with a feather when *Lady of the Moors* became a bestseller.

And therein lies the rub, as Hamlet opined.

Publishers have a habit of expecting their authors to follow up one bestseller with another. And Penelope Parish was suffering from a terrible case of writer's block.

She thought of that old saying, "Be careful what you wish for." The truth of that old saw had certainly hit home. She'd done her share of wishing as she'd slogged through her first manuscript—and there were entire days, if not weeks, when it was definitely a slog. She'd dreamed of all the things every writer does—book signings, coast-to-coast book tours, hitting the bestseller lists, royalties pouring in to swell her dwindling bank account.

And while it hadn't been *exactly* like that—her publisher had nixed the idea of a coast-to-coast book tour— some of it had actually come true.

And it had given Penelope a terrible case of nerves. She'd been raised with the strict New England ethic of hard work and was quite accustomed to it—holding down two jobs while getting her degree hadn't exactly been a picnic— but sometimes hard work wasn't enough. Ever since her success, she'd forced herself to sit in her chair at her desk with her fingers on her laptop keys for hours on end, but the words had refused to come. She'd hit a writer's block the size of Rhode Island.

Salvation had come in the form of a writer-in-residence position at the Open Book bookstore in England. She'd seen the ad in the back of the *Writer* magazine and had impulsively applied.

The application had been curious to say the least—filled with unusual and admittedly creative questions.

If you could be any character in fiction, who would you be? That had taken some thought on Penelope's part, but finally she had put down Bridget Jones. Because Bridget's friends and family liked her *just the way she was.*

Penelope's mother and sister were constantly trying to turn her into something she was not—a polished, put-together career woman balancing life and work as easily as a Cirque du Soleil performer juggled balls. Her friends were forever urging her to get it together and move on with her life. Yes, Bridget Jones it was.

If you were a type of food, what type of food would you be?

Penelope had thought long and hard about that one, too, and had finally come up with her answer—pizza. Everyone liked pizza. It was unpretentious. It was comfort food and always made you feel better. You could have it any way you wanted—with or without pepperoni; sausage; mushrooms; onion; green peppers; or even, if you insisted, pineapple.

Penelope had sent off the application without any great expectations. And for the second time in her life, you could have knocked her over with a feather when the letter came—the e-mail, actually if you want to split hairs— announcing that she'd won.

It had seemed like a heaven-sent opportunity—the quiet of a charming English village where she could write in peace in exchange for running a book group and a writers group and anything else she could think up to enhance the bottom line of the Open Book.

And the chance to get away from everyone's expectations— her mother's, her sister's, and even her publisher's. It had crossed Penelope's mind that her decision might have looked to some as if she was running away but she immediately dismissed the thought. She was having an adventure and wasn't that what life was meant to be?

Penelope had thought of herself as well prepared for life in an English village. She was an avid reader of British authors—she knew her Miss Marple inside and out—and she never missed an episode of *The Crown* or *Victoria*.

She didn't expect to be homesick. Homesick for what? An unsatisfactory romantic relationship? Her overpriced Manhattan walk-up?

There'd been objections, of course. The road was never smooth sailing as far as Penelope was concerned. Her sister, Beryl, insisted that this "sabbatical," as she called it, wasn't going to get Penelope a career. Despite Penelope's publisher springing for a full-page ad in the *New York Times*, her sister didn't consider book writing a viable occupation. According to her, what Penelope ought to do was apply for an academic position at a prestigious university.

Penelope's mother had objected, too, telling Penelope that she'd never meet anyone in Britain, and, even if she did, all the men there had bad teeth and if she thought she was going to meet Prince Harry or any prince at all, she was sadly mistaken. And as far as breaking into British society was concerned, she could forget all about that. Besides, what about her boyfriend, Miles?

Miles had seemed mildly put out that she wouldn't be on hand to grace his arm at the annual Morgan Fund investor's dinner but, in the end, he'd been the only one who hadn't vigorously objected to Penelope's upping stakes and moving overseas.

Fortunately Penelope was used to doing things that others objected to—she'd been doing them all her life—so that didn't stop her from accepting the Open Book's offer.

No, she was going to make a go of this opportunity,

because really, she had no choice. And—she could hear her grandmother's voice in her head—*the Parishes aren't quitters.*

And thus it was that Penelope had arrived on the shores of Merrie Olde England with her laptop and her battered suitcases and how she now found herself driving down the wrong (wrong in her opinion, anyway) side of the high street in Upper Chumley-on-Stoke two weeks later.

Today Chum, as Upper Chumley-on-Stoke was affectionately known to its residents, was a beehive of activity. Tomorrow was the annual Worthington Fest.

Banners, adorned with the Worthington crest and announcing the fest, hung from every streetlamp along the high street and fluttered in the mild breeze. It was a brisk October day, but the sky was cloudless and the sun warmed the air enough so she could get about nicely with just a light coat or a heavy sweater.

Upper Chumley-on-Stoke was a charming village within commuting distance of London. It was the real deal—a well-preserved medieval town that even the bright, shiny new Tesco and the curry takeaway on the outskirts of the city couldn't spoil. The quaint cobblestoned streets were the delight of tourists even if they were a nuisance to the residents, who found them rough going in any footwear other than thick-soled walking shoes.

Buildings of brick worn over the years to a rosy hue followed a bend in the road until they petered out and gave way to a narrow road bordered by hedgerows that cut through the grassy green fields beyond and into the countryside.

Penelope found the town enchanting. She felt as if she had stepped into a storybook, and even the inconveniences didn't bother her—Wi-Fi that was spotty at best, narrow streets instead of wide modern roads, an absence of large chain stores and shopping malls, save the Tesco that had opened in recent years.

The Open Book was equally enchanting. It was fusty and musty in the best possible way with books spilling willy-nilly from the shelves and arranged according to Mabel Morris, the proprietor's, unique shelving system, which Penelope soon discovered made finding a volume more of a treasure hunt than the usual cut-and-dried affair.

There was a low ceiling crisscrossed with wooden beams and a large diamond-paned front window where Penelope could imagine Charles Dickens's newly published *A Christmas Carol* might have been displayed while men in greatcoats and women in long dresses walked up and down the sidewalk outside, occasionally peering through the glass at the array of books.

Penelope negotiated the roundabout at the top of the high street and was admiring a red sweater in the window of the Knit Wit Shop when a horn blaring close by made her jump.

She returned her attention to the road and was horrified to see another car coming straight at her. She jerked the steering wheel, overcorrected, bumped up over the curb, slammed on her brakes, and came to a stop within an inch of a cement planter filled with bright orange and yellow mums.

Her heart was beating hard, her palms were sweaty, and there was a haze in front of her eyes.

The other car, a Ford, had stopped in the middle of the road and the driver was now standing next to it.

Penelope took a deep breath, opened her door, and got out.

"What do you mean driving down the wrong side of the

street," she said, still slightly breathless, as she approached the other driver.

The driver looked amused. He wasn't handsome, but had a kind, open face that was very appealing. He was an inch or two shorter than Penelope's six feet. Penelope had sprouted up early and there had been hopes that she would follow in her mother's and sister's footsteps to model; but although she was attractive enough, the camera didn't love her the way it did them. Besides, Penelope had no interest in parading around having her picture taken.

The fellow still looked amused. She knew she needed to rein in her indignation but it was her default setting and not easy.

"You scared me half to death," she said, pushing her glasses back up her nose with her finger.

"You're American," the fellow said. He had a slight Irish lilt to his voice.

Penelope raised her chin slightly. "Yes." She was about to say *what of it* when a horn honking made her jump.

A line of cars had formed behind the driver's Ford Cortina and a red VW Golf was attempting to pull around it.

Penelope's hand flew to her mouth as the realization hit her. "*I* was on the wrong side of the road," she said in a horrified voice.

"Exactly."

"I'm so sorry. I forgot . . . I thought . . ." Penelope stuttered to a halt. "I'm so terribly sorry. You're not hurt . . . or anything . . . are you?" She swayed slightly.

"I'm fine," the fellow said, his face creasing in concern. "But I'm worried about you."

"I'll be okay." Penelope took a deep breath. "It's only that I think I forgot to eat lunch."

It used to drive Penelope's sister crazy that she had to

constantly watch her diet to maintain a slim figure, while Penelope could go a whole day without even thinking about food, then devour a meal worthy of a linebacker and still never gain an ounce.

"As long as you're sure . . ."

Penelope waved at him. "I'll be fine." She gestured toward the cars lined up down the road. "You'd better get going. That mob looks ready to attack you."

He smiled. "I guess I'd better."

Mabel Morris, whose Miss Marple–like appearance and demeanor belied her former career as an MI6 analyst, was behind the counter when Penelope pushed open the door to the bookstore.

She was all rounded curves and had fluffy white hair that tended to want to go every which way and pale powdery skin. Her blue eyes, however, had depths that suggested she wasn't unacquainted with tragedy and the seamier side of life.

"My sainted aunt," she said when she saw Penelope, "you look like you could use a good strong cup of tea."

"A shot of whiskey is more like it," Penelope said as she slumped against the counter. "Not that I'm in the habit of drinking in the middle of the day."

"This is strictly medicinal." Mabel pulled a bottle of Jameson and a glass from under the counter. She poured out a generous splash of whiskey and handed it to Penelope. "Drink up and then tell me what's having you look like Hamlet's father's ghost."

Penelope tossed back the whiskey and sighed as the

warmth traced a path down her throat, to her stomach, and out to her limbs. She felt her shoulders and neck relax and her agitated breathing slow.

"I very nearly had an accident," she said, putting her glass down on the counter.

Mabel inclined her head toward the glass. "Another?"

Penelope shook her head. "Not on an empty stomach."

"You haven't eaten?" Mabel looked alarmed.

"I'll be fine," Penelope reassured her. "Thank goodness the other fellow was able to stop in time."

"What happened?"

Penelope sighed. "I'd like to say it was the other driver's fault, but I'm afraid I forgot where I was and ended up on the wrong side of the road." She felt her face color. She didn't like making mistakes.

"This is how many near misses now?" Mabel turned and put both hands palms down on the counter. "Maybe you should consider giving up the car. You can walk to the Open Book and if you need to go any farther than that, you can hire a taxi."

"That's very tempting," Penelope said, briefly reliving the horror of seeing another car headed straight at her. She raised her chin. "But I'm determined to nail this driving on the other side of the road if it's the last thing I do."

Mabel raised an eyebrow. "That's what has me worried— that it will one day *be* the last thing you do."

Gladys Watkins wandered up to the counter. She handed over a copy of romance novelist Charlotte Davenport's latest, *The Fire in My Bosom,* which featured a rather long-haired, bare-chested man on the cover and a damsel whose look of considerable distress seemed to match Gladys's own.

"I can't begin to imagine what the queen thinks of it,"

Gladys said as Mabel dropped some coins into her out-stretched palm. "I imagine the poor thing is simply beside herself."

"One can't quite imagine the queen being beside herself," Mabel said as she turned toward the register and ripped off the receipt. "She's made of sterner stuff than that."

"That's certainly true," India Culpepper said. She'd casually sidled up to the counter in order to join the conversation. "What with all that nonsense about Charles and Camilla she's had to endure. You know, stiff upper lip and all, that's her majesty's motto."

"Yes, no doubt that's embroidered on the throw pillows in the drawing room at Buckingham Palace," Mabel said dryly.

"High time the Duke of Upper Chumley-on-Stoke settled down," Gladys said, her brow furrowed fiercely. "Driving up and down the high street in that sports car of his and getting drunk at the Book and Bottle, causing no end of embarrassment to the royal family. He's very nearly forty after all."

"It's the red hair." India nodded sagely. "Everyone knows gingers are bound for trouble. Comes from his father's side. His great-grandfather was known to cheat at cards and"—she lowered her voice—"run around with loose women."

Penelope frowned. "Oh, pooh. That's an old wives' tale. Redheads aren't any more prone to getting into trouble than anyone else."

India looked far from convinced.

Penelope quashed the sudden desire to dye her brown hair red to prove them all wrong—although she was hardly the right person to challenge their assumption. Her father had often said that trouble was her middle name.

"But an American!" Gladys said, clutching her book even more tightly to her ample bosom and piercing Penelope with a laser-like stare.

Penelope stood up taller and straightened her shoulders. "Americans have become quite civilized, you know. We don't live in covered wagons anymore."

Gladys sniffed. She was as round as an apple with a ruddy complexion and large, guileless blue eyes.

"I agree with Gladys," India said, looking quite surprised that for once she and Gladys found themselves on the same page. "Most unsuitable. Of course, Arthur is barely in the line of succession, but *still*." She said that last as if it was her final word on the subject and *that was that*.

India was *to the manor born* as the saying goes, and even though the family fortune had slipped through numerous fingers before reaching her in a significantly diminished amount, she comported herself as the aristocrat she considered herself to be.

"And not just an American," Gladys was continuing, "but Charlotte Davenport—an American romance novelist." She said that last as if it left a bad taste in her mouth.

India stared rather pointedly at the book in Gladys's hand, but the significance of India's glance was lost on Gladys.

"Charlotte Davenport is actually quite a lovely person," Pen said firmly.

Gladys's eyes goggled. "You've met her?"

"As a matter of fact, I have," Pen said. "It was at a writers' conference—my first. I was positively terrified and Charlotte very graciously took me under her wing. She was already a bestselling author and my book hadn't even come out yet. I was scheduled on a panel she was moderating—I don't even remember what the topic was but I do remember being horribly nervous." Penelope shuddered to think about it. "I developed a sudden case of stage fright when someone in the audience asked me a question and Charlotte managed to coax an answer out of me."

"Still . . ." India let the word hang in the air.

Mabel turned to Penelope and winked. "How is the book coming? Do tell us."

Penelope suddenly found three pairs of eyes trained on her. She was more than grateful for the change of subject, but she really wished it had been changed to something other than her nearly nonexistent book.

"It's coming," she said as firmly as possible. "I just need to find a reason to compel my main character, Annora, to go against all her best instincts and search this creepy castle basement alone in order to find a chest that's hidden down there."

Penelope thought of some of the pickles she'd gotten herself into growing up—climbing a tree and then not being able to get down, sneaking out her bedroom window the time she was grounded and falling off the roof and breaking her ankle, hitchhiking home her freshman year in college with a knife she'd taken from the cafeteria for protection—but even she knew better than to go into a basement alone with a killer on the loose.

"That's a tough one," Mabel said.

Penelope nodded. "Tell me about it! I can't have a heroine who is TSTL."

This time three sets of eyebrows were raised in unison.

"Too stupid to live," Penelope explained. "It's the sort of

thing that makes a reader want to throw the book across the room."

"Quite." India fingered the yellowing pearls at her neck.

Penelope looked at her watch. "Ladies, it's almost time for our meeting of the Worthington Fest marketing committee. Shall we sit down?"

"Regina's not here yet," Gladys looked around as if expecting Regina to magically appear in a puff of smoke. "She's always late." She made a sour face.

"Let's get settled. I am sure Regina will be along shortly."

Penelope herded everyone to the table and chairs Mabel had set up in a cozy nook at the back of the store. Penelope used it for her writing group although her book group tended to array themselves in the mismatched overstuffed chairs and sofa that Mabel had also furnished the nook with.

The Open Book was to have a stall at the fest, and Penelope had offered to head the marketing committee with the help of India and Gladys. Regina Bosworth was the chairwoman of the fest itself.

"Shall we start without Regina?" India said, looking around the table for confirmation.

"Let's give her a few more minutes," Penelope said decisively.

It was now nearly ten minutes past the hour. Penelope opened her mouth to begin the meeting, but just then a voice rang out from behind one of the stacks.

"I'm here. I'm coming."

Regina rounded the corner, flapping her hands furiously. "So sorry, ladies, couldn't be helped. I've had such a busy morning. There's masses to get through yet before the

Worthington Fest opens tomorrow. The Duke of Upper Chumley-on-Stoke had me positively running off my feet."

Penelope noticed India roll her eyes. Hardly anyone referred to the duke by his title—around the village he was Arthur Worthington or simply Worthington and was often greeted familiarly by the patrons of the Book and Bottle, where he was known to regularly pony up for a round or two, as *Worthington, old chap.*

He and India were vaguely related. Penelope couldn't remember how, but she thought it was through India's mother's line. Of course, while India lived in somewhat straitened circumstances in a cottage on the grounds of the estate, Worthington had inherited the castle itself along with a substantial amount of money.

Regina took her seat. She straightened the Hermès scarf at her neck—the queen had one just like it, she never failed to point out—opened her Louis Vuitton handbag, and spread out her things—an expensive notebook with an embossed leather cover and a blue lacquered Mont Blanc fountain pen.

"Now, Penelope," Regina said in an officious tone, "would you like to make your report?" She folded her hands on the table in front of her.

India and Gladys turned to Penelope expectantly.

"You've all seen the banners along the high street," Penelope began and the others nodded. "We've placed posters in all the shops along the high street as well."

Gladys nodded. "We have one in our window."

Gladys's husband owned the Pig in a Poke, Upper Chumley-on-Stoke's butcher shop.

"And Regina was brave enough to volunteer to be on our local BBC radio station to talk up the fest," Penelope said. "Brava, Regina."

"As if she would have turned that opportunity down," India whispered to Penelope.

Regina looked around the table and beamed at them. "Thank you. Thank you." She cast her eyes down demurely. "And," she said, pausing dramatically, "our little fest has been written up in the *Sun*."

Gladys gasped and clasped her hands to her chest. India looked equally startled. Stories from their little corner of the world rarely made it into the national papers.

Regina preened. "Gordon—that's my husband," she said to Penelope, "places a lot of ads with the *Sun* for his business. He pulled some strings and well . . ." Regina batted her eyelashes.

She reached into her purse, pulled out a copy of a newspaper, and placed it on the table. She thumbed it open to the fifth page and tapped a headline with a crimson-manicured fingernail.

"Here it is. 'Upper Chumley-on-Stoke to hold its annual Worthington Fest on Saturday. Hosted by the Duke of Upper Chumley-on-Stoke and his American fiancée, the fest is an annual event'—well, you can read the rest yourselves." She turned the paper around so the others could see.

A stock photo of the duke and Charlotte Davenport taken at some other event was included with the article. Penelope had seen Worthington from a distance once or twice as he sped through the village in his vintage Aston Martin but had never gotten a close-up look at him.

He had a roguish air about him—in the photograph at least—with blue eyes that twinkled beneath thick, straight brows and a mouth that looked to be curved in a perpetual half smile—as if he was privy to an especially delicious secret.

Charlotte looked every inch the duchess she was about

to become in a pale pink dress with a full skirt and lace bodice. Her blond hair was in a sleek bun at the nape of her neck and she carried a tiny clutch bag in one hand. Her other hand—with its four-carat diamond solitaire—was laid lightly on the duke's arm.

"I still don't know why Worthington chose that woman," Gladys said, tapping Charlotte's picture.

"Well," Regina said, raising an eyebrow, "they're not married yet, are they? Anything could happen."

Regina folded the newspaper back up and tucked it in her handbag, and they went back to the business at hand, finishing up their meeting half an hour later. Regina gathered her things together and immediately took off at a trot, yelling over her shoulder that the duke was waiting for her and she simply mustn't be late. Everyone stood in a cluster as they listened for the sound of the door closing behind her.

"That woman becomes more insufferable by the day," India said. "Nouveau riche," she declared as if that explained it.

"I don't know why Worthington chose her to be the chairwoman of the fest," Gladys grumbled, her expression stormy.

"Quite," India said. "I understand that competition for the position was dreadfully fierce among the ladies of Chumley."

"She probably badgered him until he cried uncle," Penelope said.

India made a sound like a snort.

"I wonder what she meant about Worthington and Charlotte not being married yet," Penelope said. "It almost sounded like she was hinting at something. As if she knew something."

Gladys laughed. "What could Regina possibly know about it?"

"I don't know." India frowned. "But Regina collects secrets the way some people collect stamps. And she's not afraid to make use of them either."

Ready to find
your next great read?

Let us help.

Visit prh.com/nextread